WELCOME TO THE WORLD OF

Shallow Cove™ DIMENSIONS

I KILLED TO NUMB THE PAIN
UNTIL I SAW HER

ETERNALLY
LOST

THE ETERNALLY SERIES BOOK 6

JANUARY RAYNE

Fang v__v bang on fangbangers

ALSO BY JANUARY RAYNE

Shallow Cove™ Dimensions
The Eternally Series:
Book 1: Eternally Hers
Book 2: Eternally Damned
Book 3: Carnival of Creeps
Book 4: Eternally Cursed
Book 5: Eternally Rare
Book 6: Eternally Lost

Shallow Cove™ Dark Dimensions
The Monster Stalker Series:
Book 1: Honeysuckles
Book 2: Snapdragons
Book 3: Hollyhocks

AUTHOR'S NOTE

Blood and knife play, CNC, sadism, suicidal thoughts, knotting, mention of children being murdered (not graphic), on page murder, rough/abusive sex, degradation, masochism, pain slut, brief cannibalism (vampire feeding on vampire), pregnancy (at the very end).

DEDICATION

To all the pain sluts out there who like to get fucked so hard, your back breaks.
This one is for you.

And to Tiff,
For sticking by me through all the chaos and strife.

We survived our own Purgatory.
This series wouldn't be possible without you.

Prologue

AZIEL

I'm not old enough to know about who is fated to me, but if my heart is anything to go by, I know the woman meant for me is Elouise. She's been my best friend for as long as I can remember.

Our friendship is forbidden. If others knew, we would never be able to see each other again. Even if we have been *trying* to come to a truce with her kind for years.

She's a vampire.

I'm a werewolf.

We are natural enemies due to how dangerous a werewolf bite is to her kind, but I'd never hurt her. I'd take my own life before risking hers. I long for her more than I do the night, the moon, and the stars combined. She is my solace when my beast slashes at my chest for strife.

My werewolf has always had more violent tendencies than others, especially my brother, Anwyll. He is gentle. He wouldn't hurt a fly.

Me? I *want* to cause pain. I have a rage inside me that is so different than anyone in my family. I always feel like I'm on the edge of the disease werewolves get when they do not meet their fated mate in time.

And there are only two people who keep that want to destroy at bay.

My little brother and Elouise.

Loving her, falling in love with her, wasn't planned. Loving her is a mistake, I know that. My feelings for Elouise are a different type of pain. I can never mate her. I can never bind her to me like I truly want the moment we turn of age.

My bite would put her into a coma, and only the blood of her beloved could wake her.

I'm not her beloved.

She's not my fated mate.

If I give into my selfish feelings, I'll only have her temporarily before she is lost in a coma with no way of waking her.

But that's only if I bite her. What if we could be happy for the rest of our lives? We could grow old to-gether, choose each other, and have kids– I blush at the thought.

We could be together forever.

All I have to do is stop myself from leaving a mark. I can do that. I'm strong enough to fight the urge.

"What's on your mind, Aziel?" Mom asks, setting a plate of fresh meat in front of me. This is the deer that my father and I killed together last night. She sighs, "I know you don't want to learn about sex. Your father was the same way when he was young. Now, look at him. He's Alpha of the pack and has heirs. It's going to happen to you too when you become Alpha. You need to know these things if you are to keep the pack alive. The sex talk is awkward, but you'll need to know. Were-wolf anatomy is very different and–"

I hold up my hand to stop her. "No offense Mom,

but I'd rather learn from the pack doctor. Not from you or Dad. Especially, Dad."

Mom chuckles. "That's fair."

I stare down at my plate again, thankful I have avoided that conversation with my mother, and watch the blood ooze from the red center, dripping onto the plate. My stomach growls, reminding me I haven't eaten yet this evening. My mind is too preoccupied with the new plan to make Elouise mine.

"So? Then what is on your mind?" she prods.

Typical.

"Nothing. I think I'm just tired is all." I stab the thick piece of venison with my claw, ripping into it with my canines. My mind is still on Elouise, not even the blood coating my tongue brings me out of my trance.

I'm too excited to see her tonight. We see each other four times a week and it isn't enough, not anymore. I need more. My thoughts are invaded by her, when I open my eyes in the morning and close them at night, her name echoes on repeat in my mind.

My heart beats faster just at the mere hope of seeing her. Her voice, soft and sweet, has me breathing easier.

I'm completely in love, and I want us to be together forever. If I tell my parents or anyone else about her, they will just say it is "teenage love" and it won't last.

I don't even care.

I'll give everything up if it means I have Elouise all to myself.

Mom pushes my plate away, sits down, and takes my hands.

Oh, no.

She doesn't believe me. I know this move.

"Aziel." She dips her head then slides her fingers under my chin, giving me no choice but to meet her gaze. Her bright golden eyes shine, filled with love, and guilt pierces my gut for the thousandth time.

Not guilt from falling in love with a vampire but that I'm keeping the truth from my family.

"I am your mother, and I know you find it shocking that you think I have no idea when something is bothering you, but I can feel it. What is weighing you down, baby?"

"Mom, I'm not a baby," I grumble, irked she always calls me that.

"You'll always be my baby," she scoffs, slapping the top of my hand lightly. "Talk to me. Don't get proud. Pride is the one thing that will destroy everything you've ever wanted for yourself. Don't ever be too proud to talk about what is bothering you. It doesn't make you weak."

I swallow, the words right there in my throat to tell her. "I'm not ready to talk about it, Mom, but when I am, you'll be the first I come to."

Her eyes soften with understanding, her soft, gentle hand cupping my cheek. "You're so grown it's almost hard to believe you were once a little pup I bounced on my legs. Now you're working through big emotions because now you're an adult, and your world is so much larger. It's tough to balance them all. I'm so proud of you. When you're ready, I'll be here, okay?"

I nod, placing my hand over hers. "I know." My eyes drift to the clock on the wall, noticing I only have twenty minutes to meet Elouise at our spot.

"I'm going to go for my evening walk, Mom. It always helps me clear my head."

She stands, grabbing the curve of my shoulder before patting it. "Just be—"

"—Careful." I grin at her. "I know, Mom. I always am."

"And I want you back before—"

"—The sun rises." I roll my eyes with a smile this time. She always tells me the same thing before I go for my "walk".

"You think you're so smart," she teases, slapping me lightly on the arm. "Take your meat to go then. I don't want you to be hungry."

I stab the slab of deer flesh with my claw and lift it into the air. "Thanks, Mom. Love you!" I open the door and run outside, nearly slamming into Anwyll.

"I love you too!" she shouts.

"Anwyll." I pick him up and set him inside. He growls at me, showing me his sharp teeth. He hates it when I pick him up like a baby. "You need to be more aware of your surroundings. I could have stepped on you."

He morphs into his human form, shoving me in the shoulders. I barely move from his attempt.

"It's you who was in my way! You came barreling out of the house. Don't always put the blame on me." He stomps away into his bedroom and slams the door.

"These teen years might just be the death of me when it comes to the two of you."

I grab the doorknob and smile. "You're doing great, Mom. He's just a brat." I raise my voice so he can hear me.

He groans before yelling. "No, you're a brat! God, just leave me alone, Aziel!"

"Stop it." Mom shoos me out of the house. "Now you're aggravating him on purpose."

"He started it," I try to defend myself as she pushes me out the door.

"And I'll finish it, young man. Stop pushing your little brother. You know his werewolf hormones are insane right now, and teasing him doesn't help."

"It helps me," I mumble under my breath.

She narrows her eyes at me, shaking a finger. "I wonder what your father will think of that statement."

"I'm going." I lift my hands in surrender, backing away from the frustrated mother werewolf. "But you love me."

"Don't remind me." She gives me a crooked smile. "Now, stop causing trouble and go on your walk. I hope it helps clear your head."

I give her a final wave just as she blows me a kiss.

I'm lucky to have such great parents. Unlike my friends, I actually like hanging with my mom and dad. Our relationship seems different than the others I've seen. My family is accepting. I have no doubts that if they knew about Elouise, they would welcome her. They would be unsure, yes, but they only want my happiness.

The issue is the rest of the pack.

I take my clothes off, anchor them to my leg, and shift into my werewolf form. I'm nearly fully grown, but I still have odd baby hair around my neck, proof that I'm young. I'm bigger than most of the other werewolves in the pack, probably due to my alpha line heritage.

Once I get to the tree line, I glance over my shoulder to make sure no one is watching me. All the houses are close together, smoke coming out of the chimneys, pups playing in the distance, and a few old weres are on their porch's smoking a pipe, but they aren't paying any mind to me.

I quietly fall to my hands, careful to avoid any twigs or leaves so I don't bring attention to myself. I sink into the darkness, my night vision allowing me to see every tree or log I need to dodge.

The forest itself is quiet, the prey becoming silent as a predator invades their space. I toss the meat my mother gave me into my mouth, chewing on it loudly, the bone breaking with every hard bite.

A tree branch tickles my side as I move along the trail I've made to the other side of the forest.

Our territory ends here.

There's a meadow in between where I stand and a different forest that isn't patrolled by my pack, and that's where I meet Elouise.

Crouching, I step into the overgrown meadow with long pieces of wheat. With every step, the stems break under my heavy paws. The crickets chirping become more quiet with every second that passes.

I prowl, keeping low to the ground to remain unseen. My heart hammers when I reach the tree line. I look back to make sure no one has followed me, the long wheat swaying from the breeze and disguising the path I took.

Instead of going through the forest, I go around, choosing a dangerous path. To my right is the start of a steep cliff. The terrain becomes rocky, the tips of the rocks threatening to pierce the pads of my paws.

The small rocks turn to boulders the further I travel, and I jump from one to the other. The stars aren't out tonight, but a crescent moon is out, its glow illuminating the different shades of colors in the sky.

I stop when the scent of lilacs and citrus flutters through the air and into my lungs.

Elouise.

I jump from boulder to boulder faster, digging my claws into the rocks so I don't fall to my death.

That would really suck.

I follow the aroma I smell when we aren't together. I found if I focus on our memories long enough, her scent drifts across my nose, igniting all the times we have spent together. I could be in bed, unable to sleep, and the barest scent of her perfume drifts into my room at her memory.

I breathe in and out from the exertion, my muscles aching from the climb, but it's all worth it when I get to "The Lookout Point."

It's at the very top of the cliff. The surface is smooth enough to walk on, the ground still made of stone, and near where the cliff turns into a sharp point is an oversized log we sit on to enjoy the view.

The view that allows us to see all the territories in the area. Everything about it is beautiful, and I wouldn't share this view with anyone else. It belongs to us.

To the left, the forest creeps onto the cliff, and to the right where the edge of the cliff is, sits Elouise.

"I didn't think you'd show," she says without turning around.

She can smell me.

"Like I'd ever miss a night with you, Louie." She hates it when I call her that, but I think it's different, just like she is.

I shift into my human form, a form I don't like to choose most of the time. Werewolves have three bodies.

Human. Humanoid. Werewolf.

I personally love my humanoid form, but since I've only ever hung out with Elouise as a human, I don't want to make her uncomfortable. I quickly pull my clothes back on.

She finally turns, pressing her chin to her shoulder to look at me. A large smile stretches across her face, an expression of pure happiness. Standing, the tight curls of her obsidian hair bounce, and the moonlight falls upon the rich dark tourmaline of her skin, solidifying that she is a unique, gorgeous, one-of-a-kind jewel.

She is flawless.

Elouise uses her vampire speed, blurring to me before I can even take a step closer. Her arms wrap around me, holding me tight, and damn, I don't miss a second to do the same.

A grumble purrs in my chest as I hold her, her body fitting perfectly against mine. I never want to let her go. She feels too good, too right, too perfect.

We *will* last forever. I don't know how, but I'll make it happen.

Seconds turn to minutes as we hold one another. Eventually, Elouise pulls away first, she has to, considering it will never be me who chooses to put space between us.

She peers up at me through long lashes. Her hand lands on my chest, the touch sending my heart into a fast beat. My throat becomes dry, wondering if this is the moment that I've been waiting for.

I want to kiss her.

We have never crossed that line. It's been stolen

touches and laughs, but never more.

I tug on one of her curls, watching it stretch as I pull it straight, then let it go just to see it bounce in place. My fingers have a mind of their own, moving from her hair to the soft skin of her cheek.

Back and forth I drag my oversized fingers up her high cheekbones, watching her eyes flutter when she leans into my touch.

"Look at me," I plead desperately, needing her gaze locked on me.

When she does, I can't breathe. I can't think.

Her eyes are portals of golden sunsets, and all I want to do is travel her soul to feel what she feels.

"You are stunning. The heavens have nothing on you, Elouise. You are..." I try to think of the right word. "Everything," I whisper on an exhale.

"Aziel." My name is soft, light, and sweet escaping her lips.

My finger grazes down her jaw, so delicate, so fragile, and all I want to do is protect her.

"Elouise." I lean down slowly, daring to close the distance between us for the first time.

She inhales sharply, her fingers digging into my shirt.

I step closer, wrapping one arm around her waist to pull her against me. My free hand cups the side of her neck and she angles her head up, giving me more access to her lips.

We steal glances at each other the closer our lips become, each of us wondering if the other will go through with the kiss.

Someone will have to kill me before I miss this moment. There isn't a chance in hell that will keep me from feeling her lips against mine. I've dreamed about this moment for years.

"Aziel," she breathes, her voice shaking with nerves and uncertainty. Her palms slip down my chest and I growl, loving her hands on me.

"Elouise," I say quietly before finally pressing my lips to hers.

The entire world stops spinning as her lips give against mine, so full, so plump, and my mind comes to a complete stop. All I can focus on is her and how good she feels.

My hand drifts down her neck, swooping around her shoulder until I'm grasping her nape.

She breaks the kiss, gasping for breath. "I haven't ever kissed—"

"—Me either." I slam my mouth on her again, devouring her as if I'm seeking her soul.

Our lips move together so naturally. Nothing about it is difficult. My heart hammers in my chest, the beast inside me wanting to rip from my skin to howl and celebrate.

My tongue slips against hers tentatively, once, twice, before she gets the courage to do the same. I moan, my claws extending to grip her by the roots of her hair.

I'm losing control of myself.

She wraps her arms around my neck and jumps, wrapping her legs around my waist. Tightening my arm around her to make sure she doesn't fall; I deepen our connection.

My hands splay across the middle of her back, and we kiss until we can't breathe, barely allowing ourselves to pull away to suck in much-needed air.

Her forehead falls on mine, her hands grazing either side of my face.

"I love you," I admit, and she leans back, staring at me in disbelief.

Her eyes widen in shock.

"I do. I love you. I've loved you since the moment I laid eyes on you when we were kids playing where we weren't supposed to. Here. Right here. It all started with you in this exact spot, and Elouise, I want it to always be us. We can't be together if we choose to stay here."

"I love you too, Aziel. I love you so much. I can't imagine life without you."

Every single dream I've ever conjured when thinking of us is coming true.

"What are you saying?" she asks, her golden gaze darting across my face.

"Let's run away, Louie. You and Me. Let's be together. Forever. It can just be us. No... no rules, no parents telling us we can't be together because of who we are. No more hearing about why vampires and werewolves don't intermingle. No more negativity." I take her hand in mine, place it on my chest, and allow her to feel every beat. "I'm for you, Louie. I'm yours. Every beat, I'm obsessed with you. You don't understand how far my need for you goes. I'll do anything for us. So let's run. We can be our own family, and make our own rules. My love for you will never end, don't you see that? No matter what."

She slides off my body, standing in front of me, and she nibbles on her bottom lip as questions fly through her mind. "But what if you bite me, Aziel? We know what werewolf bites do to vampires and there is no cure. What then?"

"I won't bite you."

"You don't know that—"

"—I know." I hit my chest with my fist. "I am in control of me. I know I won't bite you because I don't want to hurt you. I won't bite you, no matter how hard it is to control myself. If I have to restrain myself for days, I will. I would never hurt you. Ever. I'd rather die, Louie."

"Don't say that," she says, tears swimming in her eyes.

"It's true." I become desperate for her to understand just how deeply I care about her. "I'd do anything to keep you safe. I'll protect you with my life. I know—" I swallow, my own emotions bubbling up my throat. "I know we aren't mates, but why does that matter? I love you. That's all that matters."

"You really love me? Really?"

"I can't remember a day where I didn't." I drop my forehead against hers, then rub the tip of my nose against hers.

"What would we do? Where would we go?"

I smile, showing my fangs. "We can go anywhere. We can do anything. I don't care where we go as long as I'm with you, I'll be happy."

She blows out a nervous breath. "When?"

"Tomorrow night. We'll meet here. I've been saving for a few years now, to get us on our feet."

"You've saved for this? You've known all this time?"

"I planned my entire life the first time I saw you, Louie. None of this world makes sense if I don't have you by my side."

"Okay."

I blink at her, rearing back in shock. "Okay? Okay, okay? Or just okay?" I search her eyes for an answer.

"Okay, okay," she giggles. "Yes. Yes! Let's go. Let's run away. Let's be together."

I shout in victory, lift her off the ground, and spin her around. My cheeks hurt from how hard I'm smiling. Tears spring to my eyes.

A sharp pain hits my back, causing me to roar in agony.

"Aziel? Aziel! What's−" Louie peers over my shoulder, the gorgeous amber tones in her skin lose their vibrance. "Dad," she whispers in horror.

Her eyes drift to red when she tugs the dart from my shoulder before I set her down gently. I snag the dart from her and bring it to my nose, sniffing to see what he drugged me with.

Wolfsbane.

I snarl, shifting into my humanoid form, and push her behind me.

"Don't worry, Wolf. I didn't put enough wolfsbane in the dart to kill you, just enough for you to pass out, so I can get my daughter away from you."

"You'll..." My head begins to swim. "You'll never take

her from me."

"Dad, I love him! He's a good man, please."

"It's okay." I take her hand in mine just as I fall to my knees, the wolfsbane pumping through my veins. "We'll be okay."

"Aziel? No. Look at me. Aziel?" She shakes my shoulders, and just as I open my eyes, her dad is behind her.

"Louie," her nickname is gravel in my throat as I try to warn her.

"Let's go, Elouise. You're forbidden from seeing this fucking wolf again, do you understand?"

"Dad, no. Please, you don't understand," she sobs, fighting the hold he has on her, and she wins.

Elouise runs to me, falling to her knees, and she holds my hands. "I love you. I love you so much."

"Elouise, that's enough!" Master Durand, her dad, orders her.

"Dad, please. I love him." She presses her cheek against my chest and with the little strength I have left, I kiss the top of her head.

"You'll learn to love someone else who can't damn you to a forever sleep. I won't risk my daughter because her heart is tricking her." He wraps his arms around her, yanking her away, and her hand slips down my arm to grab me.

My claws do the same, only I rake them down her forearm to grab a hold of her. Blood fills the air, and four gashes appear on her flesh.

"Aziel!" she screams for me. "Aziel!" My name is a brutal, soul-wrenching cry from her chest.

"Elouise." My entire body sways, my vision unreliable either due to the tears or wolfsbane, I'm not sure.

Most likely both.

"Elouise," I repeat, falling to my hands and knees.

I drag my body across the solid rock of the cliff, willing to do anything to have one less inch between us as her father takes her away.

"I love you! Aziel, I love you. Always!"

"I love you," I roar to the sky with every ounce of strength I have left, ending my proclamation on a savage, grief-stricken howl.

"Aziel!" she cries for me again, cries for me to save her, but I can't.

I fall to the ground in a hopeless, worthless heap. Tears break free, rolling down my cheek to quench the dry rock. "Elouise," I rasp her name, my claws grinding against the stone.

A foot lands on my back, flattening me to the ground. I manage to look up to see her dad's second-in-command, Dahveed, staring down at me with a smile. He has another dart in his hand, rolling it between his fingers.

"You are a stupid dog if you thought for one minute you'd ever have a chance of a life with her. You promised you wouldn't bite her, and that was not your promise to make." Dahveed grabs me by my hair, yanking my head back and off the rock's surface. "If you loved her, you'd stay away. And when she's of age, I'm going to make sure she is mine. Maybe when I'm fucking her, she'll think of you. That's the closest you'll ever get to feeling her body."

I snarl, snapping my jaws at him, and he stabs me in the neck with the dart.

"That should be enough for you to come to your senses, pup. When you wake up, she won't be here, and she'll never be here waiting for you again. Pretend you never met her because you will not see her again." He shoves my head against the rock so hard, I hear bones break. "You're lucky to make it out of this with your life." He stands, kicking my side for good measure before his footsteps become quieter.

Until I'm left alone, my mind drifting into darkness.

There is only one thing on my mind.

What life do I have now?

Without her, my life has no meaning. I'd rather die

than live another day without Elouise. We're young, I know, but love knows no boundaries. Being young allowed us to live the rest of our lives together.

If I can't have that, if I can't have her, then I want nothing this world has to offer except death.

And I won't hesitate to do it myself.

Chapter One

AZIEL

Purgatory

There was a brief moment when I could hear my brother calling for me. I heard his voice, and I tried to get back to him, but the moment my body healed and I landed in Purgatory, his pleas stopped. And so did most of the pain. Finally.

I'm not sure how long it has been since I heard him but Purgatory has become a place of comfort and rage. It's become home. I'm not sure if I want to go back to the coven. I didn't belong there, even if I do crave their presence.

Here, I'm able to release every ounce of anger I've had inside me. Here, I can ight without consequence. Here, I can be myself.

Twisting my neck from left to right, it pops loudly, causing me to groan in relief when that one spot finally gives. I drop the rock in my right hand and my weapon in my left, massaging the nook of my shoulder.

Carrying Uri around on my back is really starting to irritate me. Life would be a little more convenient if

I were at home, and then Luna could give me one of her massages.

I could be with my brother, his wife, his kids...

"But I'm not, am I?" I whisper to myself, bending down to pick up Uri, my weapon that I made after spending my first night in this void of a place.

I pick up the rock again, laying Uri over my thighs, and begin sharpening the giant mandible.

Coming to Purgatory, it's kill or be killed, and if there is one thing I know I am good at, it's taking a life. I did it for fifteen years under a curse, and I remember every slash of my claws, every drop of blood on my tongue, and every scream.

My brother was eaten alive with guilt, and that is where we are different. I do not feel guilty, but it did harden me to a life I can't escape from.

I'm a fighter. I always have been.

I always will be.

My mind wanders as I drag the stone across the massive jawline of the creature I killed the first night in Purgatory.

Night One

"Anwyll?" I shout in the abyss, spinning and turning to see if anyone is there.

If anything is there.

"Aziel? Aziel!" Anwyll's voice is far away. It echoes.

"I'm here!" I yell to him. "Anwyll, I'm right here!" My eyes search the darkness, but no one is there. Only the skinny fingers of naked branches from the trees. "I'm here," I whisper, the words a frozen cloud on my next breath.

I still, a cold draft wrapping around me. The hair on

the back of my neck stands up, the brisk air traveling down my spine. I growl, calling onto my werewolf, I shift.

My entire body grows beyond my human skin. My flesh turns to a charcoal grey, hair sprouting on my arms, my clothes splintering from my body into piles of useless cloth on the ground, and I roar by tossing my head back.

I'm at least ten feet tall in this form, larger than most werewolves, and I have no idea why. My biceps bulge, my giant elongated feet plant against the ground, my heels in the air, and my pointed ears flicker when I hear the quietest of sounds.

A twig snapping. Nothing important.

Usually.

My eyes sharpen, sweeping the darkest shadows of the forest. A chitter echoes around me, the debris on the ground rustling. Slowly, I follow the shape disappearing behind the trees. I drop my chin, snarling loudly in warning.

The fear of the unknown is gone and replaced by the bloodthirsty beast I was born to be. If I'm honest, killing is easy, killing comes naturally, and there are days when I crave the warm liquid of blood dripping from my claws.

I've had barely controlled rage living inside me since I was a young werewolf. A low thunderous rumble is continuous in my core. The air changes into something thick and heavy making me work harder to breathe. It's as if all the air is being sucked from around me, forcing me to struggle.

I gasp, one of my clawed hands lying flat against my chest, feeling the wild beat of my heart in panic. My vision begins to blur, my peripheral darkening more with every passing second.

The chittering becomes louder above my wheezing, above the blood rushing through my ears, above the burning in my lungs as they fight for air.

Something cold wraps around my neck, gripping with vigor, with the promise to kill me. Gasping again, I inhale deeply, squeezing my eyes shut before opening them again.

What I see has my gaze widening. My entire body freezes in shock. The creature is double the size of me. It reeks of rotten flesh, its skin only made up of other beasts. Looking closely, the hide is stitched together with hair. The vision of him disappears just when I think I'm about to pass out, but I inhale again, allowing myself to see him.

It has no face, just a giant skull with oversized black eyes. The jaws are giant, and from what I can see, they have no teeth, just the sharpened inside edges of the mandibles. The bone is stained red from its past victories.

It chitters again, the sound reverberating loudly off the trees.

And I can't help but chuckle.

I snag its wrist in my hand, the need to kill flowing more strongly in my veins than my blood.

"It's going to take a lot more than that to kill me." I rip its hand away; the stitched meat falls from its arm in a disgusting plop to the ground. I try to break the bone, but even with all my strength, it won't crack.

The creature releases a high-pitched scream and I dive to the right, barely dodging its boney fingers as it slices its hand through the air. The ability to breathe is still difficult, so I try to run to gain some space so I can finally get some clarity.

It screeches again, the leaves and brush rustling as it chases after me. I'm able to get far enough to inhale a deep breath, finally able to string a thought together. The ground shakes with the creatures' every step. The air gets tighter as it catches up with me. I glance over my shoulder to see it reaching its boney hand out, the tips of its fingers grazing my back.

The pain is unlike anything I've ever felt. My skin

slices open like butter, the warmth of blood dripping down my spine. I roar, the simple gouges burn like wildfire. Every motion of my muscles causes more pain.

I drop to all fours, gaining speed as I sprint through the forest. The ground is wet, the mud trying to grip my hands and feet to slow me down. I leap over a fallen tree, the branches grazing my underbelly.

The air becomes heavy again, the oxygen being ripped away from me, and I stumble. Knowing I'm going to lose my footing and fall, I suck in the deepest breath I can before smacking against the ground. My shoulder hits first, taking the majority of my weight, and I do my best to hold my breath in, but naturally my mouth parts in a grunt.

I slide through the mud, my fur covered. The creature flips me onto my back, its inhumane jaws spreading, inhaling the air from around me. I choke, gasping for any trace of oxygen remaining.

Its breath makes my stomach turn, bits of flesh flying from its mouth as it screeches, my ears ringing from the high-pitched noise. My vision blurs. My strength dwindles.

The creature comes closer, hovering just above my mouth, and I feel the air in my lungs being sucked out.

Remembering I've been through too much to die like this, I use the last bit of strength I have and shove my hand through its chest. Bones in my hand break punching through the sternum, but regardless of the pain, I can't stop.

If I do, I die.

My growl morphs into a painful roar, wrapping my hand around its heart. With a snarl, I yank it free. The screeching slowly stops. The luxury of being able to breathe returns and I suck in a breath, getting the creature's rancid blood into my mouth.

"I told you it would take more than that, motherfucker." I squeeze the heart, the rotted grey organ oozes black goop that burns my skin.

I toss the organ to the right, wiping my hand in the mud just as the creature falls on me, blood pouring from the hole in its chest lands on my own. Howling in agony as my skin begins to burn, I shove the disgusting beast off me.

I lie there for a minute, sucking in the air this damn *thing* tried to take from me. Swallowing through the pain, I focus on breathing, taking long deep breaths to feed my oxygen-starved lungs. I lift my mangled hand; my pinky is bent to the left while my index finger is touching the top of my hand. Burns taint my wrist and forearm, the skin charred and raw.

I swallow thickly, thirst kicking into high gear. I don't even know where I am, so how am I supposed to find water?

"Okay, okay, you can do this," I chant to myself, gripping my broken index finger. "Fuck!" I shout, taking a deep breath in, I snap it in place, roaring from the pain of fixing an un-natural break. Before I can talk my-self out of it, I do the same to my pinky finger, watching as my healing abilities kick in.

I let out a relieved breath, the bones, joints, and knuckles fusing again. My skin becomes flawless again, the burns gone as if they never happened.

But they did.

I flex my hand to make sure I have the same mobili-ty as I did before.

"Fuck," I groan, having to work harder than usual to sit up from the mud.

When I do, I rub my neck and glance down at the creature I just killed somehow because what the actual fuck was that, and where the actual fuck am I?

I stand and shake my fur, mud slings from me and smacks against the trees. Shoving the creature with my foot, I flip him to his back and the flesh falls from his bones, showing nothing but his skeleton.

"What the hell are you?" I whisper, staring into the void of black eyes.

"That creature is called a suffogrim."

I spin, claws out, fangs bared as someone steps just a few feet away from me. A doomed-filled growl is a beast beating in my chest.

He lifts his hands. "I'm not here to hurt you. I'm here to help you."

"Help me? I'm in a fucking nightmare. Where the fuck am I? What is a Suffogrim? And who are you?" I narrow my eyes at him as he steps closer. He seems familiar. "Do I know you?"

"Briefly." He dips his hands in his pocket and pulls out a cigarette. "Want one?"

I stare at him in disbelief. "Do I want a fucking cigarette? Are you joking? I just had acidic blood burn me and you're asking if I want a cigarette."

"Well, it sounds like you need one. For the love of wolfsbane, man, you are nothing like Anwyll."

I snarl again, taking my battle stance. I cock my head. "How do you know my brother? Keep his fucking name out of your mouth. You don't know a thing about him." My understanding and my ability to think vanish. I launch myself at the stranger, needing to kill someone else.

Wings burst from his back and he easily dodges me. I slide through the mud and nearly hit a tree when I come to a stop. I turn around, the stranger gone in one instant then nose to nose with me in the next. With one hand, he snaps his fingers, and I am slammed against a tree trunk.

I snarl, doing my best to fight the invisible hold he has on me. Parts of him are stitched together, certain areas of his body are his beast while half his face is human. It's as if someone sewed people together to create him.

"You better calm down, Aziel, or Purgatory will be your death sentence." He strikes his finger against the tree and the tip catches fire.

He tucks a cigarette between his lips, lighting it.

"Now that we have that out of the way and you're…" he hums thinking of the word, "settled. I can talk and you can listen, so if I were you, I'd fucking cool your temper. You're in my territory now, where I thrive, and pissing off one of The Horsemen will kill you in the end. Be careful of your next words. Understand me?"

"Kill me, then," I urge him. "You think I'm afraid of death? I'm not. I've faced it and lived through it too many times to count, so do your worst."

The stranger's eyes come to life, flames overcoming his irises. "You should be afraid of me because I am Death. I have been the one to bring you to the edge and back. I have been the one to dangle the hope of dying to the curse of life. So you better listen to me, because if you don't, you will die."

I struggle against the tree, wanting to tear his head from his neck. "Why do you want to help me? You don't know me." I stop fighting against the sheer grip he has on me. There is no use. Whatever magic he holds, I'm not stronger than the power it brings.

He cocks his head, his pointed ears flicker, and his black hair sways in the breeze wafting the putrid scent of my dead friend over there.

"We've… met briefly but you were in a maddened state, if you remember. You might not considering your circumstances."

"My what?" I ask, confused, looking around to see nothing but darkness and dirt. "Where is Anwyll? Is he okay? Is he safe?"

"He is fine. It's you who isn't safe, Aziel. I'm Death, one of the Four Horsemen. This is my home when I can be here, and right now, I'm here to help you. Are you finally willing to listen to me?"

"Death…" I search my mind for him but I remember nothing. Regardless, I nod, yet I stay in my werewolf form.

The invisible hold he has on me fades and I'm freed. Tripping over the tree root, I right myself and put some distance between me and a man who could kill me with a wish.

"I'm in Purgatory?" I question him, glancing around my new prison.

"I'm afraid so." His footsteps thud against the ground before I find him next to me.

So much for that space I wanted.

Smoke fills the air as he drags on his cigarette. I usually hate the smell, but that Suffogrim reeks.

"Do you remember getting treatment for the sickness?"

I nod. "I do. I said horrible things to Anwyll, things I wouldn't want him to forgive me for. It's hard to forget my behavior." I give him a sad, forced smile.

"The medicine saved you, in a sense. Your physical body is there, at the estate, but your soul is here. You aren't dead but you aren't alive either, and because you're paranormal, you were brought here. Purgatory is a place filled with the worst of the worst. Some aren't bad, but this place changes all the time. It uses your deepest desires against you. It can make you believe you're seeing what you want when truly, you aren't seeing it at all. It's kill or be killed here."

"How do I get back to my body?"

"You have to find it yourself. You have to understand, there's only one way out of here, and that's only if you find an avisseus. Only they can cut the fabric of time and space to create a portal to send you home. They are born here, but they aren't easily seen. I haven't seen one in a few years."

"Years? How much time do I have?"

"You need to get to your body before the Lunar Moon. A Witch's Moon, when they can draw the most power from it. You know it as the full moon on Halloween. They only happen once every fifteen years. Purgatory receives all the blood of those who have died over those fifteen years. When the moon *here* turns red. The sky will rain blood for three straight minutes, bringing out the worst creatures. If you don't get out, before then, your soul will be stuck here. It's a power shift in the universe."

"And when is the next one?" Caution ripples through my voice.

"Three months."

"Three months? Three fucking months!" I shout at him. "How am I supposed to find this avisseus in that amount of time? In a place that changes and tricks my mind, that's not enough time."

"I can't interfere too much with your journey. I have to be careful, but I can give advice. Search for a place called The Graveyard, say Death sent you. Every win, you get a clue of where an avisseus is. I recommend taking the bone of the Suffogrim as a weapon. They are hard to destroy."

"It would help to know what those creatures are." I rub my eyes, wondering when Fate will finally give me a fucking break and let me die. "Three months until the Lunar Moon. I'm in Purgatory. I have to somehow survive this and–" Something in the wind has me sniffing the air. I know that smell.

Where do I know that smell? It reminds me of–

"The creature you killed– Aziel– you with me?"

I snap out of it, my nose still tingling from the scent. "Yeah, what are they?"

"The creature you killed is called a Suffogrim. They suffocate you by sucking all the oxygen from their surroundings. They are part grim reaper, so once you die and they get to take your last breath, they steal your soul. I say steal because they aren't my voids. Only my voids are given permission to handle souls to and from."

"What do they do with the souls?"

"Bet them, trade them, fuck them, whatever they want."

"And an avisseus? What do they look like?"

"A big skeletal bird with a giant silver beak. Many try to hunt it to grab the beak as there are rumors that the beak can open the portal back to where you need to be." He shrugs, flicking his cigarette. "I don't know if that's true or not."

"But you're Death. This is your home. I'm assuming you created all these creatures?"

He eyes me with humor before blowing out another cloud of smoke. "No, this was the place that I was given to rule. Everything is brought or born and somehow raised here. Avisseus's are rare. It's your best bet to get back to your body and don't forget The Graveyard. The dragon who runs it seems to have all the information." He flicks his cigarette away before stepping on it with the tip of his boot. "If you want to live, you'll kill."

He gives me a smirk before vanishing, leaving me alone and lost in this place.

"Killing comes easy. Won't have to worry about that," I say to no one but myself.

"Oh and—"

Startled, I drop down, kicking my leg out to trip the person who decided to sneak up on me. Death lands flat on his back with a groan.

"You're quick. Christ, I'm too old for this shit. You can't do that."

"Popping in and out like that is bound to get you killed one day."

"I'm Death. I don't die. Well, it's hard to kill me."

Instead of carrying on a conversation, I squat next to the Suffogrim, curling my lip in disgust at how horrible it smells.

"I'm glad you don't smell like death," I mumble, ripping the femur bone away from his body.

He scoffs. "Even I have standards."

With a grunt, I twist the creature's skull off. The skull is heavy, and I twist it in the air to get a good look at it.

The first thing I notice is how the blood no longer burns my skin.

"He's dead. His blood is no longer acidic."

I stare into the large, empty eye sockets, wondering how this thing has sight. Analyzing his remains, he has no teeth, but the mandible is sharp. I hiss when I slide my finger across the edge, my skin slicing open like butter. It heals in the next second, but my eyebrow quirks as an idea runs through my head.

I tilt my head up to speak to Death, "What did you come back for?"

"I wanted to warn you again. Be careful. This place fucks with your mind. It knows your innermost desires to use against you. Question everything, Aziel."

I nod in understanding. "Thank you for letting me know."

Death straightens as if he hears something calling him. "I need to go. Good luck, Aziel."

He is gone in a cloud of black smoke, once again leaving me alone. I don't mind being alone, but I am lonely. I've never been the kind of werewolf who didn't crave the company of someone else. Like now, the alpha inside me wants its pack.

Wants the coven.

Wants to be near his brother.

His family.

And I will do everything I can to get back, but if I don't, I know I'll be okay here. Killing is something I'm great at and if that's something I have to do for eternity here, I will. I've been a bloodthirsty beast once and I don't mind needing to be one again.

I search for anything I can use to tie the skull and femur together. The trees are all different. So many different kinds. Some are dead, black, with bare branches that resemble bones. Staring at them closely, they move, curling and stretching like fingers.

Other trees seem normal with full green leaves that are probably deceiving. I bet if I ate one, I'd die because, well, Purgatory.

"Cedar," I whisper when I see the tall trunk. I rush over, using the mandible to cut long strips off. When

I think I have enough, I sit down, lacing the ropes of strong fibers through the eye sockets, wrapping the natural strings around the femur until it's nice and tight.

I stand, testing the weight of my new weapon in my hand, then swing it against the trunk of the tree to see if the femur and skull stay intact.

They don't move. Grinning, I swing the weapon onto my shoulder, eyeing the darkness to see what my next move will be.

Presently—One week left to The Lunar Moon

I toss the stone I use in the leather pouch I made from a little nuisance of a creature called a Zowlyn. They seem small and innocent with a thick hide, but the little fuckers have large sharp fangs with red eyes and when they bite, their mouths triple in size and take a huge chunk of flesh from your body.

I sliced its head off with Uri, my weapon. It's short for Purgatory.

A hot, humid breeze drifts, and the scent of something amazing and wonderful teases my senses for the thousandth time. I try to put the delicious scent out of my head like Death said, knowing this place is fucking with what my heart wants and misses the most.

Elouise.

My beast whines inside me, wanting her, missing her to the point my chest tightens. Memories of us sneaking off to be alone together play like an old worn-out film in my head. She feels like a lifetime ago, moments that never happened.

Did she? Did I make her up in my head? Am I completely dead?

No. No, I'm not. She was real. My love for her was real– is real. Nothing will stop me from getting back to her. I'll find her.

That's my goal and if the attempt kills me, so be it, at least my soul will finally be at peace.

Fog rolls in, drifting through the eerie trees, and violence swells in my chest. The menacing fog curls around the branches, heading toward me slowly like a wave waiting to crash over me. Purgatory fog is much different than the kind in my dimension. Sometimes, the fog holds an electric charge or even the ability to burn you to death depending on if it's stormed recently.

Getting distance from it is hard, but doable. It tends to stick to the east side of Purgatory which means I try to get as far west as possible.

The rules of The Graveyard are simple. When the fog hits, the fights begin. Securing Uri over my shoulder in the sheath I made from Zowlyns, I drop to all fours in my werewolf form. It's quicker to run this way. The earlier I get to The Graveyard, the earlier I get to fight, and the more I win, the closer I get to getting out of here.

The part of me that loves the fight, that loves the kill, doesn't want to leave Purgatory. I fit in well here— too well.

And that's why I know I need to leave and get back to my body, even if I am torn. This place blackens the soul, poisoning it slowly until you have no choice but to stay. I fight the toxicity and it's the hardest fight of my life.

I leap over a fallen tree, grunting when I hit the ground. My claws sink into the ground, the dirt flicking behind me with every stride as I head to The Graveyard.

My air begins to turn from heavy and hard to breathe, to cold and thin. Every exhale leaves me in frozen clouds, frost inching its way up the whirling misshaped trunks of the trees. I can hear the crackling of ice as my surroundings begin to freeze. The leaves curl, the silence dangerous, and the chill seeps into my bones, trying to make its way into my soul.

A whoosh of air sounds from my left, and I slow to a stop, standing on my hind legs to my full height. I snarl, growling low in warning. I've made my name in this place and not many choose to fuck with me, but when they do, I make it worth their while by enjoying their pleas.

A vampire with red eyes comes out of nowhere, standing in front of me, hissing. His fangs are small, nothing compared to Master Monreaux's, proving how weak this vamp is.

My gaze quickly sweeps his body to analyze if he has any weapons. I'm not seeing any, but that doesn't mean they aren't there. Vampires have weapons of their own, the biggest ones are speed and strength. This one seems feral or rogue. His veins are ashen, traveling through his arms, neck, and face. His hair is patchy, showing balding spots on his scalp that are raw and oozing.

He must have been bitten by a spidorion. Half spider, half scorpion, and one hundred percent from Hell itself. These creatures are in for the hunt. They bite and their venom doesn't hit you right away. It's a slow build and the longer your heart beats, the more the venom spreads. Spidorions can smell the infected and slowly hunt them until their prey is paralyzed from head to toe. Then, they wrap their victims in a thick layer of webbing, stab their chests with their scorpion tails, and take their meals to their nest where they feast.

Sick, sadistic bastards.

I'll be doing this vampire a favor when I kill him, so he won't have to go through the pain and torture of the spidorions process.

The vampire slashes his extended grey talons at me. I lean back, missing his strike. He continues to come at me, grappling the air, throwing his hands one after the other in hopes of getting me.

If he does, I'll be as good as dead too, spidorions venom will enter my bloodstream. All I have to do is bide my time until he gets too tired from the venom.

I dodge right, then left, then duck, using the opportunity of being low and whip Uri from the sheath. I slash Uri through the air, slicing the vampire's legs at the knee.

His screams are loud and piercing. If I weren't tainted by so much death, I might have cared, but this poor vampire crawls on the ground to continue his attack on me.

With one final blow, I take his head off, his body falling with a hard thump against the ground. His head rolls a few feet away and the red in his irises fades as his existence ceases. His blood is black, killing the leaves on the ground from the venom in his bloodstream.

I wipe Uri on the ground, making sure his blood is off my weapon before sheathing it again. Looking around for spidorions, I begin to sprint away from the crime before they arrive.

The Graveyard calls my name.

Yet so does the breeze that holds the tantalizing scent of Elouise.

Chapter Two

ELOUISE

I can't remember how I got to this place, and I know I'll never find a way out. It's the same with most of the creatures here. Sure, there are rumors of finding a way out, but no one has been able to get out of Purgatory.

The best anyone can do is find others to live out this odd existence with and just come to the realization that this is our home now. There's no leaving. There's no escaping.

Anyone who believes otherwise, well, I wish them the best when they realize their expectations are unrealistic.

Or maybe it would be best if they just get themselves killed from existence.

I rub my head at the dark intrusive thought. I don't mean that. No one deserves that. Everyone deserves to hold onto a sliver of hope. Mine disappeared a long time ago and when I feel it creep inside again, I remind myself that hope dies, and all that is left is realism.

Reality tells me there is no hope.

I sit on the edge of the cliff, the view somewhat

reminding me of where I grew up. As I stare into the blood-red horizon, the onyx sky bleeding into the crimson trying to mix. It's the closest thing to a sunset I'll ever see. I shouldn't find such beauty in it considering the red is blood waiting to rain down on us, blood from all who have died and are here now.

The wind blows the familiar scent of my teenage love, pulling on my heartstrings, and my eyes fill with tears. I rub my chest to ease the ache, knowing he isn't real, knowing there is no world, no universe, no dimension where I will ever see him again.

Aziel.

I squeeze my eyes closed when the scent becomes stronger as if he is standing right next to me. I do something I shouldn't, I revel in the scent, allowing this place to seep further into my heart to mess with my head more.

At first, I cared, but after being here for so long, I've learned to ride the waves of chaos.

I inhale, smiling when not only do I smell him, but the phantom touch of a hand on my cheek has me leaning.

"*Louie*," the depth of his voice carries in the wind causing goosebumps to arise on my skin.

I hate that nickname, but I'd give anything to hear him say it in person. I'd give anything to feel his touch one more time.

I'd give my existence to experience him one more time.

"*I miss you*," the hellish grip this place has on me whispering one of the many things I've been craving to hear from Aziel.

Tears well in my closed eyes when I swear, I feel the warmth of his breath on my cheek, the tease of the tips of his talons lightly tickling my neck, and his lips brushing against mine.

My heart stutters, forcing me to open my gaze to my life without him, this place tricking my mind successfully for the thousandth time thinking he'd be standing in front of me.

He isn't.

And he never will be.

I wonder every day if he is okay, if he is alive and well, if he is mated and in love. God, the thought of him giving his love to anyone but me feels like I'm driving my own dagger into my chest.

That love is meant for me. It's for me to experience, to feel, to touch, to laugh, and to cry.

Does he have kids? If so, how many? Where does he live? Is he happy?

"Elouise?"

I'm startled out of my thoughts, turning sharply to the left and tossing one of my daggers through the air.

"Woah!" My friend Iggy, short for Ignatious, dodges out of the way.

My knife lodges in a nearby tree, the amber handle shining in the low light of the scarlet sky, reminding me of Aziel's eyes.

Everything reminds me of him, and it only makes me ache for him more.

"Iggy," I blow out a breath. "You scared me."

"You? I'm the one that nearly had a knife in his head."

I point my other dagger at him. "You would have lived." I roll my eyes. "So dramatic."

He snags my weapon out of the tree, strolling over until he takes a seat next to me. Grabbing the sharpened side, he flips the blade around to give it back to me.

"Thanks." I tuck it in the sheath.

"You let this place get to you again, didn't you?"

I blow out a breath, narrowing my eyes at the "sunset" before nodding. "Every now and then I do," I admit.

"You have to stop doing that. Every time you do it—"

"—I get one step closer to losing my mind, unable to decide between what is real and what isn't," I finish for him. "I know."

"Then stop acting like you don't. I understand you miss him but—"

I blur in the blink of an eye, pressing my freshly sharpened dagger against the pulse of his neck. Iggy isn't a vampire, he is a bear shifter, so it wouldn't take much for me to take the little life he has here.

Even if he is my best friend.

His skin doesn't burn from the silver like mine does or like a werewolf's.

My eyes flip red, my fangs lengthen, and every part of me wants to kill him for talking about Aziel. "How dare you speak of him when you have no idea who he is." The hiss that leaves me is lethal and it causes his Adam's apple to bob as he swallows. "I do not simply miss him. He is not a pet. He is not food. He is more, so much more. He is a craving that can never be satisfied. He is the only one who has ever sated my hunger. He isn't someone I simply miss. He is someone who is an intricate part of my very being and if you can't respect that, I have a quick solution to what can." I press the dagger slightly harder against his neck until the scent of blood carries through the breeze.

I drop my knife, allowing his skin to heal so the smell of his blood doesn't have creatures clawing their way from the darkness to get a taste.

He raises his hands in surrender. "I'm sorry, Elouise. I didn't mean to upset you. I worry about you. If you lose your mind, it's me who will have to kill you. I don't have it in me."

I nudge his elbow. "You wouldn't have to. I'd kill my-self before I became a burden to you. I'd never ask you to do that for me."

We fall into a lull of silence, it isn't uncomfortable or anything, just quiet. Our legs swing over the cliff as we stare into the blood-ridden horizon. It's at that moment more blood enters its system. The ominous clouds swirl, the red becomes brighter, sparks begin to fly, and I make believe they are shooting stars.

Because the truth is just too hard to stomach.

"I know you loved him but I'm wondering if he was your fated mate."

I shake my head, then lift a shoulder. "I wouldn't know. We were just kids, Iggy. We didn't know if we were fated mates. We were ready to run off together, did I ever tell you that?"

He gasps. "No! You would have run off with a man who wasn't your mate?"

I smile, biting my lip, remembering the night Aziel asked me. "We weren't allowed to be together. His bite would have put me in a coma, so vampires and were-wolves never mated. It was too risky." I tuck my hair behind my ear, my cheeks hurting from how hard I'm smiling. "He asked me to be with him, to run away and never look back, and I agreed."

"So what happened? Why didn't you?"

"My father found us at our secret hiding spot. He was the Master of the coven and shot Aziel with wolfsbane. I was dragged away while I watched him fall unconscious." My smile turns into a frown, those valu-able tears begin to run down my face. "I saw him try to crawl to me. To get to me. I saw him drag his body across rocks, his claws extended, his roars of pain echoing for me, and that was the last time I ever saw the werewolf I loved. We were only kids, seventeen. We didn't know anything about the world, you know? We just knew we wanted to be together. That's all that mattered to us." I pick the lint off my shorts with one hand, wiping my tears with the other.

"It's the hearts that we want most that always cause us the most pain," he states, not looking at me.

His jaw ticks as if he is reliving a memory of his own. I loop my arm through his, place my head on his shoulder, and point.

"This cliff is somewhat similar to the spot Aziel and I would sneak away to. The view was– well– prettier than this."

"No," he teases. "You mean the view you had didn't have dying trees that like to reach out and snag you? Or creatures that have crawled out of Hell itself? No kidding? What was that like?"

I chuckle. "It was a little different, yes. The sunset and sunrise always seemed so close, like we could reach out and touch it. Mountains as far as the eye could see with the greenest of nonviolent trees," I add, igniting a small laugh from Iggy.

"That sounds nice. What was Aziel like? You've only mentioned him in passing a few times."

I sit up, breathing in and releasing it slowly, trying to think of the best way to describe the only man who has ever made me want to risk my life for love.

"He had your typical werewolf qualities of an alpha. Massive in size–"

"–Hot." Iggy winks.

"–So hot," I giggle before continuing.

"Brave, courageous, daring..." I trail off, his scent teasing the bottom of my nose again. I hold in a sob. "Funny. He was so funny, but at the same time, so serious. Protecting me was all he cared about. He loved his brother too. He would have done anything for Anwyll."

"We love a family man. Okay, keep going." Iggy crosses his legs, places his fist under his chin, and bats his lashes at me playfully.

"He was a leader. He wanted what was best for everyone. And Aziel was..." I try to find the words, the big heavy emotions washing over me. "Compassionate and loving." I glance up to the sky, hoping it will help dry my eyes. Alas, it doesn't work. "He was the kind of guy to love you first and want to kill you next. He'd give anything to protect the ones he loved. He'd give his life. He was my best friend, and I think my biggest issue is I have no idea what happened to him, Iggy." I cut my eyes to him, letting my tears show.

His bear's eyes turn to their brilliant yellow, hide fur sprouting on his arms before he holds them out. His omega nature senses my distress and this time, I lean into him, allowing the peace he exudes to wrap around my grieving heart.

"What if he is dead," I turn, kneeling between his legs while gripping his worn, stained shirt. "What if I'll never know if he had a good life? I need to know Iggy." I clutch onto him, burying my nose into his neck.

His blood doesn't entice me, yet the calming low purr coming from his chest helps me catch my breath.

"And I can't because I'm here. I have no answers. I can't keep living like this. I can't be here day in and day out, missing him, and thinking he is right near me. I can't anymore with the phantom touches, words, and scents. It's driving me mad, Iggy. I'm going mad—" I whisper, sniffling when I realize just how true that is.

Iggy rubs my back, the purr becoming more intense, wrapping my insides in a tight hug too.

"We will figure it out. No matter what, okay? I'm here for you. We will find your answers somehow. Maybe we can go to The Veiled Library. Sometimes creatures slip through—"

"It's too risky." I lean away, wiping my cheeks with a small, appreciative smile. "Thank you for wanting to do that for me."

"You're my best friend. I'll do anything for you, even if you did place a dagger to my neck. Rude, by the way," his bear huffs at me instead of Iggy.

My mouth parts. "Did your bear just huff at me?"

"He may have. He is a needy bitch, you know this." He swirls his finger up and down. "I mean, duh."

I stand, offering him my hand, when the temperature falls. I look up, hearing Iggy get to his feet, my sights searching the trees with what is making me uneasy.

My eyes widen when I see what it is.

"Fog," I whisper in horror.

"Fog never comes this far south, not here. It also means the fights are happening, if we can make it."

"Iggy. Elouise! We need to move before the fog hits. We can't risk staying," Flynn, the unspoken leader of our little group, shouts at us from across the valley. "Let's go to The Graveyard. It's the one spot we won't have to worry about."

I nod, giving him a wave to let him know we heard him.

I hold onto Iggy, taking a few steps back to jump over the valley. I only need a running start.

He latches onto me. "I really hate this part."

I grin, not giving him a warning before sprinting and jumping. Iggy shuts his eyes, but I don't. While I'm running at a speed most can't see, I can see everything.

I look down, the valley becoming rockier the further into the dark it goes. Rumors say this crack leads to Hell, but no one has ever been willing to find out.

Me included. Being in Purgatory is close enough.

We land with ease. Iggy, like always, sways before finding his feet.

"It doesn't get better. Every single time," he murmurs.

"Come on. We have to catch up with the group. They will leave us."

"Why do we bother going with them? You know they are going to try to sway you to fight like they always do. What if you agree? What if I have to be there without you?"

I bring him to my side, pressing my head on his shoulder. "I'll never say yes. When was the last time we watched a fight? We usually just explore around the area. Though, it has been a while since we have been at all. Even when the fog hits, we have traveled too far away to make it to The Graveyard. Maybe this time we can actually watch a fight."

"It's not like we will ever find out enough information to get out of here. Someone from the group always dies besides Flynn."

"I think the information is fake. It's a way to get creatures killed and for the ones who run Purgatory to get paid. Why would we get to win a way out when the entire point is to keep us here?"

He grips my arm and tugs me to a stop. "Then why risk it at all? One day Flynn will throw you into that arena because of how skilled you are. You and me, we can break away from the group. It's always us anyway. I'm okay with losing them if it means you're safe. Please, Elouise."

His big bear eyes swim with tears, pulling on my heartstrings.

"You want us to strike out on our own?"

Iggy nods, and for some reason, I feel relief. I don't trust the others in the group. They would use Iggy for leverage if it weren't for me. Iggy is worth so much because he's a male omega. The demons here would have too much fun if given the chance. I wouldn't put it past them to use him to get out of Purgatory.

"Okay," I say, happily, turning us southwest instead of tagging along with the group. "But I still want to see the fights. The smell of blood is something I need."

"When was the last time you fed? I didn't want to say anything, but you seem... different."

I've felt different too. The taste for blood lessens every day, but my need for it becomes stronger. It makes no sense. Blood has been impossible to stomach.

"I'm fine. I promise. While we walk, I'll look for a razorhopper, okay?"

He curls his nose. "God, those can't taste good. They have silver for teeth for fuck's sake."

"Exactly." I lift my dagger into the air by the handle. "I need more blades. They taste awful, but they do what they need to, and I get a weapon out of it."

"If the damn thing hops on me again and its little

metal claws scratch me all over, I'm burning you at the stake."

"I'm trembling in my boots, Iggy."

"As you should. I'm fucking vicious."

"So scary," I pretend even if he believes what he is saying.

"One swipe of my paw—"

I mouth quietly, knowing what he will say, "—I will fuck you up."

"I need to make sure I don't get on your bad side."

"That's right. One roar from me and—"

I lift my hand in the air to silence Iggy, scenting something that has me peering west.

"What is it?" he whispers, freezing in his tracks to not make a sound.

My heart lurches forward and immediately my mind thinks of Aziel. This scent is his but stronger. I feel his energy.

It's him.

Or the more realistic answer, I am losing my mind, and now this torture chamber is becoming better at yanking all my desires to the surface.

What's sad is that I no longer care. Put me out of my misery.

I'm unable to do it myself.

Chapter Three

AZIEL

"Aziel, My Junkyard Dog returns. My undefeated champ," says Scorder or "The Lucky" as others call him.

He's a dragon, so he loves to hoard his winnings from these fights. There aren't a lot of money-making opportunities here in Purgatory, as one can imagine, but when there is, everyone shows up.

For instance, the fights at The Graveyard. Everyone in Purgatory comes to them. Either for entertainment or in hopes that they can be a winner so they can earn a few eerie. At least, that's what everyone in this fucking place calls the black matte coins with an avisseus on one side.

And Death on the other.

I growl in warning, wrapping my humanoid hand around Scorder's throat, and for the hell of it, I give it a good squeeze. "Do not." I seethe through tight teeth. "Call me a dog."

He gasps, slapping at my hand. "It is a compliment."

"Find another compliment or I'll kill you too, Scorder."

"So mean to the one who gets you closer to freedom."

I snarl, smashing him against a tree, then lean down until our noses almost touch. "Freedom seems hard to come by. I'm starting to think you're leading all of us on, so your hoard gets larger."

Releasing him, I take a step back, allowing him the space he needs to catch his breath.

He coughs, rubbing his throat. With every huff, sparks and smoke fly from his mouth in annoyance.

"I'm doing everyone a favor by allowing these fights. Everyone—" he rethinks his words. "Ehh, okay, not everyone because let's be realistic, in order to win, everyone else has to die. It isn't easy earning freedom from here, Aziel. Either fight for it or watch, resigning yourself to be here forever. Those are your choices."

I really fucking hate him because he isn't wrong.

Grunting, I dig into my bag and grab my mask. It's a skull from one of my first kills at The Graveyard. I don't know what creature he was. I didn't care to ask. He came at me with red eyes, antlers to the sky, and charged me in hopes of sinking those sharp points through my chest.

Luckily, I was stronger, quicker, and had much more experience in fighting to kill. I ripped his antlers from his head, broke his back, and watched as he faded from existence. All that was left in his wake were his bones, additions to the many others that pad our feet as we fight.

I grabbed his skull and decided it would be my shield, a way for me to be the killer I was with the warlock who cursed me. The skull allows me to sink into that headspace again, watching everything happen in front of me from the inside of the mask.

Scorder cracks his neck and smiles, spreading out his arms as if he is a showman. "How many fights do you think you have in you, Junkyard?"

I close my eyes and take a deep breath, retreating

to the killer I have been for most of my life. "As many as needed," I reply, my voice deepening while I push my humanity a little bit further inside myself. "And don't call me Junkyard. You better find a different name when announcing me."

"I've been calling you that all day in my head! That only gives me two minutes, Aziel."

"Then you better think better than you fuck, Scorder." I check to make sure the skull is secure on my face before heading to the ring.

There's already a good crowd forming, leaning against the bones that make the ribcage arena. It's a good size, enough to run around, back away, or fuck with your opponent. Scorder loves a show, and he expects every fighter to put one on.

The bleachers are made of dirt, piled to create different levels. Watchers are already filling the seats. So many different creatures are waiting to see who dies from existence. I'm not sure if that's sick and fucked up, or sad.

There's nothing else to do here in Purgatory but survive. Entertainment is few and far between these days. You have to take it when you can get it. Even if it means watching someone fade away from the universe.

I stop in my tracks when Elouise's scent teases my heart. This fucking place using her against me has me murderous. I narrow my eyes, searching the shadows of the trees, and the movements of the branches because maybe she's here in the darkness Purgatory casts.

I don't want that for her. I don't want her here, trapped, fighting for her life, and miserable. I want her happy in the real world. Purgatory isn't a place for someone as beautiful as Elouise. Her soul is too bright to be tainted by the evil Purgatory brings and creates.

Selfishly, I'd spend eternity here if it meant getting to hold her. Selflessly, Elouise deserves to be alive, laughing, and living in a world surrounded by life, not death. I want her to be in love with a mate. I want her to have children like she always talked about having. I want the life she dreamed for herself.

Even if it means I'm not a part of it.

"Fuck you, dog! I hope he rips your tail from your ass and fucks you with it."

I'm just about to open the cage where I wait to be called into the ring when I hear the person disrespecting me. My entire body tenses and I turn to look over my shoulder, noticing a man staring at me with black eyes and a hateful expression.

"Dogs like you deserve to be put down," he continues with a hiss.

I sniff the air, still inhaling Elouise, and if anything, that only pisses me off more because her scent should never be tainted by creatures like this guy. Facing him has me grinning behind my mask. He is bald, a burned symbol on the top of his head to show how he was banned from his pack and disgraced.

No pack would take him in with a mark like that. He must have done something truly unforgivable.

Which makes what I'm about to do so much easier.

A low growl thunders in my chest. I squat, then launch myself in the air, and land directly in front of him. My fist barrels into his throat, I snag his cervical spine and rip it out.

"Dogs like me don't get put down." I spit on his corpse before it fades away, leaving nothing but his bones behind.

His spinal cord is in my hand, giving me a morbid idea to attach it to Uri somehow. Weapons aren't allowed in the arena. It's body against body and whoever has the strongest, wins.

The crowd murmurs before most of the spectators slide from the dirt bleachers to make their way to Scorder.

They are placing their bets.

Scorder looks up at me, sending me a wink as he smiles and takes money from his audience.

Cracking my neck, I sneer, stomping back over to the cage. Bones crack under my weight with every step, the sky darkening even more as the trees move closer together to create a canopy.

Opening the door to the cage, the hinges creak, and I step inside, knowing damn well this could be the last fight of mine if I lose. Part of me thinks it wouldn't be so bad being wiped from the memory of the dimension I'm from.

Then, I think of my brother, of our new pack, our new Alpha taking a chance on us, and I know I can't do that to Anwyll. Thinking of the ones I love forgetting me is a different type of pain. It creates a void in my chest, one that fear creates and hope tries to fill.

Hope tells me I'll win this fight and I'll be a step closer to going home.

Fear tells me there is a good chance I'll die.

Then, there is Elouise, and wherever she is, whatever she is doing, whoever she is with, I don't want her to forget me. I want her to remember me in every detail and every moment of her life.

When she kisses another— I growl at the thought of another man's lips on hers— does she think of me? When she's lying in bed, waiting for something amazing to start her day, is she waiting for me? When she's outside looking at the stars, does she remember when we used to stargaze for hours some nights? Flirting, stealing touches, wishing things could be different.

Does she miss me when she thinks of me?

My heart slams against my chest, and I catch myself on the fence made of bone, curling my fingers from the need exploding in my chest.

I can barely breathe and when I try to inhale a deep breath, all I taste is Elouise. Her aroma sinks its way into my lungs. My head becomes dizzy. My cock thickens and I don't even try to hide my want or need.

Fuck.

This place is really getting the best of me.

I lean against the cage, grip the wall with both of my hands, and hang my head. My shoulders rise and fall as I try to regain my composure. My growls become louder. Saliva drips from my fangs. The hunger for blood coats my tongue.

And the need to claim her sends me over the edge.

That's impossible.

She isn't my mate. I would have known before, wouldn't I? Maybe I love her like Severide loved his mate who passed away.

I toss my head back and roar, releasing the pent-up energy, hoping somewhere, Elouise hears me. The bones rattle together from the vibrations of my howl.

Every breath that escapes me is loud and filled with fury. My claws extend and my muscles bulge as I change into my werewolf form. My cock jerks, a bead of liquid dripping from the slit and lands in the middle of someone's skull.

I probably killed them too and now their bones will be haunted by me.

Something about that turns me on even more.

"Hey, are you ready to fight? I have a cobra shifter that's getting antsy."

Scorder slaps me on the shoulder, his touch sends a rage of poison through my muscles. I whip my head to the right to look at him, eyes blazing amber, and he takes a step back.

"Don't fucking touch me," I warn, holding myself back from attacking him, from slicing my claws into his skin and feeling his warm blood drench my hands.

"What's going on? I've never seen you like this before a fight. Are you good?"

"This place is fucking with me. I'm fine. I just need a minute—" I growl again when I get a stronger whiff of Elouise's scent. I tilt my head back and groan, my orgasm threatening to explode from me. It's as if her scent is being stroked over every inch of my body, licking and sucking me in all the right places.

"Fucking hell. You can kill the guy just by swinging that—," he mumbles, looking to and from my cock.

I narrow my eyes at him. "Stop looking at my dick," I bite.

He scoffs, throwing his arm out in the direction of my cock. "It's literally right there. Get yourself together. It would be a little weird to fight for your life with an erection."

"You don't think I know that? You're very close to being my next kill if you don't leave me the fuck alone, Scorder."

He raises his hands in surrender. "I have a lot of money on you. Don't fuck this up for me because your mind is somewhere else."

I growl, taking a step in his direction. "Don't threaten me. It won't end well for you."

He has to look up at me to meet my eyes, a bead of sweat threatening to fall from his temple. "Just win this fight, Ripper."

"I always win." The fog of needing Elouise fades with her scent. I'm able to take a deep breath to right my mind and body.

I unhook the straps that hold Uri and place it on the bench. "I'm ready," I tell Scorder, staring at my opponent across the ring.

The annoying menace slaps his hands together, rubbing them like an evil villain. His eyes morph into swirling rings of fire, smoke billowing from his nose like a chimney.

"You better fight for your existence." He opens the cage door, stepping into the ring, and raises his hands in the air to get the crowd going.

They scream in excitement, drumming the bones with sticks or stones, anything they have brought to sound the alarm.

When Scorder gets in the middle of the arena, he

blows a ring of fire around himself. The flames are tall, nearly covering the betting man in the middle of The Graveyard.

The crowd chants his name, "*Scor-der. Scor-der. Scor-der.*"

A microphone is lowered in the middle, the cord made from an elephant shifter's trunk, and the mic itself is made from a mocking horned goat. The horns naturally enhance voices.

Mocking horned goats mimic everything you do and say. I've killed a few for meat while being in Purgatory and that damn goat had me believing I was about to kill myself.

I hate the bastards.

"Welcome to The Graveyard!" Scorder announces, throwing a ball of fire into the air. The flames hit the edge of the ribcage, shocking the crowd from the fire getting so close to them, yet they cheer for more. "Thank you. Thank you. I appreciate you all being here. When the fog comes, you all never disappoint to show up!"

The creatures shout victoriously as if they are doing Scorder a favor. He could sell fake gold to his own kind and live to tell the tale.

"To the left, we have a deadly opponent. He slithers when you aren't looking. He'll strike when you least expect it. He will crush your body with his form and swallow you whole. Make some noise for Crusher, our cobra shifter!"

The crowd goes wild, shaking the cage or drumming the bones. Roars echo, fueling my werewolf.

"And to the right, we have our champion. Ten times in a row he has fought for his existence and won!"

Instead of cheers, I get silence, and I tilt my head down, grabbing the fence made of vertebrae, and snarl.

"He's massive for a werewolf. Standing just above ten feet tall, weighing in at one thousand one hundred pounds, a beast no one would ever dare to go up against. A creature with fangs that would rip you in half before you had a moment to think. A monster so vicious, that not even I would risk my life. Please give a loud welcome for the one, the only... Ripper," Scorder bellows, throwing his arm out to my cage.

I roar, letting him know I'm ready.

He speaks into the horn one last time. "Opponents, you know the rule. Fight–"

The crowd finishes his slogan, shouting, "–For your existence!"

The microphone is reeled up and away from Scorder. The cages automatically swing open to reveal the arena and I take a step forward, standing tall on my hind legs.

"Good luck," he whispers to me like he always does as he runs by me.

I plant my feet in the pit of bones. Femurs, skulls, and ribs crunch under my weight. I spread my arms out, stare at my opponent, and roar so loud, that the dead under me rattle.

Crusher slithers out of his cage, hissing at me. The hood behind his head expands wide, giving the illusion that he is bigger. His forked tongue flicks out, his pupils turning to slits.

My humanity fades, ceasing to exist, and all that is left is rage.

Rage for losing my mind. Rage for what I've done to my brother. Rage for Elouise.

So much fury for a love that will never know how much it deserves to be had.

Nothing else matters but killing.

And if I'm not careful, I'll kill everyone at the arena. Without hesitation. Without regret.

I'll turn and walk away drenched in their blood.

Crusher slithers around me, his scales dry and cracked. A few spots are raw and bleeding causing me to wonder how long he has been in Purgatory fighting for his life.

I have no mercy or empathy for beings I do not love. I find they take too much out of the little I have left of my soul.

And I will protect the bit that is left because that is saved for Elouise. I refuse to let anyone take that from me.

If it's between me and him, it will be him who dies.

I look around, eyeing the crowd, letting the energy rush over me. Closing my eyes, I listen to the threat. He is fast but loud, and that's the only leverage I need to have.

He strikes again and I lean to the right, missing the heavy weight of his tail. Crusher slashes his arms out in front of him, hoping his claws scratch the expanse of my chest.

Two fingers manage to dig into my flesh, slicing me from my right shoulder to my left hip.

Roaring, I leap into the air and land on his back, dragging my claws down until five long grooves spill blood. The snake hisses in agony, his tail wrapping around my torso. He tightens the hold, constricting me until I can't breathe.

He grins thinking he has the upper hand.

Leaning down, I sink my teeth into his tail, biting down until I feel my bottom row of teeth clink against my top. I rip the chunk from his body and spit it out, allowing the blood to stain my fur and drip down my chin.

He screeches, tossing me through the air. I smack against the ribcage of the arena, and it knocks the breath out of me. I roll to my stomach, lifting myself on all fours, circling Crusher.

Blood pools under what is left of his tail. The color from his skin fades but the anger becomes brighter in his eyes, spilling onto me like molten lava. He can't flick his tail anymore so he has to count on his upper body.

Slashing his body through the air, his mouth opens to swallow me whole. Catching his jaws in time, my right hand grips the top while the left holds onto the bottom, spreading his jowls wide. My entire body shakes, every muscle working harder than they ever have to beat the snake's strength.

He inches closer, the stench of his breath swaying the fur on my cheek.

Then the scent of the one I love possesses my body when I inhale, fueling me to end this fight. The thought of her, her beauty, her soft fucking skin against mine, her smile, gives me everything I need.

I rip his head in two with a howl so loud, I wouldn't be surprised if my brother could hear me on the other side. I keep hold of the top half of his head while his body drops to the bed of my victories before him.

Blood drenches me and with shaky hands, I snap his fang from his mouth before Purgatory takes everything but his bones from him, wiping Crusher from existence.

I gasp for air, staring at what's left of my trophy. Raising the fang in the air, the crowd cheers for my win and Scorder runs to me with a big smile on his face.

The microphone lowers again for him. "Creatures and Creaturess', I give you your champion! He has earned fifty eeries and the last location of the avisseus."

I roll my eyes at the last part. Every time he gives me a clue, it leads me nowhere. I will take the eeries and go to Purgatory Pins to grab a beer though.

I allow the attention, slowly analyzing the crowd and waving every so often in appreciation.

Elouise's scent becomes overwhelming. Automatically, I search for her in the dirt bleachers, even though I know she isn't there. The uncontrollable need to have her debilitates me.

"Here." He hands me my winnings. "Meet me in my office in a few minutes for that location, Ripper." He winks, staring at the fang in my hand.

"I thought we had more fights after this one?"

"The others backed out," he grins, then shakes his finger at me. "And there will always be other fights."

I don't say anything as I walk away, my mind becoming a tangled mess. The crowd's murmurs blur together, my vision darkens around the edges, and her fucking scent becomes stronger.

It's as if she's right next to me, her cheek leaning against my shoulder, her giggles sounding in my ears, her breath tickling the fur on my arm, and her eyes peer up at me, golden as the sun.

With a frustrated grunt, I strap Uri onto my shoulder, wanting to get this blood off me and catch some sleep, maybe then Purgatory will give my heart a rest from playing tricks on me.

"Aw, we missed the fight!" a deep yet feminine voice pouts from the distance.

"It's okay, Iggy. There's always next time."

Elouise.

And that's what ruins any control I have on my beast. Hearing her voice so close sends me spiraling into the same madness that got me here in the first place.

I fall to all fours and run towards the sweet melody of the song I've only heard in my dreams for the last fifteen years.

Chapter Four

ELOUISE

A familiar scent hits me like a brick wall, an aroma I have only been getting teases of since I was seventeen, sneaking off with a werewolf I had no business sneaking off with.

The smell burns into my skin like the cold on a frozen winter day, burrowing into my bones to make itself at home.

I follow the mouth-watering scent, turning where the wind is blowing it the strongest.

"What is it?" Iggy asks, tugging at my elbow to bring me to a stop.

"I smell him again. This time, it's overwhelming." My eyes roll to the back of my head as I inhale, and my fangs drop, preparing to sink into meaty f esh.

Only this time, the scent is different. It's stronger. My body reacts. My blood heats. My want becomes unbearable.

"Beloved," I whisper in shock and immediate lust.

"Beloved?" Iggy gasps, snagging my arm tight. "But here? In Purgatory? Is that possible?"

I shake my head, opening my eyes to a tint of

red when I see a massive werewolf with a skull mask running toward us on all fours. He must be the biggest werewolf I've ever seen. The muscles in his shoulders flex with every leap he takes, his claws fling dirt into the air, his growls awaken goosebumps on my skin, and his eyes glow a brilliant shade of amber.

I know those eyes. I know that body, those muscles, the ones working so hard to get to me. I've memorized his form in my dreams, the way he moves, his voice, and that's how I know this place is using him against me.

He's in physical form now.

I'm going mad.

I shove Iggy so hard, he flies twelve yards through the air. Slipping my daggers free from their holsters, I somersault to the right, just missing the massive paws of this beautiful wolf.

I know this can't be Aziel. He *can't* be here. He isn't real. Purgatory is pulling a sick joke, bringing every wish and every want to life. Every desire is staring me in the face, every dream, every tear I have ever shed, is snarling at me.

The Purgatory's version of Aziel turns to Iggy, snapping his jaws at my best friend.

"You motherfucker. Don't you dare go after him when you know it's me you want." I crouch, preparing to fight the demon embodying my one true love. I know it's him. He's the only one who can make me feel this way.

Hopeful. Beautiful. Strong. Resilient.

Aziel has always brought out the best in me, but I refuse to let this monster take the best *from* me.

I even feel the pull of my soul to him. The one that binds us together for eternity. Is it real? Would this mean if I were in his dimension, that we would be together? That we were meant to be?

Twirling the daggers in my hands, I launch myself at him, twisting through the air over his impressive form. The freshly sharpened blades slice between his shoulders, the flesh burning from the silver, and he shouts a call to the sky in agony, reaching for the bleeding wound.

The blood licks its fingers like a lustful lover. The mirage of Aziel sneers at me, his golden eyes glowing, swirling to the same shade as mine.

An occurrence that only happens when a werewolf meets their mate.

If this demon's goal is to hurt me, then the plan is working. Staring at Aziel for the first time in all these years, knowing it isn't him, it's as if I'm bleeding internally, and there's nothing that can be done to stop it.

Except death.

I land on my feet, throwing the dagger through the air with precision. It lands just to the left of his shoulder blade— I want to maim not kill.

He tosses his head back, roaring so loud from the agony, that my ears begin to ring. We begin to gather the attention of other doomed creatures here, the ones who were just watching the fight.

The beast cuts his eyes to me, a feral gleam twinkling in them. He reaches behind his head, wraps his fingers around the handle of the dagger, and without taking his eyes off me, he pulls it free from his body.

He doesn't even wince.

My eyes begin to burn with tears, and I refuse to let them fall. I toss the other dagger at vampire speed, and yet, he catches it before the metal tip makes contact with his chest. His palm smokes from the metal eating away at his skin. He drops my dagger onto the ground, kicking it away.

I'm without weapons now. I'll have to depend on myself, my speed, my claws, and my fangs.

"I'm not afraid of you," I tell him, slowly circling him.

He smirks, his tongue licking his own blood from his finger. A visceral desire stirs within me, my gaze dropping to how his tongue swirls, staining itself red.

My throat becomes dry, my fangs throb, and hunger twists my insides.

"You should be," the thunderous timber of his voice has me catching my breath.

He leaps again and I try to run away, to use my speed against him, yet he is shockingly fast. One arm wraps around my waist, tugging me tight against his firm chest.

"Elouise!" Iggy screams for me, shifting into his bear form.

He lumbers after me, the small brown bear moving his legs as fast as he can, but he gets lost in the crowd dispersing from the fight.

Iggy has no chance of catching this creature.

This is it for me. Purgatory has won.

After all this time fighting the little whispers of Aziel, I have lost.

Since I'm on my own without my daggers, I ball my fists and begin to wail onto his shoulders, back, anywhere I can reach. I hit him with my vampire strength. If this imposter was a human, one punch would explode the insides of his body just from the force.

I lean into him, getting close to his ear, and tears tickle my eyes again. My vision blurs and this time, the dam breaks. Warm wet drops fall onto my cheek. The heartache is unbearable.

He still has me clutched to his chest; his giant arm wrapped around my waist to keep me safe against him. We're in the depths of the forest now. I don't see the ribcage where the fights are or the crowd.

Or Iggy.

"You will never–" I sneer into the demon's ear, the salty tears rolling down my lips. "–Be him." I fight so many urges at once.

Desire. Need. Hope. Anger. Sadness.

They all swirl inside me, but I know what I need to do.

I have to kill the creature posing as my beloved.

These Purgatory demons are smart to take him from my memories, and then add the cherry on top by pretending he would be my beloved.

It's sick and twisted, yet there are no better words to describe Purgatory.

I sink my fangs into his throat, preparing to rip his jugular out, when his blood flows across my tongue.

My eyes widen in shock when I don't taste the rancid blood demons usually have. A sweetness travels across my tastebuds instead, reminding me of a cool night when thunder rolled across the sky and I became so scared, I jumped into Aziel's lap.

"*I got you,*" he whispered that night, wrapping his strong arms around me. "*I'll never let anything happen to you.*" He kissed the top of my head. "*I got you.*"

And right as I sank into his embrace, rain poured down on us, sending the scent of fresh water and flowers into the air. Thunder kept growling. Lightning kept striking.

But I was no longer scared because I knew Aziel would keep me safe.

Now, as this creature's blood pours down my throat, I taste that night. I taste the rain, the wind, the terror of thunder, the crack of lightning, and the sweet scent of flowers.

I sob, stealing another long deep drag of blood that tastes so fucking good. I didn't know Purgatory could go so far as to mimic Aziel's blood. I know this place isn't Hell, and yet, I've been living in my own worst nightmare since arriving here.

Smelling him.

Feeling his touch.

Hearing his voice.

It's this place's plan, isn't it? To slowly drive me insane until I'm nothing, not even someone's memory.

Just... gone.

The beast under me groans, skidding to a stop to toss me to the ground. The soil is cold and almost feels damp under my fingers. The small grains of dirt become trapped under my nails. Soggy leaves stick to my forearms as I back away from the largest werewolf I have ever seen besides Aziel.

He whips a large weapon from his back, slashing it out until the edge is at my neck, promising death.

Please.

I welcome it.

Blood stains the side of his neck, the small rivers trickling to his chest. My mouth waters for another sip of him. Just one more little lick up his neck so I can gather what is being wasted.

"Who the fuck are you? Because I know you can't be her." His chest rises and falls as he tries to catch his breath.

A cloud of warm air escapes his nostrils with every huff, his snarl warning me not to wait a second longer to answer.

My heart stops beating. It must because the blood rushes from my face. I have to be looking at a ghost. Gently, I push the weapon from my neck and hold out my hands in surrender as I stand.

"Don't move another inch!" he yells at me, his body betraying every word he speaks.

My eyes fall to his cock, long, hard, and thick. There's a bump at the base and I know that's the knot that will form during the first full moon of mating.

Swallowing my nerves, I take a step closer.

He seethes through his fangs, twirling his weapon in the air. "Don't take another step. I swear, I'll kill you. Who are you?"

His voice is deeper than I remember. There's a constant rumble after he says every word, almost like a constant growl.

"Who are you?" I ask of him, hope blooming like the flowers that used to surround us on our favorite cliff in the spring.

He lifts his weapon which has got to be made from

someone he has killed here and lifts it to my neck again.

"Who I am doesn't concern you."

Again, I push the weapon away from me, following the pull to him that Fate has created until I'm standing directly in front of him.

This has to be Aziel. Purgatory demons aren't great at copying deep heartfelt emotions.

Pressing my hand against his chest, I gasp when his warmth seeps into my palm. He growls in pleasure, dropping his weapon to place his gargantuan hand over mine.

"Kill me already," he whispers, his eyes all I can see through the mask. "I can't fight the demons that look like the woman I love."

My bottom lip trembles as I reach for his mask, standing on my tiptoes, and still, I can't reach. He's so tall.

"Killing you is the last thing I want," I reply just as a tear breaks free of my lashes.

He bends down, allowing me to remove his mask. I hold my breath, afraid of what could happen at any moment. This could be the only second the demon allows me to have peace before making his move.

He turns his head before I can take the mask off, closing his eyes. "You feel so good," his breath catches when I turn him to face me again.

If he is demanding who I am and if I'm demanding who he is, then maybe... maybe he isn't a demon after all.

Gripping the edge of the skull, I pull it free, showing more of his dark grey hide.

When his face comes into view, my fingers lose all their strength, and the mask drops from my hand to the ground.

I gasp, covering my mouth, and scramble backward until I hit a tree. I point to him, a crying mess at this point because I don't know what's real or fake anymore.

"Tell me something about yourself that no one here would know," I yell at him, the kind of shout that comes deep within someone's soul when they don't know up from down, left from right.

Sorrows I've kept buried deep in my heart, in the depths of my mind, break free.

"Tell. Me," I sniffle.

His eyes become round wide moons as he slowly steps closer, a glisten in his irises when tears fill them too.

"I never wanted to be the Alpha of my pack. I only ever wanted you." He stops in front of me, leaving enough space for us to process what is happening.

Silence falls between us as we stare at each other, not knowing what to say or do. I'm wondering if I'm really standing in front of him after so much time apart.

He lifts his arm, stretching it out, and his fingers graze my cheek. "I'm dead, aren't I? That's the only explanation for me seeing you. It's the only heaven I've ever wanted."

I sob, leaning into his touch, and shake my head. "This isn't heaven. You aren't dead." I kiss his palm, over and over again, until I work my way up his forearm. "Oh God, please let it be you. Please," I beg to someone, anyone who will listen.

"Louie?" He chokes out my nickname and for the first time, I'm not bothered hearing it.

"Aziel," I release his name on a breath, but then crimson tints my vision, remembering the most important detail. "Beloved." My fangs drop, my gaze meeting his.

His nostrils flare and he snags me by the waist, yanking me against his hard cock. "I always knew you were mine. My mate." He shifts into his hybrid form, his skin the color of rain clouds.

"My fucking mate." He wraps his hand around the back of my neck and tugs me against him as he leans down, stealing my lips in a searing kiss.

It isn't like the first time when we were kids and uncertain where it would lead. Now, Purgatory isn't the time or place to give in to our instincts, but if we don't, it could mean we die.

He lifts me into the air effortlessly, and my legs wrap around the body that's built for pure destruction. Against me, he feels like less of a weapon and more of someone who was built just to please me.

Aziel slams me against a tree, the power of him causing the trunk to splinter in half. He knows he doesn't have to worry about hurting me.

I'm a vampire.

I can take whatever he gives.

"Let me see your human form," I whisper against his lips.

He shakes his head, capturing my lips again in a wicked, desperate kiss. "Not in Purgatory. I have to be able to protect you." He grips my shirt by the hem and tugs it over my head, tossing it to our left.

I grip his face, forcing him to look at me. "I can take care of the both of us if anything happens. It's been so long since I've seen your face. Please, Aziel," I beg of him, rubbing my thumbs over his sharp cheekbones.

He tugs on one of my curls, smiling softly before inhaling and closing his eyes. His grey skin recedes. The small amount of fur lining his arms disappears and turns into a dark brown dusting of hair.

His jaws shrink. His fangs become smaller, but they don't vanish. The cuspids are sharp, the point pressing against the dusty pink flesh of his bottom lip. He loses a few inches of height, morphing from his hybrid form to his human, but it doesn't make him less impressive at all.

The man before me is strong, still taller than most, and his wide chest flexes as I rub my hands across it. His skin pebbles under my touch, his nipples beading tightly as I tease the left side. Aziel growls in pleasure.

I finally bring my eyes from the middle of his chest, noticing for the first time just how many scars riddle his physique.

There aren't many things that can scar a werewolf like this. These scars don't look random. They seem too precise. I open my mouth to ask him, unable to drag my eyes from his chest when his fingers slip under my chin. Aziel tilts my chin up and for the first time in years, I'm able to see his face.

My breath catches when I finally see *him.*

Not his hybrid.

Not his werewolf.

But *him.*

And don't get me wrong, I love all his forms.

I *want* all his forms.

"I'm okay," he tells me.

Tears cloud my vision, a storm waiting to burst with relief at finally having him in my arms and not my dreams.

"I've tried to put you in the back of my mind for years thinking I'd never see you again," I admit with a broken heart. "The memory of you was so painful." I drag my fingers through his long, shoulder-length hair. The strands are wavy and a mess. There is a strip of silver hair that frames his face. When he is in his werewolf form, that silver is a small patch on his chest.

An overwhelming surge of heat cramps my stomach. I tighten my legs around his waist, pulling myself closer to him until the tips of our noses touch.

We don't have much time.

"And I've kept you in the forefront of my mind because I knew it was the only place I'd ever see you again," he whispers, his breath ghosting over my lips that are still tingling from our kiss.

I press my forehead against his, wishing we had more time to talk, to be together, to relish in this happiness I've been begging for ever since I was forbidden to ever see him again. The mating heat is acting fast.

I can feel it. My veins are beginning to burn. My need for him is becoming too hard to ignore, and with him looking at me as if I'm his next meal, makes my control that much harder to maintain.

My fingers trace over his defined jaw, his scruff a bit wild. I like it, though.

Because he is wild, and I wouldn't want him any other way.

"I missed you. It isn't supposed to be like this. This isn't how we were supposed to be together."

"I don't care how we are together as long as we are." He wraps a hand around my throat, pinning me against the tree again. The wood splinters from his strength, the trunk threatening to snap in half. His gold eyes swirl, matching the color of mine, and everything settles in my soul.

"And I won't let anyone, or anything take you from me again. Do you understand me? You were mine then and you are mine now. This time, Fate made sure of it. There's nowhere you can go, Louie. I'll find you. In any dimension. In any hell. In any life. I'll travel the stars even if it means embracing your bones."

I've been fighting in Purgatory for so long, I forgot what it felt like to completely surrender.

"I'd eat them," he snarls against my lips.

"My bones?" I ask, horrified, my eyes widening in fear.

He licks my lips, a feral gleam in his eyes, the kind that tells me our time to talk is nearly over.

"So I know you'll always be with me. In my blood. In my own marrow. And then, I'd die without you. Our ashes becoming one."

I grip him by the back of his hair, forcing his head back, and he has the audacity to moan. His lips part and he grins, his fangs urging me to force them into my neck to mark me.

"You've made death sound more romantic than it should be." I lick from the bottom of his chin to his lips.

"There's something really fucked up about that, Aziel."

"Then I'll bring you as close to death as possible, so you get to experience it."

I wrap his hair around my wrist, forcing him forward. His lips own mine once more, our tongues swirling, his hands gripping at my curves. There's a lawless desire as he touches every inch of exposed skin. There's no more hiding. We aren't kids anymore. We aren't forbidden.

And yet...

The same emotions swirl inside me from when we were teens, that panic of being found and sneaking to see one another.

Our love for one another has no rules anymore. Fate decided we are to be together and that's enough for me.

I pull away, his face a vision of red as my eyes shift, proving my carnal desire. Licking my palm, I reach between his legs, wrapping my hand around his thick cock. My fingers don't touch.

And we both gasp for very different reasons.

Chapter Five

AZIEL

"Fuck," I groan, my gaze locked onto her hand stroking my cock. So many times I've dreamed of this. Her touch is all I have ever wanted. My body is always on high alert for her, my skin extra sensitive to every graze she gives.

"I can't wait for you to fuck me in this form," she nips at my chin, her fangs causing me to bleed before dragging her lips to my ear. "And in all the others."

My breathing becomes ragged, my control becomes untrustworthy with every fucking stroke she gives.

And she licked her fucking palm? Filthy fucking girl.

A wave of her heat coming on full force hits me like a ton of bricks. Reaching behind her, I unhook the makeshift bra made of cloth and claws for clasps.

Clothes in Purgatory are hard to come by. It's easier for me to go without them. When I'm in my other forms, my cock is protected by my werewolf's fur hide.

I scratch my claws down her arm, not hard enough to break skin but enough to show her how much I want to make her bleed.

Her thumb slips over my slit, gathering a bead of pre-come. Her tantalizing eyes lock onto mine before she sucks her finger into her mouth and moans.

Sneering, I pick her up by the back of her thighs and slam her on the ground. The ground craters beneath us from the force, the dirt cracking, and the nearby tree falls from the roots being splintered.

"Aziel," she moans my name, cupping her breasts. "I need you. I need you. I can't wait any longer. It's different for vampires."

I smother her words with a kiss, fighting my impulse to rip her clothes to shreds. She needs them. I won't have her walk around naked so everyone can see what is mine.

She's for my eyes only when she's on her back, nipples hard for me, and her fangs dropped.

I cover her, curling my body over her as I take her into a wild kiss again. It's been so long since I've felt them that if it weren't for the mating heat taking her, I'd take my time and kiss her all night. We could memorize each other's lips, the flicks of our tongues, and how we taste.

There's no time for that.

"Do you…" her words are cut off as I tug down her pants, then toss them to the side where her shirt is.

Growling in appreciation, my hands gently glide down her legs, so soft, so goddamn smooth, and I wrap my fingers around the thin band of her makeshift panties.

I swallow my nerves, trying to hide the tremors in my body. I'm nervous. I feel like I'm seventeen again and have no idea what I'm doing, not that I'm going to tell Louie that.

"Do I what?" Her panties slip free, revealing more skin until I have to hold my breath as her pussy comes to view. I lick my lips, doing my best not to come just from the sight of her.

The delicate material of her underwear is finally free from her body, and I can't help myself– I bring them to my nose. My eyes flutter shut as her scent invades my lungs.

"Aziel." My name a breathless surprise off her lips.

"What?" My question is nothing but a muffled rumble in the fabric. "You smell so fucking good."

"Maybe I taste even better."

My eyes fly open, gazing upon her body. She spreads her legs, showing me her glistening cunt. The growl that escapes me is louder than thunder, bigger than any storm that could be brewed.

I forget the panties, tossing them somewhere over my shoulder, and yank her to me. Picking up her legs, I place them on my shoulders, then slip my hands under the thick of her ass, squeezing the flesh so hard, she'll bruise. Pushing her body up, I bend down, licking her down her lips.

"Yes. I've waited so long for this." She stretches her arms above her head, beckoning my eyes to her breasts.

Sucking her clit into my mouth, she cries out, sliding her arms down to roam her hands over her chest. My mate plays with her nipples, lightly pinching them.

I kiss her pussy, circling my tongue over her clit just as I slip a finger inside her. She lifts onto her elbows, gasping, her lithe fingers slip up my arm, tightening them around my wrist when I push in deeper.

"You're so tight, Louie." I moan, pressing my cheek against her leg. "Fuck, I can't wait to feel you. At last. All this time you could have been mine." I kiss her calve, slipping my finger in and out, taking my time, enjoying the fucking warmth and softness of her.

"Aziel–" she whimpers when I slide a second finger inside, wanting to prepare her for my cock.

"What is it, Louie? My Light, tell me," I beg of her, rocking my body to the thrust of my fingers. My cock sweeping across her inner thigh and leaving a trail of sticky pre-come.

"I haven't–" she groans, tossing her head back before gripping my wrist even tighter. "I haven't done this before." Louie stares up at the darkened sky, no noises around us but our own breaths and sighs.

I pause in my next finger stroke, staring at her with wide eyes before slumping in relief and laughing.

"It isn't funny." She covers her face with embarrassment.

With my free hand, because I am not removing myself from being inside her when I've dreamed of this day, I take her hands from her face. Curling over her, I kiss her gently, the movement causing my finger to slip in further.

I press against the barrier, the one that makes her gasp, and try to squeeze her legs together on instinct to tell me to stop.

And I do.

For now.

When she gives me the okay, I won't ever be able to stop.

I catch her shy gaze, our eyes finally locking, and I cup her cheek. "I haven't either."

Her bold shapely brows pinch together. "You haven't? What– why?"

"I've only wanted you, Louie. Just you."

She gives me a bashful crooked grin before biting her lip. "Really? But all this time–"

I press my finger against her lips to silence her.

I didn't want to get into why for so many years, I was unable to do anything but kill. Not yet. Even if I wasn't cursed for fifteen years, I know in my heart I wouldn't have wanted anyone else.

When the sun touches the sky, I think of her, and when the moon rises and the sun sets, I dream of her.

No other woman could have me, not when I knew who I've belonged to since I was seventeen. I wouldn't give her claim away for a woman who would mean nothing to me.

"All this time, I knew who claimed me," I whisper against her lips, brushing my thumb back and forth across the plump clouds. "Don't be foolish to think I'd ever allow myself to be owned by anyone else, My Light." I crash my mouth against hers, Louie's arms wrapping around my neck to meet my exuberance.

She groans into my mouth, and I swallow the vibrations eagerly, wanting her sounds to be a tune my body memorizes.

Louie presses her palms against my chest, shoving me with her vampire strength, blurring us until I'm flat on my back. The boom of my body hitting the ground echoes for miles, a warning to all of what is happening.

My fingers grip the tight curls of her hair as she kisses her way down my body, swirling her tongue around my belly button before the blonde suns of her irises peek at me through her long lashes.

"Fuck. Fuck. Fuck. You looking at me like that is going to make me come."

She pauses at my cock, smirking, peering up at me again.

My mate knows exactly what she is doing. I growl, my fur sprouting on my arms when she spits on my cock. Louie licks her palm again, then wraps it around the base before she dives down to suck the crown into her mouth.

I punch the ground, creating a fist-shaped hole in the ground, and shout, "Oh my fucking God, Elouise. Your mouth—" I'm unable to finish the sentence because she strokes the spot where my knot will swell, then sucks me down halfway, effectively stealing my breath.

Struggling to breathe, I pant, staring down at her while she sucks my dick. Her free hand cups my sack before tugging and rolling them in her palm.

My eyes roll to the back of my head. "Don't fucking stop. God, Elouise. If you keep going, I'm going to come." Sweat beads across my forehead, a continuous thunder rolling in my chest.

Louie doubles her efforts, her fangs scraping across the vein that floods my cock with blood. She settles between my legs, lying down in the dirt, uncaring.

"That's what you want, isn't it?" I grip her neck, stopping her mid-suck. Her mouth is full, spit dripping from the corners, my cock stretching her lips, and her eyes flip red. "You're daring me." A snarl curls my lip. "You want to choke on my come? You want your stomach full of me while I fill that fucking virgin cunt? So greedy. I'll give you what you want but only if you sit on my face so I can eat that pretty pussy, Louie."

Her nostrils flare before giving me a small nod. My cock falls from her lips with a soft pop. Louie kisses her way down my shaft to my inner thighs. I gasp when she forces my legs apart, then presses more kisses to the sensitive flesh near my groin.

"Mmm, I love the feel of your lips on me," I praise.

"Good. Since they are the only lips you will ever feel," she replies, sinking her fangs into my femoral artery.

I have to hold in the urge to shift into my werewolf, her bite alone making my cock spasm. Stream after stream of come lands on my stomach and chest, tangling in the coarse hair. She whimpers, one hand dropping between her legs to make herself orgasm.

"Does sucking my blood turn you on, Louie? I bet you're so wet right now, aren't you?"

She nods, continuing to take long drags from the vein. Retracting her fangs, Louie tosses her head back as her orgasm tenses her body. My mate lifts onto her knees, her hand still working her clit, blood dripping from her mouth down her chin, her lips parted in ecstasy.

She is a fucking vision, more than my imagination has ever conjured. My blood drips down her lips, staining her beautiful skin, and creating a painting that encompasses my claim.

"Yes! Aziel! You taste so good. I want more. I want

so much more," she growls with a newfound hunger. "So much more." Louie brings her fingers from her slick pussy, the tips glistening, and with fire-red eyes, she sucks the digits into her mouth.

And fucking moans from her own taste.

Bending down, her onyx claws rake up my thighs. Her tongue flicks the corner of her mouth, cleaning the blood away. Louie pushes her ass into the air, crawling ever so slowly over my body.

I've never felt like prey before. I'm always the predator, but the view of her naked and savoring me?

I have a feeling I won't ever mind being preyed upon.

Her hand blurs in a typical vampire fashion, squeezing my cock yet again, and I suck in a needy breath of air.

"Such a big cock, Beloved. What if I need your knot now?" She lowers herself, the pink of her tongue gathering the come decorating my torso. "What if I need to be full right this moment? My heat needs to be sated," Louie pouts, licking another rope from my chest.

I can't seem to focus. Every fucking nerve-ending is sensitive and on fire from her touch. "I- I don't know. I want to," I growl, watching as she spits the come she gathered from my chest, onto my cock. "You're a dirty fucking girl, aren't you?"

She settles herself over my cock, her pussy hugging the girth before she rocks back and forth. The slick sound of her desire against mine has me holding my breath, focusing on anything else other than losing control. Her body rolls gracefully, entrancing me with every gorgeous curve as she uses me for her own pleasure.

The crown rolls over her clit with every stroke. Her hands fall onto my chest, propping herself up to gain more momentum. My hands become travelers, gaining a mind of their own as they caress her body, my thumbs flicking the delicate peaks of her nipples.

"Oh, fuck, Aziel." She runs her fingers through her hair, tilts her head back, and bites her lip. Sweat begins to drip down the middle of her sternum, the scent of her heat tingling my nostrils, and I snarl. I sit up, licking the middle of her sternum to gather the drop. "Oh God, I need more. It's getting worse. How do we know we can do this?" She rides me faster, her cries of pleasure becoming louder. "What if you bite me? What if... what if I die, Aziel? What if I need your knot and you can't?"

I hear the frustration of tears brimming, her valuable, beautiful tears, and I can't have them fall. Not when we are in a place that would take advantage of them. Vampire tears are worth more than anything in every dimension.

"I need your knot, Aziel. I can't wait. Please," she begs, moving faster, slipping and sliding along my cock.

The wet sounds of us seeking pleasure only add to my burning desire to claim her, to make her mine, but I know I won't be able to give her my knot. I wish I could. I want nothing more than to give my mate everything she needs and knowing I can't in this moment, it's as if I have failed her.

Being a werewolf, I can only knot her for the first time on the first full moon of our being together. Any werewolf who meets their mate can have sex with them, but won't be able to knot them until the full moon rises, solidifying their bond. I can also knot her any time I fucking want after the full moon, after the hunt where I chase, claim, and mark Elouise. When I breed her.

Once all that is complete and the moon sets so the sun can rise, her body is mine to do anything I want with.

"Please, Aziel. Please, give it to me. I need it so much. I ache. You know you want to fill me. I want your come inside me. Breed me, Aziel. I need it so much." She bends down and I cup the back of her head, forcing her to crash her lips to mine.

"You're going to make me come again if you keep talking like that. Be a good fucking girl and wait for my knot like a good mate."

Pressing her harder against my cock, my fingers dig into the plump flesh of her ass, slipping her faster along my shaft.

"I'm not even fucking you yet and you want my knot. You're going to be such a slut for my cock, aren't you?"

She chuckles, leaning down to tease her fangs over my jugular. "Just like you'll be a whore for my pussy, My Big," she kisses my throat "Bad," then wraps her arms around me and with her strength, blurring us to another spot in the woods where she is flat on her back and my cock is at her entrance. "Wolf."

A wave of uncontrolled shifting tremors through my body. My head rolls over my shoulders, a savage growl escaping from my chest as I fight the urge to shift into my beast. My ears lengthen, my fangs become longer, and my feet grow far past their normal size as they plant themselves into the ground.

I rake my claws next to her head, digging deep lines into the dirt. My muscles shake, wanting to give in to my beast. Taking a deep breath, I reel the beast back in, morphing into my human form like she wants— for now.

"I can't wait until you're in your werewolf form, Aziel, fucking me like the beast you are."

Wrapping my hand around her throat, I pin my mate to the ground. Her nostrils flare and the sweet, wicked smell of her desire saturates the air, so I'm forced to breathe in her scent.

"Do it," she tempts me, fighting against my hold to lift her head off the ground. "You know you want to." Her nails rake down my back until her hands are clutching my ass. "I know I want you to. Are you really going to make me wait longer than I already have— than we already have?"

I slip my hand down her body, clutch her left hip, and drive forward with the need of the last fifteen years. Elouise cries out in pain while I moan in pleasure. The tight, wet heat is all too much for me. She hugs me from every angle, taking every inch of me just like she is created to do.

Curling over her, a confession of a dark whimper falls from me for her ears only.

"Even in this form, you're so much to take. I don't know how I'll live through the others." She squirms under me, her muscles tensing around my cock which draws me closer to coming for a third time.

I can't ruin this so fast. I wish our first time wasn't like this. I want to know what I'm doing. I want to give her nothing but pleasure. I only knew the basics before the curse stole so many years of my life.

Staying still is the most difficult thing I've ever had to do, but having Elouise under me for the first time gives me the strength and control I need so I give her time to get used to me.

To ease the pain and discomfort, I kiss her neck, taking my time to show how much I love and care for her. With my right hand, I trail my fingers lightly down the side of her body. Her skin reacts, rising in goosebumps from the feathery touch.

I drag my lips up her neck and to her mouth, delving my tongue deep, and wanting nothing more than to taste her insides. She moans with every flick of my finger against her breast. Our tongues wrap around one another in a slow, seductive dance.

One that has me closing the space between us so every inch of our bodies touch. I don't wait for her to say a word. Instead, I listen to how she moves against me. Her hands begin to roam, stroking up the divot of my spine.

Everywhere she touches, the werewolf inside me shifts, sprouting grey skin and hair in Elouise's wake. Then, the beast disappears again. I have a feeling all of my forms are going to be greedy for her touch.

She presses herself down against me, the tight grasp has me breaking the kiss to groan. Snarling, I lock eyes with her before moving my gaze down to where we are connected.

I need to see us. I need to make sure this isn't some sort of fever dream I'm having in my death.

Gliding my cock out until all that is left is the wide head, spreading her pretty cunt to the brink. There is the smallest hint of red staining my shaft and with my finger, I gather the liquid and bring it to my mouth.

"Aziel," Elouise gasps.

I groan when the sweet elixir of her virginity coats my tongue. "I had to know what it tasted like."

"What, what tasted like?" she sounds so confused.

I inch back inside her, causing her to hold her breath while being filled. "My claim," I growl so deep, that the ground shakes beneath us, and Elouise's eyes flip red.

Bending her knee, I hold her leg against me while setting a pace. In and out, my cock vanishes inside her to the base where my knot will inflate.

"Tell me," I pant. "Tell me what to do. Teach me to please you." I kiss her knee, squeezing my eyes shut. Fuck, she feels too fucking good. I can't last. Not like this.

Not with Elouise taking me.

That in itself is enough to make me come.

"I can't... Elouise..." I warn her, thrusting quicker. "I can't hold back. You feel too fucking good. Oh fuck." The whines and whimpers that leave me, I'm not proud of.

My claws extend, digging into her leg hard enough to make blood bead on the surface.

I slam into her harder, our bodies sliding across the ground from the force. If she were human, the amount of strength I'm using would kill her.

But she isn't human.

She's a vampire and even if I split her open, she'll heal.

The thought of that, the thought of being too much for her, has me driving into her with more force. My feet slip causing me to lose traction, so I shift them into my beast's form for more stability.

She wraps her arms around my neck, wrapping her legs around my waist, then slams me against a nearby tree. The breath is knocked from my lungs, and the trunk splits in half, yet I don't really fucking care because Elouise is on top of me.

She whimpers with every downward stroke, roaming her hands down my chest.

"Mmm, goddamn it, Elouise." My head thumps against what's left of the tree. My fingers grip her hips, helping her grind harder against me.

I lick my lips, tasting the bite of salt from the sweat beading just above my mouth. I can't look away from her body, how she moves, how her skin shines, and her tits bounce with every rock and sway of our bodies.

I'm entranced.

"You tell me what you like." She grips my chin, her long claws digging into my skin. "Goddamn it, tell me?" A gasp interrupts her interrogation when I hit that spot inside her.

I flex my hips again.

And again.

She cries, clawing her nails down my shoulders so hard, that blood spills free. With a purr, she bends down, sucking and licking the blood from the wounds she created.

Wrapping my hair around her wrist, she yanks my head to the side and without warning, she bites me. Elouise sinks her fangs into my neck and this time, it's a bit painful.

She isn't careful.

She growls as she takes the blood that rightfully belongs to her. "I said tell me." She repeats herself, the words lost in a mouthful of liquid.

I can't say another word. The need to orgasm finally wins. I snap my eyes open, the new gold hue to my vision taking its permanent place now that she has mated me. A guttural howl fills the air until my throat is raw.

She's still drinking from the freshly tapped vein.

Spasms wrack my entire body as I fill her cunt with every ounce of come I have.

"I still want your knot," she whispers into my ear, licking the lobe with her blood-ridden tongue. "Give it to me."

"I can't," I barely manage to say through tight teeth as she continues to fuck me, slamming herself down onto my cock. "I want to, but I can't." I glance down, wishing my knot would inflate but it stays the same.

No amount of wanting or wishing will give us what we want because that is not what the moon wants. Elouise isn't the only woman in the world who has control over me. The moon is locked into my werewolf's soul and anything she gives, she can take away. I have to listen to her.

And my knot won't form just because my vampire mate needs it to. I have to wait until the moon is high, my humanity is gone, and every care in the world vanishes.

Except one.

The craving to hunt Elouise.

The thrill of capturing her.

The desire of pinning her down and knotting her cunt.

The visceral need to breed her.

The thought of that night has a thunderous boom vibrating my throat. I flip her onto her stomach, my claws threatening to plunge into her back as I hold her down, and my free hand slaps the round cheeks of her ass.

"This pussy is mine, isn't it? It's always been mine.

Tell me." I drive into her so hard, she loses her grip on the ground, and her arms give out. I tilt her ass up, holding her in place while I use her hole.

Glancing down, I see our orgasms combined, slicking my cock, dripping from her entrance onto the dirt, and I want nothing more than to mark her. I'll be able to the night I hunt her down like the prey she'll be. She won't be able to heal any of the wounds I give her.

Her body will be ruined for everyone else yet designed just for me.

"You know I'm yours. I've always been yours." With her vampire speed, she escapes my grasp, leaving my cock without her warmth.

Thick drops of come fall from my shaft and onto the leaves. I glance around, sneering slightly, wondering where she went.

I can't hear her.

"Come out, come out, wherever you are. I'm nowhere near done with you," I say, my voice deepening.

A snap of a twig has me grinning to myself. The whoosh of her speed gives her away and I stretch out my arm, slam her against another tree, wrap her legs around me, and in one hard thrust, settle home.

"You are out of your mind if you think you could ever get away from me. Smelling this good, your heat is in full swing, do you know how many males will want you?" I wrap my hand around the back of her neck and lift her from the ground, still using her hole to milk another orgasm from me.

I bring my lips to her ear, slowing my pace to make her beg me for more. "I dare anyone who tries to touch you or take you from me. I dare anyone to try to claim what is mine. You have no idea what I am capable of now, Louie. I will rip anyone apart, drench myself in their blood, and over their dead bodies, I will fuck you so they can crave you from Hell."

My claws rip into the tree trunk as I drag them down, the wood splintering into tiny pieces.

"You are havoc on my control. I'm already close but that's okay," I say softly, breezing my lips against her neck. "I'll just fuck you through my orgasm since you're so intent on making me come. You're just going to have to deal with me dripping down your thighs all day every day."

Her mouth parts, those beautiful white fangs glistening with blood. I bend down and suck her nipple into my mouth, her erotic pants and groans becoming louder. The scent of her heat becomes stronger, urging me to fuck her harder and faster.

I give her everything I have.

"Aziel, oh God, yes, I knew you'd feel so good. I dreamed about this so many times. I have ached for you. Give me your cock. Make me hurt. Oh, God."

"Fuck, Louie. You're going to make me come if you keep—"

"—Good. Come with me." She sucks her tongue over her teeth with a lustful smile. "Don't stop."

"I won't."

"Don't fucking stop," she cries, struggling to catch her breath.

"Only death could stop me." I drive into her with every ounce of paranormal strength I have, thankful she is a vampire.

"Fill me, Aziel. Give me more. Fill me up and don't let any escape."

The words alone have me tipping over the edge again, giving her exactly what she wants.

"Aziel!" she shouts my name loud enough for the entire Purgatory to hear as she comes, her muscles pulling me deeper. She rocks slow and steady, letting her orgasm run its course.

When she can catch her breath, her red glare focuses on me before she strikes the other side of my neck, feeding and marking me once more.

Slipping my hands under her thighs, I carry us away from the tree. She groans softly as she drinks and I cup the back of her head, wanting to keep her there.

"Good girl. Take all you want. Drink."

I check for a decent spot and sit down, pressing my back against a tree we didn't manage to break. I hold her to me, my cock still buried deep, while she takes what she needs from me.

Too many years have gone by. I've yearned too much to have this moment come to an end.

The power of the mating heat subsides, for now, but I know it isn't over. Sitting here with my mate has peace settling over me like a warm blanket. I might be in Purgatory. We might be fighting for our lives, and yet, this is the happiest I've ever been.

Because no matter where or when, the only thing I've ever wanted is finally in my lap with my blood in her veins.

I have six days until the full moon but I'm not sure if I really care about getting out of here now. Wrapping my arms around Elouise, being with her is all I have ever wanted, so why bother fighting when everything I need is in my grasp?

Chapter Six

ELOUISE

I wake up surrounded by a ton of heat. There's a heavy weight thrown over me, so I pat the area, wondering what the hell it is. My eyes snap open when fur touches my fingertips. I panic knowing I don't have my daggers but then the tingly ache between my legs reminds me that it isn't a stranger next to me.

It's Aziel.

Burying my face in my hands, I blush, wanting to squeal with happiness, but I don't want to wake him up.

Did last night really happen? It all feels like a dream. A delicious-too-good-to-be-true dream. I turn over to my side. He must have shifted at some point in his sleep because not only does he have his arm around me, but he has me tucked against his side.

He's always been a big werewolf but being against him like this makes me realize just how small I am. I lift onto my elbow to get a better look at him in this form.

God, he is so handsome, even as a werewolf, there is something so primal that calls to me.

I drift my fingers along his inner wrist before

trailing down to his fingers. Pressing our hands against one another, I give a slight shake of my head when my palm is practically swallowed by his. I walk my fingers up his arms, loving how his soft fur slips against my skin. My mating mark is scarred on his neck. Reaching, I trace the small pinpricks with my fingertip, a warmth spreading through my veins and up my arm.

His grey skin is familiar as I explore his body. The soft drag of my finger migrates down his impressive chest. Width-wise, he must be two or even three of me. The size of him makes my heat return, my pussy wet, and my hole aching to be filled with him again.

I bend down and kiss his defined pec, then his nipple, and continue on my trail over his ribs. A release of warm breath drapes over his abs as I pay attention to all eight.

The dips. The valleys. The way the V is sculpted into his hips, leading straight down to his cock.

I am obsessed with him.

God, he is beautiful. I've always thought that. From the first moment I saw him, I was never scared. I never felt the urge to run away or to fight him. I only ever had the need to get closer.

I still feel that; the pull of our souls, the tug of our hearts wanting nothing more than to be as close as possible.

He grunts, yawning so wide, that I'm able to see every single sharp tooth he has. I swing my leg over his lap and still, I need to crawl up his body to be closer to him.

"How's My Light today?" he asks, wrapping his arms around me before carefully trailing the sharp points of his claws down my back.

"Mmm, you remembered," I whisper, pressing my cheek against his shoulder. "I'm good if I can wake up to you every day."

"I remember everything when it comes to you and there is no way I'm ever letting us spend a night apart again, Louie."

"After all this time, I still can't stand that nick-name." I tweak his nipple, teasing him.

He flips me onto my back, grabbing me by my arms, and pinning them above my head. "You're just going to have to deal with it."

His arousal is pressing against my stomach, firm and thick. It nearly touches my chin in this position.

And I want him inside me.

"No," he grumbles, rolling off me and shifting into his hybrid form as if he can read my mind.

The best of both forms? Yum.

"Why not? Aziel, I can take it. I'm not a delicate human. I'm a vampire."

"Because I don't want to hurt you, and you need more of my come first. It relaxes your muscles and prepares you for the full moon night."

"Is that why it tingles?"

He grunts in confirmation, his attention focused on my body.

"So you're saying I can have you in your beast's form on that night?"

"Yes," he growls. "And even if you say stop, I won't. I won't be able to. All my humanity will be gone." His claws tickle my skin as they descend on my arm, his brows pinching together when he finds the scars he left on my forearm the night we were caught together.

"Then I can't wait until you chase me and hold me down, using me until you get your fill."

Those gorgeous eyes heat before a confused ex-pression pinches his face. He pushes off me, his grip still tight as he analyzes them. "I hurt you all those years ago?"

"They healed."

He curls his lips. "This is not healed. This showed everyone that a werewolf marked you."

I slip my hands down his chest, both of our lips parting when I slip further south and wrap my palm around his cock. "That's right, Aziel. Even then, you marked me as yours. Everyone stayed away from me. I was isolated. No one wanted a ruined vampire. I waited and waited and *waited* for you to come back to me, but you never did. You marked me for all to see and then you didn't come back for me." I kiss the middle of his sternum. "Why didn't you come back? I was so lonely." I stroke him in his werewolf form, lazily gripping him up and down.

He is heavy, my hand not even close to wrapping around him, so I tease him with feather-light touches, the scrape of my claws, and a firm grip every so often.

"I wanted you just like this, you know." I pepper an open-mouth kiss on his nipple before flicking it with my fang. "I've dreamed about you in this form. Hunting me down, howling at the moon, killing anything in your way when it comes to catching me, using me, fucking me until you get your fill. Scarring me, ruining me, splitting me in two, breaking my bones to get what you need."

A constant vibration lodges in his throat. "I would never want to break your bones."

"Why not?" I nip at his chest. "I'll heal." Tugging my hand from his hold, I glide over the ridges of his abs, ignore his heavy throbbing cock, and tug on his sack.

He hisses, latching onto my hip to keep me still.

"Who knows," I flatten my tongue on his stomach and lick upward until I have to stand on my tip toes just to reach the top of his chest. "I might even like it."

With a brutal snap of his fangs, he snags me by the throat and lifts me off the ground until our eyes are level. "Do not tempt me, mate, or I'll be tempted to break your fucking back when I claim you."

I moan, holding onto his arms for balance. "Don't make promises you can't keep, *Wolf*."

Tossing me to the left, I hit the ground with a hard thud, my shoulder cracking out of place.

I roll to my stomach, groaning in pain when I pop

it back in place. I glance behind me, watching the big beast leap into the air until he is on top of me. He shifts into his hybrid form, the perfect combination of his human side and his werewolf. If I can't have his wolf yet, I'll take what I can get.

Monsters fucking monsters makes it so much easier to be as rough as we want.

He shoves my face into the dirt, bends down, and inhales. Aziel buries his nose in my pussy before grazing up the crease of my ass. "Is this what you wanted? You smell like you need more of me. Is your mating heat getting the best of you? Because you're starting to reek of being my whore and I have to say—" he lodges his cock at my entrance "It fucking seduces me." He slams home, pounding relentlessly, forcing me to grasp at nothing but the ground.

I'm at his will.

And I have never been able to fight it.

Not that I would want to. He gives as much as he takes and I spiral into a headspace where there are no worries, no stress— just pleasure.

Those lethal nails dig into my skin, keeping me still as he rails into me with a vengeance.

Clawing against the ground, I try to pull away from him, but he applies more pressure between my shoulder blades, threatening to break my back.

"Keep trying to get away from me. Keep trying to pull this cunt from my cock. And see—" he slams into me. "What—" he plants himself as deep as possible, his giant paw landing next to my head. "— I fucking do to you."

I turn to the left, needing to inhale a deep breath when his hand covers my mouth, silencing my cries.

His chest aligns with my back as his lips graze my ear. The tips of his fangs bite against the outer shell. My moans are internalized, burning through my veins like a U.V. ray injection.

My eyes water from being so full, so stretched. The

inability to breathe and cry out only adds to the delicious pain. His tongue dances upon the apples of my cheeks, gathering the tears others would kill him for.

His speed quickens. His pelvis slaps against my ass. He becomes stronger, holding me down with a force that almost hurts, that almost has me begging him to stop.

Almost.

"Right here." He digs a claw into my shoulder so hard, that he breaks the skin, and I shout behind his palm. "I hate that it heals." And he scratches me again.

And again.

He continues his assault before licking the blood from my skin. "You won't be able to heal from my marks soon. Every time I get too carried away, I'll find a part of your skin to claim as mine. The scars on your wrist are nothing compared to what I will give you under the moon."

He pushes me further into the ground, the dirt swallows my body. He rams into me, his forehead pressing against the back of my head. My werewolf moans, "That's it, Mate, My Light, take my cock. Mmm, fuck, you feel so good. Ah, goddamn it, this cunt will always keep me feral." His breaths are broken. He is out of control. His fingers lace through mine and with every push against me and every pull away, the nerve-endings in my body light with pleasure, a fire Aziel has caused.

I am gasoline and I have drenched myself with it to tease my mate only to underestimate the size of the flaming torch he holds inside himself.

Now, I'm a blazing wildfire, getting hotter, searing me from head to toe as my orgasm builds.

"You smell so good," he groans for me. "Fuck, your heat is too much. How will we survive another round when the moon comes? Are you going to throw me into a rut?"

"I hope so," I whine in return.

I want us to die just like this. I want our skeletons to be tangled as we decompose into nothing. I want others to stumble upon what we used to be. They won't be able to see my skin to prove Aziel's claim, but they will be able to see every spot where my bones healed when he broke me with every fuck.

He growls into my ear, my spine tingling from the vibrato. "No, you don't. You better hope I don't rip you to pieces."

The threat makes me wetter. My body aches across the ground, the pressure of his body, his strength, threatening to shatter me into pieces.

"Aziel! Oh, fuck, God, yes, don't stop. Don't stop. I'm so close. You feel so good. Give me your come. Are you going to fill me up again? Make me feel it, Beloved. Give me every inch, every drop, make me drip of you for days."

With primal snarls, he thrusts deep three more times, trying to reach my womb that won't take his come just yet. He claws at the ground, stretching his arms above my head, before smothering his grunts into the wound on my neck.

His cock thickens as it spurts every jet of come. The heat of the liquid pours into me, his shaft jerking as he empties himself.

"I'll never get enough of you. I'm going to be inside you every day. Before you open your eyes to see the day and right before you close them to dream of me."

I hum as I turn my head. "And what makes you think I'll be dreaming of you?"

He flips me over, pinning my arms to my sides, and the movement makes his cock slip free. Come spills from me and he growls in discontent before taking his dick in hand and sliding inside me again.

"Because if they aren't of me, I'll kill every person who walks into your dreams."

I lift my head off the ground, sucking his bottom lip into my mouth before releasing it with a pop. "And how–" I nudge his nose with mine, breezing my lips over his without giving him a kiss. "–Would you even know who they are?"

"You'll tell me."

"You sound so confident that I would. What if I like playing with you? What if I want to tease my wolf with a bone?" I smirk, knowing how much he hates being compared to a dog.

"Then I'll chew the bones of anyone you dare to think of, killing everyone you used to know as I feast on the weakness of their marrow."

"Aziel." My fangs begin to throb, needing to drink from him again. My pussy pulses around his cock, another wave of my heat threatening to take us under again.

I can't remember a time when a vampire and a werewolf were mated. I trust in Fate but no one knows what will happen. Vampires always go through a mating heat the moment they meet their mates yet were-wolves have to mark, claim, and knot under a full moon.

My hope was that he'd be able to knot me during my heat, but Fate is a wicked bitch making me wait.

"Give me your neck, Beloved. I'm so thirsty," I practically cry for him.

He shifts from his mid-form to his human, his long hair falling down his shoulders. Smiling, he gathers the wild strands to get it out of the way. He lowers himself until his chest is against mine.

When I can smell the sweat on his skin, the tip of my tongue gathers the salt.

Aziel lifts his head just as I'm about to feed. I watch his gaze narrow and turn calculated.

"What is it?" I whisper, feeling a small amount of his unease through the bond we have. We will be able to hear each other's thoughts and feel what the other feels at all times once we are fully mated.

He covers my mouth with his hand, pressing a finger against his lips, signaling me to stay quiet.

I nod, realizing he senses a threat.

He slowly slips out of me which has me holding in a moan and by the expression on his face, I know he isn't happy about being interrupted. Because of the threat, my heat subsides enough to allow me to think of something else besides Aziel.

"Get dressed," he mouths. "Fast."

Blurring to the first tree we broke, I slip into my pants and then find my bra and shirt. Having my holster for my daggers gives me a sense of safety even if it is false sense considering I have misplaced my daggers.

I'm dressed in less than thirty seconds, taking my place next to my Beloved. Aziel shifts and even with being on alert, I watch in fascination as his body does the impossible. His bones grow, not just in length, but in size. His skin darkens to a haunting ash color, and his muscles bulge in places that have beads of sweat dripping down my temples.

I wipe my forehead, urging my heat to remain under lock and key. The warmth spreading in my veins that has me wanting to drop to all fours and present myself to Aziel turns from a violent heat wave to a simmer.

"Stay behind me," he informs me, stretching out his arm to keep me safe.

I shove his arm away. "No. I'm either beside you or in front of you, but never behind."

He huffs, his nostrils flaring in anger before taking a step closer to me. "Fine but be careful. Stay close to me."

"Aziel, I've survived Purgatory without you, I can survive this too."

"But I can't survive if something happens to you."

My heart melts and I'm caught in his gaze, the love and desperation there urging me to be safe has me giving him exactly what he wants. "As long as you are careful too."

He scoffs, analyzing the darkened tree line for enemies. "I'm always careful."

"Says the guy who goes to The Graveyard," I grumble.

"Good thing I did, or I wouldn't have been able to steal you from that other guy.

"Other guy? Iggy? He is gay and my best friend and if you care about me at all, you'll help me find him in this place. He can't be left alone for long because he is a male omega. He is rare, Aziel. Please, nothing can happen to him."

He snags me by the wrist and tucks me to his side. Aziel cups my cheek and leans all the way down to press a kiss to my forehead. I expected more of a fight or him demanding more information about Iggy. I know paranormal creatures are very possessive, but werewolves are much more feral.

"Nothing will happen to him. I'll make sure of it, Louie. Okay? I promise." His thumb strokes my cheek, sending my heart into a wild frenzy.

A slow clap reverberates from the trees, catching us off guard. That's what we get for being so lost in one another.

"Aww, isn't that adorable? You two are just so cute."

Everything about Aziel changes. The kindness and gentle nature in his face vanishes. The air around him becomes heavy to breathe, nothing but pure rage flexing every muscle in his body. He turns to our guest, spreads out his arms, and roars so loud, so deep, I have to cover my ears. The guttural thunderstorm lasts longer than the fights at The Graveyard.

The newcomer leans against the tree, arms crossed, and a smirk tilts his lips.

I want to kill him. His confidence has my fangs

itching for violence.

He snaps his fingers, nodding. "I remember you now. You had an impressive howl, very menacing. How are you doing, Aziel? Do you and your brother miss me?"

Aziel's breathing sounds more like a raging bull. Every inhale and exhale becomes faster. His shoulders rise and fall in a rapid beat. His lips are constantly curled, showing the large sharp teeth. My Beloved is rabid and whoever this person is, they are about to be on the receiving end of it.

A silent beat passes but, in the silence, the anger is so loud.

The man smiles at me, giving me a small bow. "We haven't met. Aziel didn't have a mate when I knew him. I'm Brenden."

"Aziel, who is this?"

Brenden feigns being hurt, placing a hand on his heart. "You haven't told her about me?" He tsks, taking a step closer before his smile fades. A cold, menacing mask falls on his face making me wish I had my daggers. "That's so hurtful, Aziel. After everything we did together, you would think telling her about the most important part of your life would be essential."

"You never held an importance in my life, and you never will," Aziel finally speaks.

"I don't know—" Brenden taps his chin "—I would think keeping you under my influence for fifteen years and having you kill, torture, and eat innocent people would be enough. I mean, I cannot believe you killed children, Aziel. The poor little children." Brenden spins in a circle before a sick bubble of laughter escapes him like the maniac he is.

"Aziel. What is he talking about?"

Aziel doesn't answer me. He leaps through the air, snags Brenden by the throat, and slams him against the ground. He roars while taking Brenden's neck in his hands, squeezing so hard I know any moment it is about to break.

Brenden doesn't seem bothered.

"You don't have it in you, Aziel," Brenden seethes and taunts. "You couldn't then, and you can't now because while you fucking hate me, you're still somehow dependent on me. Aren't you? You want me to die but then what would that mean for you? Would that mean you deserve death too? After all, you're just like me." He lies down, settling into the ground before clearing his throat. "Okay. Okay, I'm ready. Kill me."

Aziel lifts a hand in the air, preparing to strike, when Brenden says one last thing, "Just know if you do, your precious little pack will never be able to walk in the sun again. Because once you kill me and I cease to exist, so does everything on my body, including page 576."

Aziel's eyes widen and to my shock, he releases Brenden.

"What are you doing? Kill him, Aziel. Kill him!" I yell, not understanding why he is allowing Brenden to live. It makes no sense. Whatever happened between the two is serious and unforgiving.

"I can't," Aziel whispers, watching Brenden get to his feet. "I can't do that to them."

"Them? What about you?" I can't let Brenden leave here without dying. I refuse. He hurt Aziel and while I don't know all the details, I protect what is mine, and the last I fucking checked, Aziel belongs to me.

"My pack is more important."

Hissing through my fangs, I blur to grab a stake from one of the trees we broke and sling it through the air. Brenden, to my shock, uses his own speed to dodge the spear. I didn't know he was a vampire. He doesn't smell like one.

It lands in the tree behind him with a hard thud and he nods his head, impressed.

"Impressive. You would have made a fine warrior if I didn't love werewolves so much. Isn't that right, Aziel?"

Aziel slashes his claws through the air, and I gasp

when five scratch marks appear across Brenden's face. Blood oozes down his face and he screams in agony, stumbling backward. His hands reach for his face, only when he pulls them away, his palms are covered in red.

Next, my mate grabs Brenden's left arm, spins him around, and bends it back so far, it breaks.

"Fuck!" Brenden shouts, trying to pull away from Aziel.

I bite my lip, my lust for my beloved awakening my heat once more as I watch him become someone I have never seen before.

Aziel lifts Brenden into the air with his broken arm, only to snap it again in another place. Lifting his leg, he kicks Brenden's thigh. The force alone would typically send Brenden flying but due to Aziel's grip on him, I flinch when I see the bone break as his thigh caves in.

"You need to remember something," Aziel begins to state, folding Brenden in two before there is a loud crack as his back breaks, leaving him limp.

He'll heal. Unfortunately.

"I might not be able to kill you because I care about others who are outside of myself, but I can still cause you pain and suffering. You'll never know what it's like to have a family surrounding you. You'll always use your hate and anger to try to control people." In one quick slash, Aziel's long sharp nails cut into Brenden's throat.

Brenden is wide-eyed and gurgling, holding his free hand to his neck.

"You won't die easily, I know that," Aziel whispers, his eyes dancing over Brenden's surprised face. "But I will make sure you suffer every time I see you. You are not strong. You aren't what you used to be. You don't control my beast anymore. And God, the day I can kill you—" Aziel turns Brenden's pale face to me.

He gasps and coughs, his mouth turning red as it fills with blood.

"—I'm going to fuck my mate in your blood."

Brenden dares to grin. "Lucky me to have died and my blood still taint your skin."

Aziel snaps Brenden's neck, rotating it all the way around and breaking his jaw in the process. He stands there staring at his body. He's thinking about killing him. He has the chance.

He drops Brenden onto the ground. "We won't have much time before he heals. I have a feeling this won't be the last time we see him. I should rip his fucking heart out or cut off his head. I really should, but what would it change? Anwyll and I would still have the weight of the crimes we committed on our shoulders."

"What happened, Aziel? How do you know him?"

He shakes his head, placing his hands on his hips as he tilts his head back to look up at the sky.

"Aziel." My tone is demanding. I'm leaving no room for escape or argument. "I deserve to know. I want to know all the dark and horrible things. I want to know your secrets. I want to know everything."

He steps on Brenden's body, the bones crunch under the weight. "I don't want you to know!" he shouts at me, shifting from his werewolf to his human form.

His hair falls in his face, hiding the most beautiful part of him— his eyes. It's where all his emotions are shown, swimming inside his soul. They are his windows where people can peek in and get a glimpse, but he has only ever opened them for me.

"I don't want you to know what I became. I don't want you to know how horrible of a man I am. I don't want you to know how my werewolf has changed. I am not the same man from when we were teens. I'm broken." He cups my cheek, lowering his voice to a hushed breeze. "I'm nothing but pieces of who I used to be. I'm angry and I am undeserving of you. If you knew me, you wouldn't love me. Who I am and everything I have done makes me unloveable."

"I love you because of those things. I love you for who you were and who you are now. I know you aren't the same. I don't expect you to be as I'm not either. Life makes us harder, Aziel, but we don't have to be with each other."

"I'm afraid you would rather choose death than life with me."

"Silly wolf." I hold his face in my hands and smile. "I have experienced both and I can say both are much better with you at my side." I place a soft, firm kiss against his lips. "You are not the worst thing you have ever done. Do you hear me? Look at me, Beloved. Look at me." My eyes water when he finally lifts them from the ground to meet mine. I press my hand against his heart. "All your scars, all your pain, you don't have to carry them alone again. I love you because I see you, Aziel. Not the werewolf, not the fighter, not the killer, but you."

"But those are who I am," he tries to explain.

"Those explain what you have done, but they don't explain you. They don't show how much you love star-gazing or how much you love being touched– it's your love language." I skim my fingers over his cheek. "Or how you always loved bringing me flowers and I knew you would now if Purgatory had them. Or how you love your brother, you have always done everything you could to protect him. Let's not forget you had your enemy in your grasp, and you chose your family first. Your soul is beautiful, Beloved. If I have to remind you of that every day for all eternity, I will."

His eyes search mine, darting back and forth to see if I'm telling the truth. I don't waiver in my stance. I want him to know a strong woman stands beside him when he feels weak.

To my surprise, he lifts me from my feet, smashing his lips against mine. His oversized palm cups the back of my head, controlling the kiss in a way that has his tongue slipping into my mouth at the perfect angle. He growls down my throat, the vibrations awakening the mating heat once more now that the threat of the enemy has been dealt with.

Well, it has— for now.

It will take hours for Brenden to heal from the damage Aziel caused. I need answers from him, I want answers, but I know my feelings for him won't change once I know his truth.

That's all I want. I want to know him. If that means learning heinous atrocities, then I will treat them with the love they deserve so he can have peace.

In the poisonous waters he creates, I will gladly swim in the rough waves if it means bringing him to my shore.

Aziel unsnaps the holster that holds my daggers before tugging my shirt off. "I want you," he manages to say between kisses. "I want your pussy right now and I expect you to give it to me." He sucks and nips at my throat, shoving his hands down the front of my pants.

His fingers graze my clit before slipping down. Aziel moans when he feels how wet I am, then dips them inside me before gently pulling them free.

"Taste yourself."

"Make me," I taunt.

He traces my lips with the same two fingers, glossing them with my own slick.

"I'd love to." Aziel shoves them into my mouth until they hit the back of my throat causing me to gag. "That's right. Gag for me. You better get used to it too because I plan to choke you every fucking day."

I lick his fingers clean as he tugs my pants down. I step out of them, slipping on the red-saturated grass. Aziel doesn't ask if I'm okay. He doesn't even notice we are in a pool of his enemy's blood, his body right next to us.

My hand ghosts over his chest and in a blink, his human flesh fades away, and the hybrid takes charge. Hair fills his arms and shoulders and stops at a point at his sternum. His pecs are able to be seen with smooth skin and no fur. His entire front is bare except for the charcoal-happy trail leading to his cock.

Reaching for his shaft, he snags my wrist, snarls, and twists my arm until it breaks. The bone snapping is loud in the quiet forest, and my vision flips red as a painful yet pleasurable roar explodes from my chest.

"Try to touch me again when I only want your pussy and see what else I break." The blood under me is slippery. I can't gain any traction. "I'll tell you if I want your hand around my dick." He yanks my head back by the thick of my curls, the ends dipping into a deep pool of crimson. "And usually I do, but right now, I want to fuck you in his blood—" his tongue flattens against my cheek just before he grips my chin, forcing me to turn left.

Aziel slams into me, my body slipping against Brenden's.

Brenden's eyes are open, pupils blown wide, and all the color has left his face. If it weren't for my enhanced hearing, I would think he was dead. The slow slur of his heartbeat is there letting me know he is watching us.

"—So he can know what it's like to witness someone drawing pleasure from his death."

"Aziel!" I cry, my claws digging into Brenden's arm.

"That's right. Scream my name into his ear, mate. Let him hear what he has never had, and never will." Aziel reaches over, yanking Brenden's broken neck back, forcing his hooded eyes to look at me. "Look at her. Isn't she fucking gorgeous? How does it make you feel knowing that the beast you controlled is controlling you now?"

His revenge is an aphrodisiac and I want to commit it with him.

My wrist finally heals giving me the strength I need to flip Aziel onto his back.

"Fuck," I groan, sliding my blood-ridden palms up Aziel's body, painting him in his vengeance. "That feels good, doesn't it? Knowing you can always make him bleed now that he can't control you. You can do this every time." I bend down, tracing his lips with my tongue before I dive in. Our fangs grind against each other, our growls colliding into a deep moan from the roughness of the kiss.

I grip Brenden's shoulder, puncturing his skin with my claws. I don't know what he did to Aziel, and I don't need to know the details. If My Beloved was wronged, then I'm at the forefront of the battle to have them meet Death.

Aziel flips us, forcing me to my hands and knees. To stop myself from sliding, I grab onto Brenden's broken thigh. I apply too much pressure, snapping another section of bone as Aziel drives his fat cock into me.

He grips my shoulder, using my own body as leverage to pound as hard as he can into me.

"Ah, oh, Aziel—" I hang my head, taking the pleasure he is giving me. "So fucking good."

He slaps my ass, driving his long length into my pussy, growling with every wet thrust.

We're covered in blood, sweat, and rage.

And nothing has ever felt better.

"Look at me," he demands, his nails threatening to break my skin.

I refuse.

"I said—" he snaps my head to the right, breaking my fucking neck, the bones cracking in my ears, "—To fucking look at me!"

I'm barely able to move. My gaze follows every flex of his abs, the furry happy trail exposing the base of his cock.

"I can't wait to claim you under the moon, mark you as mine, and add more scars to your body. You know what I think this is?" He grabs the wrist that is scarred from when he tried to pull me away from my father. "I think I imprinted on you. I think my soul knew you were mine so I did what I could to make sure no one could ever have you but me."

"Werewolves scar vampires anyway," I remind him with a slur. Drinking werewolf blood has me healing quicker, I notice.

Tugging on my hair, he bends my head all the way back until I touch the middle of my shoulder blades.

His force has an orgasm rippling through my ragged, used body. I moan to the empty branches of the trees up above, needing something more.

"Not when we were fated the entire time." He presses his pelvis against my ass, planting himself as far as he can before curling his hips. Shoving my head down to the ground, my cervical spine begins to mesh. The bones pop into place and the senses that were dull are now extra sensitive.

He reaches between my legs, blood coating his fingers from Brenden, and circles my clit. I rise onto my knees, looping my arm around his neck, urging his throat to my mouth.

"Are you thirsty, My Light?" He purrs, teasing my fangs by rubbing his stubble against them. "Go ahead. Take what is yours because I survived *him* just for you."

I ease my fangs into his flesh, humming as his delicious blood warms my throat.

"Louie," he snarls, unable to remove himself from my grip as he fills me with his come again, easing my mating heat. With every stream, he tries to get deeper, shoving our bodies closer together so that not an inch of flesh isn't touching. "That's it. That's a good girl. You're doing so fucking good for me. You're full of me, aren't you? My blood. My cock. You're a slut for both."

When I have my fill, I lick the wound, gathering every drop of blood.

He eases from me, his come flowing out of me like a river. He gathers it with his finger, sucking it into his mouth before he snags Brenden's face.

I watch as I lie on my back trying to catch my breath.

Aziel spits on Brenden's face, a mixture of saliva

and come. "Fuck you. Count your days because you will die by my hand. That's a promise."

And if there is one thing I know, it's that My Beloved never breaks his promise.

Chapter Seven

AZIEL

"We don't have much longer until he is healed. We need to find a place to get cleaned up." Louie stands, her thighs shaking and smothered in my come.

I smirk with pride at how unsteady she is. And to think our sex life is only going to get better when our bond is fully formed. How it could get any better than this, I'm not sure, but that's what has been told to me. I know Maven and Alexander only want each other more every day. Comparing them to Louie and I has me wondering how explosive we will be since we have so much time to make up for.

"We can go to Purgatory Pins. It's the only place where we can get decent food, drinks, even clothes. We can pay to shower too."

I stand, brows raising when I take in the damage we created. So many trees are broken, some worthless stumps now. Blood is everywhere. It drips from the leaves above and coats our skin.

And then there is Brenden who looks like a pretzel. I have no regrets.

Elouise stands with her hands on her hips giving

the appearance of someone who has been to battle. I suppose in a way she has.

I'm the war she will never conquer and the battles she gives me will only make me stronger.

"You are beautiful," I say, tugging on one of the spiraled curls. "You've always been the most breathtaking woman I've ever seen. The moon has nothing on you, Louie. You are and will forever be, my favorite moonlight."

"Is that where 'My Light' comes from?" she asks. "You're comparing me to your moon?" She bops the tip of my nose with her finger.

I take her wrist and bring it to my lips, kissing the inner part where the soft, smooth skin is. "What's to compare? Your beauty is brighter than her light will ever be."

"Always such the romantic." A teasing tilt of her lips and me licking my own.

I snatch her throat and growl as deep as I can. "Only when I want to be. You'll do well to remember that."

No longer am I staring into golden hues but bright red gems.

Her fangs peek from under her top lip. "Maybe when I'm not behaving, you'll do well to remind me of that."

A continuous purr vibrates my chest. "My Light," I tsk. "Eventually, the only thing you'll ever remember is me."

The crack of bone sliding into place has us turning to see Brenden's ribcage is healed. We're running out of time.

"Let's get you dressed and head out of here." I bend down, picking up her shirt, then her pants, bra, and everything else I happily stripped from her body.

They are covered in blood and dirt.

"I'll get you new clothes," I tell her. "But you have to wear them or I'll kill too many people for seeing you."

"Maybe I should stay naked then."

"Elouise," I growl in warning.

"What?" She rubs her hands down her delectable body, grinning as her nails rake clean lines through the blood drenching her flesh.

"Louie." Her nickname is a cross between a hiss and a snarl.

She winks at me, the flirtatious gesture has my cock twitching. I don't know how I'll make it out of the full moon alive with my body intact. I already want her. The heat, the pull, the lust between us is so strong, and mixed with all the years we had to be without one another– we are a bomb waiting to go off.

I shift into my beast, shaking off as much blood as possible from my fur before gathering Uri and strapping him over my shoulder. I pat the small pouch I have, double checking to make sure the eeries are in there. That's what will pay for food, drinks, and anything else we will need tonight.

And then, it's time to try to find the avisseus. Or try to.

So we can get the fuck out of here and live the rest of our lives in my pack, surrounded by love, and maybe, I'll be able to put the past behind me. Because then, I'll have everything I've always wanted.

A future.

And I will not let my past ruin it.

I frown when she pulls her shirt over her head, a short white tank top that shows her stomach.

"What? You don't like my shirt?"

I shake my head. "I fucking hate it because now I can't see your body."

She giggles, lacing her boots. "You can see it whenever you want, Beloved. You don't even have to ask." Elouise begins to walk away from me, swaying those hips I was just clenching onto five minutes ago, driving my cock as deep as I could.

I snag her wrist and tug her to me, outlining her body with my hand until I'm cupping her cheek. "Don't ever walk away from me without giving me a kiss."

"We are going to be walking together, Aziel."

"I don't care. Anytime you walk away from me, you kiss me because I won't ever miss an opportunity when I can feel you. Ever."

Her eyes soften in understanding. "I like the sound of that." She leans in, giving me a quick, deep kiss. "Now, let's go before you have the urge to rip his head off."

"Climb on my back?" I fall to my hands and feet, expecting her to argue with me about how she is capable of walking.

She reaches onto her tiptoes, petting under my ear. "I am in love with every single inch of you."

My ears flatten as I hang my head, rubbing my snout against her neck. "You say that now—" I gently lick her cheek "—Until I tell you what happened." I crouch lower to allow her to grip the fur at my neck and swing her leg over to mount me.

"We have a few hours until we are at Purgatory Pins. How about you tell me on the way?" She strokes my neck. "And I promise, there's nothing you can say that would make my heart cease the love I have for you. I want to know everything about you, Aziel. The good and bad."

A heavy sigh deflates my lungs. I begin to walk away, stepping on Brenden's body so it takes him longer to heal.

"Hold on," I tell her. "I want to get us as far away from him as possible."

She leans down, wrapping her arms around my neck. She curls her fingers into my fur, holding on to me for dear life as I leap through the air.

"Oh my God! You could have warned me!" she screams, but through the faint bond we have, her happiness and excitement fuel me. Elouise laughs. "This is so freeing! Aziel, this— you're amazing."

I leap over fallen logs, my paws splashing into creeks. The skeletons of the trees reach for me, wanting to snag us with their branches. Certain trees engulf creatures into their trunks forever embolizing them in wood. I dodge to the left when two branches swing out like they are about to hug us.

The bark groans and squeaks with every stretch toward me.

"Aziel!" Elouise screams when a branch hits her across the chest, sending her flying off my back.

I skid to a stop, growling with the intent to kill. I sprint, using my momentum to jump onto a tree, only to use it as leverage to push off it. My claws grind against the trunk as I twist my body, launching myself into the air to snag Elouise. The branch is wrapped around Elouise's ankle, the root beginning to shrink back to its natural state— taking Louie with it.

"I'm not losing her to fucking firewood—" I sneer, biting the wooden tentacle where it grasps her leg.

The wood snaps and the tree screeches in agony. Water pours from the broken root, the leaves trembling in pain. Picking Elouise up by the back of her shirt with my teeth, I run in a direction where the tree can't reach us before veering left.

"You can put me down now," Louie grumbles.

Yeah, I knew she wouldn't like being carried away in that manner.

I slow to a stop, checking my surroundings to make sure we are safe before putting her down. Only, she doesn't make it easy. She starts wiggling to get free of my hold. When she twists, her shirt catches on my right fang and it fucking hurts, so I open my mouth naturally.

She plops to the ground, smacking it with a hard thud that makes me flinch. Elouise groans, pushing herself off the ground. She narrows her eyes at me and the way her anger is pointed directly at my soul has me wanting to lay my claim all over again.

"Really? You had to pick me up like a puppy?"

"Not like a puppy. I would have gripped you by your neck or the middle of your back. I chose to pick you up by your shirt. That's very different."

She gets to her feet, hissing when she twists. "Ow, fuck." She raises her arm and right at the curve of her hip is a large bleeding gash. "Damn, that hurts."

"Why aren't you healing?" I panic. "Louie, why aren't you—" A relieved breath fills the air when I witness her skin meshing together.

"You have to give me time to heal," she chuckles, touching the spot that is as good as new now. "Doesn't even hurt. This wasn't a paper cut. You have to remember, the bigger the wound, the longer it takes to heal."

"I know. I'm just irrational right now. We are only half-mated. I can still taste your heat on my tongue. I can smell my claim, my come, and my possession on you. I feel your love for me and— I don't deserve it— but there is no way in hell I'm ever letting it go. So yeah, I thought you were about to become a tree trunk and that scared me. You scare me, Louie."

"Me? Scare you?" She blinks in confusion, tilting her head and probably wondering how.

"You terrify me because if anything happens to you, I'll go mad. Did you learn about werewolf sickness after we weren't allowed to see each other?"

Her brows furrow as she gives me a slow nod.

"I'll spiral into madness for you because I've already done it once. I have no doubt that I would do it again." I walk away. I need a moment to calm down.

She tugs on my tail hard enough to bring me to a stop. "What do you mean you have had the sickness? You seem fine. What are you talking about?"

I shake my head, not wanting to talk about it. "Come on. We don't want to waste time in these woods, Louie. We need to get to Purgatory Pins."

"Aziel, don't you dare try to sweep this under the rug. We have put off talking long enough. Plenty has happened over the years, and we can't ignore it. Talk to me."

I stand on my hind legs, frustration— and once again, fear— lead my heart. "Because I don't know how to talk about it!" I yell, hitting my chest with my fist. "What is it that you want to know? That the moment you were dragged away from me, the moment I knew I would never be able to have you again, the moment your father's second in command threatened to fuck you when you were of age, that it changed me forever? Yes, it fucking broke me, Louie. Losing you broke me. I didn't care what happened to me after that."

Her eyes brim with tears at the same time her bottom lip quivers. "Aziel—"

I take a few deep breaths as my emotion builds and cut her off, "—You want to know what happened to me? You were taken from me, and I no longer cared about anything. I had images in my mind of you belonging to someone else, being in someone's arms that weren't mine, taking someone's cock that wasn't mine, having someone's children that weren't mine. The thought of you tortured me."

"And you don't think I had the same thoughts? The same fears? You think I didn't think about—" her breath catches and one tear drips down her cheek "—I thought of you with your mate, laughing, having kids, loving her, giving her what I always wanted. Do you really think your feelings were one-sided? I nearly died when they took me from you. I refused to eat, to sleep, to do anything. I held a stake to my heart more times than I'd like to count but something always stopped me. My love for you tortured me too."

I cup her face with both of my palms, my beast's hands engulfing the delicate bones. I've killed too many with these hands but with her, they are gentle and at ease. "A stake? Louie," I choke on her name, thinking about a world where she no longer existed. "I had something similar, but it wasn't a stake."

"Tell me." Her small hand hidden with strength presses against mine as she leans her head into my palm.

"Brenden, the vampire back there. He used to be a

warlock. A very powerful warlock. He was evil, stealing power from other witches, and it made him unstoppable. He captured werewolves, destroyed our homes, and put us under a curse that made us kill for him. I was trapped inside my beast for fifteen years. I did...” I take a deep breath, my teeth grinding together as flashes of the people I've killed flash through my mind. Their screams ringing in my ears. Their pleas for death make me struggle to breathe.

“—It's okay.” Louie rubs soothing circles on my chest. “You're okay.”

“I'm not okay. I killed women and children. I ate other shifters in war because Brenden wouldn't feed us. I'm a fucking monster, Louie. And I have to live with what I did forever. I can do that. I lost myself a long time ago, and I never planned on finding a way back.”

“How did the curse break?” she questions, kissing me on the chest where my heart is racing against my bones.

“My new Alpha or in your case, Master. Alexander Monreaux and his beloved Maven Wildes helped end the curse by changing him into a vampire. The curse lifted but I think parts of me were still trapped in the age when I was seventeen. I missed you. The majority of my life was taken from me, and I didn't last very long in the new life Alexander and Maven gave to me. I swear, I smelled you on the property.”

“Oh, God. Aziel.” She wraps her arms around me the best she can. They don't wrap all the way around. I'm too big. Her shoulders shake as she cries for me.

“Smelling you sent me into sickness. I had gone without you for far too long and that's what happens. All those years ago, we were supposed to be together, and we were forced to be apart. I have no doubt that's what pushed me into sickness. I nearly died. I was terrible to everyone, especially Anwyll. I said hateful, unforgivable things, but Maven found a treatment.”

“A treatment? For werewolf sickness?” Louie takes

my hand, tugging in the direction of Purgatory Pins, and casually leads me to where we need to go.

"Yeah, I didn't know it existed, but Anwyll and his mate went on a journey to get all the ingredients. It worked, in the sense it cured my sickness, the feral and rabid rage."

And the pain... God the pain. Every so often, it likes to roar its ugly head, reminding me of what I felt when I was going mad.

"Physically, I'm fine now, but according to Death, my soul got lost fighting between life and death, so I got sent here. I have to find my way back to my body before the lunar moon which means *we* have to find our way back to the surface. I am not leaving here without you, Louie."

She stops, sighing, and it's the kind of exhale that lets me know that I won't like what I'm about to hear. "I don't even know how I got here. I can't remember anything other than complete darkness."

The familiar fire of fury boils my blood. What happened to my mate that sent her down here like me?

"What do you mean you can't remember? What events lead up to it?"

"I– I don't know." She drops her hands to her sides and bends down to pick up a fucking stick, poking at the ground. "I remember screaming but that's it. I have no other answers for you, Aziel."

"I'll find them."

"You don't know that."

I jump in front of her, cutting off her line of escape. "I swear to you. On my soul's life, I will find those answers because I'm not living my life without you again. I will happily live in Purgatory for the rest of my days if it means I get to be with you. If you stayed here and I found my body, I would die anyway. Why would I choose death when I could spend the rest of my life right here with my mate?"

"Wait. If you can't go home because you'll die, and I

don't have a body that means—"

I take her hands in mine, giving them a firm squeeze. "—It means we stay here."

"But we could die. We could get killed and then what? We wouldn't be remembered."

"Why would I care about being remembered by anyone who isn't you? I don't think you understand just how far my need goes, Louie, how far my love goes, how intense my obsession is with you. I'd do anything for you. There isn't a line I wouldn't cross. There isn't a life I wouldn't take. Nothing could stop me from being with you in this world or any other world."

I lift her by her shoulders, inciting a yelp from Louie while she kicks her feet.

"Aziel! Put me down."

"No. Now. Give me a kiss."

She quirks a brow at me before crossing her arms over her chest. "Excuse me? You want a kiss after you manhandled me to be ten feet in the air?"

"I can make it eleven." I stretch my arms above my head, grinning when she kicks more, but it's the constant laughter coming from Louie that lets me know she doesn't mind.

"Okay. Okay. Okay." She reaches for me, planting a kiss right on my werewolf lips. "Better?"

"For now." I set her down on the ground and the moment her feet touch Purgatory's floor, she slaps me on the arm. "Ow. That hurt."

She rolls her eyes at me. "Please. I bet you didn't even feel it. My feet belong on the ground. Got it?"

I lift a shoulder and shrug. "I guess that rules out you straddling my face, your legs over my shoulders while I eat that pretty cunt of yours."

Her mouth drops open. "In this form?"

"This one," I echo in agreement.

She pouts her lips before nibbling the bottom one. "I guess heights aren't really that bad. Plus, you'd never drop me, right?"

"Never, My Light."

She becomes bashful before taking my hand again. "Come on. We are close. I want a shower to rinse all this blood off."

"I thought vampires loved blood?"

"If I was covered head to toe in your blood, that would be different. His blood kind of reeks."

"It's the evil," I mutter while looking straight ahead. Nothing but dead trees and black grass in sight. "He might have changed forms, but his blood is still as toxic as ever."

I'm not too sure how far we are into our journey, but my stomach begins to growl. I can't remember the last time I ate. I've been too busy feasting on my mate. I lick my lips when my mouth waters. If only she were enough to sate my actual hunger, I'd never need food again when I could live off her.

Louie stops, the blood on her skin no longer gleaming, and sniffs the air.

"What do you smell?" I place my hand on her lower back, my gaze trying to follow hers.

"Iggy!" she shouts, blurring away from me and heading straight ahead before I can stop her.

"Louie!" I growl, worried she isn't hearing her friend at all, but a demon pretending to be him. "Louie!" My legs stretch with every stride as I run.

I'm going to spank her for running away from me.

I follow her delicious scent that's muted by Brenden's blood. My paws leave indents in the ground, landing with weighted thuds. I'm closer to her scent. Chirps and hisses sound in alternate rhythms around me. Small glowing eyes appear in the shadows of the trees, watching me.

An uneasy feeling takes hold, and my instincts scream for us to get out of here. We are predators, yet there is something in here that sees us as prey.

"Louie! Where the hell are you?" How far could she

have gone? This vampire speed gives me a headache. I'm going to have to put a bell on her, so I know where she is. I'll do the same with the vampires in my pack.

When I get to the edge of the tree line, I skid to a stop when I see one of my worst nightmares come to life. Louie is standing next to a feminine man. He's short with big round eyes and from here I can smell his fear— and his nature.

And so do the skelewolves surrounding them.

They are similar to hellhounds only instead of being born in fire, they are birthed in darkness here in Purgatory. They are skinny, their skeletons on the outside of their bodies, encasing their organs tightly under their skin. Their hair is patchy, and their eyes are bottomless pits of coal, something most creatures seem to have in common here.

I slip Uri from the holster. Louie must hear me because she lifts her head and stares in my direction. She has a dagger in hand, one arm stretched around Iggy to keep him safe.

These skelewolves don't want Louie. They want Iggy.

He is a male omega and if they get to him, they could force him to birth their pups. He'd be used until he died and then the wolves would hunt down someone else.

They snap their jaws, acidic spit dripping from their jowls. The ground sizzles and steam rises.

"What is it with this place having acidic fucking fluids?" I mumble, giving Louie a nod so she understands what I'm about to do.

I rear Uri back. Louie's eyes widen before the realization dawns on her. The warrior she is replaces her fear. Her stance changes. Sights narrowing. Dagger firm in her grip.

Twisting to gain more momentum, I swing Uri once, twice, and on the third, I let it go. My weapon flies, cutting through the air by flipping in a straight line. The skelewolves whip their heads to me, giving Louie the chance she needs to lunge.

The crunch of bone and the spew of blood creates an orchestra when Uri hammers a skelewolves head.

Right. Down. The. Middle.

Its head splits in two and the body falls limp. That gives Louie the split-second chance to shove her blade through the temple of another wolf. She blurs, fighting as fast as she can so the wolves won't get to Iggy.

I run, eating up the distance between me, my mate, and her friend. Iggy stabs the air missing the creatures as they dodge and nip at his ankle, toying with their food. One of the wolves manages to slip by Louie on her quest of killing and I'm soaring through the air to tackle the one closest to me when Iggy screams in agony.

The wolf begins to drag him away through shallow murky water. His scream is drowned out by dirty water and not even that is enough to cover the stench of Iggy's arm burning from the acid.

Carnality takes over. Louie hops on the back of the wolf I'm fighting, plunging her daggers in on either side of its neck. A loud screeching howl from the skel-ewolf sends shivers through my bones, almost causing me to howl its pain in return.

"Get Iggy! Please! I'll take care of them." She jumps over another wolf, twisting her body in the air, and lands perfectly on her feet.

"Louie…"

She gives the skelewolf a come-hither motion with a confident smirk. Louie doesn't look at me. Her eyes are locked onto her target, waiting for the beast to make its first move. The daggers dance across her knuckles before she spins, flicking the knife. It lands in the abyss of the right eye. Black smoke oozes from the orbital bone.

"Aziel. I'm fine." She rips the blade free before plunging the other into the wolf's chest. "Please, go!"

Louie yells at me, killing yet another wolf by herself.

Dropping to all fours and taking one last long look at my mate before I dash to save Iggy. The wolf is snarling, still dragging him through the murky water only this time, Iggy has shifted into his bear.

He's small which isn't unusual for omegas, and he is doing his best to fight. He bites and swipes his paw at the wolf, landing one good hit on the side of the wolf's face. It's enough for Iggy to be freed. He runs through the shallow water, staring at me with big, wide eyes that are full of fear.

He bellows for help, and I roar in reply, so he knows I'm on my way. He's halfway across the field of death weeds. The grass can come to life whenever it wants, wrapping its blades around its victims to squeeze until all the life is gone. All Iggy and I can do is hope the weeds remain still.

Just as the wolf hurls itself through the air, arms wide to land on Iggy's back, I sink my claws into Iggy's back, slinging him behind me. I take the brute force of the skelewolf's weight. Its paws push against my shoulders, pushing me under the disgusting water they drink.

I relax, making the creature think he has won, and when I feel him ease up on his power, I rake my feet down his underbelly, punch my fist into his chest, and rip out his heart.

Breaking the surface of the water, I gasp, inhaling as deep as possible before standing on my hind legs. I hold the heart in my hand, watching it beat slower and slower until the pulse ceases to exist.

I throw the useless organ to the side, the water splashing from the thunk of it.

"Iggy! Iggy, I have you. It's okay. You're okay. You have to be okay."

I don't have time to catch my breath, not when I feel the soul-aching sadness from Louie. Iggy has shifted and is lying in her lap, struggling to breathe, and clutching his mangled arm. The acid did damage.

All that is left is bone.

Iggy shivers from shock. His hair drips with muddy water. His cheeks and lips shake from his tremors. His mouth is blue, and all color has drained from his face. I know Louie can smell it— the seconds ticking towards death.

"Iggy? You're okay now. I have you. You'll be okay. Please, be okay." My sweet mate runs her fingers through Iggy's hair to try and comfort him.

"I'm okay, Elouise. I'm not in pain." He smiles, moving his head back to look up at her. "Never would have thought some fucking wolves would get me— no offense—" he says to me before coughing.

"I'm not a wolf so no harm no foul," I make sure to return his light-hearted nature with a sad smile.

"No. You're going to be fine. You'll be just fine." Louie takes a deep breath, blinking her tears away. "You're my best friend. Please, Iggy, don't go. I need you here with me. You're my best friend. I can't— I can't do this without you. It's been us since day one."

His attention drifts to me and an understanding passes between us. "I think you'll be just fine now that you have your beloved, Louie. You'll be okay. He'll take care of you."

Louie shakes her head, lifting Iggy into her arms to clutch him tighter. His heart rate begins to slow, his eyes fighting to close.

"You were a light in this place, Louie. You made my existence worth it when I never thought it could be," he whispers, losing the battle of staying conscious.

"No, no, no! Iggy! Wake up. Please wake up!" She shakes him, holding his face in her hands. "Iggy!" A scream built upon pain and suffering swims for miles around us as she lets her friend go.

A tear falls from her jaw to Iggy's chin, and I've never moved so fast in my life. I drop to my knees and take Iggy from her, his heart losing its strength with every wasted second.

"No! Give him back! Let me have this. Let me say goodbye," she shouts at me.

I wipe the glittering tears from her eyes, rubbing the silky liquid between my fingers before showing her. "Your tears, My Light. Give him your tears."

She stares at me dumbfounded and frozen. "How could we have forgotten that?" Louie rushes to scoot closer. "We are so damn stupid." A relieved emotional cackle barks from her before she leans her head over Iggy's mouth, a single tear dripping free from her face and right onto his tongue.

A second passes without anything happening but I still hear his heart beating. It's a dragged-out pulse, one that proves how close he is to death's grip.

"Come on, come on," Louie begs the universe.

But we aren't in that kind of dimension. The universe can't hear our pleas. Her cries for help have no reply.

"Why isn't it working? Aziel, it should be working. My tears fix everything, anything, everyone. I don't understand."

I lift his arm for her to see what I do. "Look," I say, easing my tone to a more soft and gentler level in hopes she can hear my calm and feel my hope. "It is working. He is healing. Life takes time to create." I reach for her, and she falls into the crook of my arm, wiping her wet cheeks on my fur.

"Thank you."

"For what?" I drop my gaze to her just as she peers up to me with tear-stuck lashes. I love her eyes when she cries. I know it's horrible to say but the gold in them seems brighter, almost like they are glowing. I hate her sadness, yet I find it beautiful all at the same time.

"For making me think clearly. I was so caught up in pain, in the grief of losing my best friend, I forgot I could save him."

I run my claws through her hair which is a bit tangled with blood just like my fur is.

"It's what I'm here for, to help you when you can't help yourself. You're the strongest woman I know, Louie. The bravest. The wildest. It's okay not to have it all together all of the time. You don't have to. I'm here now. You can relax that part of yourself. I never plan on going anywhere."

Her gaze drops to my lips as her fingers play with the fur on my cheeks. I bend down to catch her lips in a searing kiss when Iggy's voice stops us.

"Ugh, God, kill me all over again. You two are sickening—" he coughs, inhaling a deep breath.

"Iggy! Oh my God. You're okay." Louie gathers him into her arms, manhandling him a bit with her vampiric strength, and squeezes him too hard.

"I can't breathe," he croaks, eyeing me to save him.

I shrug, silently telling him he is on his own.

She releases her stronghold, dusting off the dirt on his torn shirt. "Oh. Sorry. I'm sorry. I'm just so happy. I was so scared. I haven't felt that in a long time." She brushes Iggy's hair back. "I thought I lost you."

His face is still pale, but his heartbeat is normal. There isn't a mark on him. Vampire tears are special. More so than their fangs. I know there are hunters out there who want the fangs to prolong their orgasms and the ability to perform, but the real salvation is the tears. They heal diseases, add to someone's lifespan, and increase libido.

I hope the last one doesn't hit Iggy. That would be awkward. I wouldn't be able to help him out with that. The vampire back home, Greyson, he'd like Iggy. Greyson thinks he is covering up his secret so well, but everyone knows he likes males.

Iggy tugs her into another hug. "Thank you for using your tears. I thought I was a goner. I know how sacred the teardrops are. I would have never expected—"

She pulls away, snagging him by his shoulders. "—I

would do anything for you. If you need more tears, I'll give them to you. You're my best friend, Iggy. Your death isn't allowed."

My stomach lets out a long, loud grumble, and if it were possible for me to blush in this form, I would.

"Way to ruin the moment," Iggy teases, knocking my knee with his elbow. "Thanks for coming after me, Aziel. I know you didn't have to."

"Any friend of Louie's is a friend of mine. If you died, she would be sad. I can't have my mate unhappy."

"So for selfish reasons. I can live with that. And also—" he turns to Elouise. "Louie?"

I grunt, not really knowing what to say. Saving him was selfish. I also know it was the right thing to do.

"He loves calling me that even if I hate it," she mumbles with a sigh.

"You love it." I snag her neck and yank her to me. It's been too long since I've felt her lips. I break away, leaving her glassy-eyed and by the scent of it, aroused.

"Okay. Remember, I'm here." He waves the air away from his nose, the smell of lust too much for him. "What's the plan?" Iggy cracks his neck from side to side, groaning. He does the same to his back, fingers, and ankles. How does someone crack their ankles? "Hey, Aziel? Can you just tug on my leg?"

"I'm afraid I'll rip it off, and I won't shift to human form, not when we are vulnerable."

"He's a shifter, Beloved." Louie grabs his ankles, giving his legs a good yank, and a loud pop from his hips makes me flinch. "He'll be fine."

He moans. "God, that feels so much better. Thanks."

"We are going to Purgatory Pins. We'll wash up there, eat, and be on the way to look for the avisseus. Hopefully, no fog hits and I don't have to go back to fight for more information."

"You aren't fighting," Louie objects, getting to her feet.

I stay seated, tilting my head back to appreciate my

angry mate. Her finger is in my face, shaking it as she speaks.

"You will no longer fight, Aziel Monreaux. Do you understand me? We are half-bonded. You won't risk that."

Hearing my pack's last name behind my first shocks me. I've never thought about it before. I know we take the last name of whatever pack we pledge to and it's a reminder of how I was packless for so long. I didn't have a last name. Not until Alpha Monreaux took me in and gave Anwyll and me a chance. I'll do my best to live up to the Monreaux name.

"My Light." I tug her hand causing her to fall into my lap. "I have to if we want to get out of here. All of us. Iggy too."

"I don't know if I can," he admits. "I'm dead. I died in my dimension when they wanted to kill all male omegas. I don't think I can go back. I don't have a body waiting for me."

"– But you have bones."

Louie unsheathes her daggers and takes a stance while I drop in front of Iggy, growling at the intruder.

Only to see it's Death.

"You," I growl.

He lights a cigarette. "Hiya. How are y'all doing? Me? I've had better days. Someone's mate just died so that really sucked. I really hate the sadness. I really think love is so beautiful, ya know?"

"Death?" Iggy peeks around my back. "Like the Four Horsemen, Death? You brought me here? You could have saved me, you know!" Iggy launches himself at Death and I snag him in time. He is kicking and reaching for the Horseman.

Death casually stands there in his beast form, his wings tucked behind his back, and the stitches that sew his face together crinkle when he takes another hit off his cigarette. "Feisty little thing, aren't you? I was doing my job, little one."

"Don't call me that. I might be little, but my attitude and anger are your size, bucko."

Death snickers, flicking the ashes off the cigarette. Humor flashes across his eyes. "Noted." He takes another puff. "Little One."

"Oh, I'm going to fucking—" Iggy tries to attack Death again and I roll my eyes, clutching his shirt to keep him in place.

The bear still swings, missing Death by— let's just say— so much room.

"So, you were saying he can come back with us?" I ask, tugging Iggy back. "Stop it," I grumble. "He could kill you."

"He already has." Iggy narrows his eyes and crosses his arms.

"Brat," I say under my breath, exhausted by this day. When will it end?

"If you three manage to escape and his soul is freed, he will find his bones. He'll be alive and well. Loopholes, am I right?" Death holds out his fist for knuckles. "Come on," he urges. "You want to."

"I don't."

"Yes, you do." He shakes his fist. "Come on. Give me some knucks."

Louie slaps a hand over her mouth to smother her giggles.

Sighing, I roll my eyes and lazily clench my fist, bumping his fucking knuckles.

"There it is! You're welcome for the advice by the way."

"I thought you weren't allowed to help us escape?"

"I didn't tell you how. I said if you managed. Loopholes." He blows smoke into the air. He checks the time on the watch he isn't wearing. "I've got to fly. Someone else died. Every fucking second. So depressing. Smell ya later." He holds out his fist again, and I bump it for good measure before he flicks the cigarette away, vanishing in a black cloud.

"That was... that was..." Louie is trying to find her words to explain that meet and greet.

"–Something. I know. All the Horsemen are like that."

"Well, then I'm going to have words with all of them," Iggy says.

"Okay, Killer. How about we make it to Purgatory Pins alive first? If we don't get there soon, I'm going to have to have some bear."

Iggy and Louie gasp in horror.

"I'm kidding. Jeez."

Kind of. They don't need to know I'm a little serious. I've eaten shifter before in desperation. I have no issue doing it again.

"Not a funny joke," Louie whispers out of the side of her mouth so only I can hear.

I lift my finger and thumb, pressing them together to make a small space. "It was. Just a little bit."

A howl sounds in the distance and the hairs on my body stand up in warning. "We need to go. Skelewolves are coming. They probably sense some of their pack is dead."

"Iggy. On Aziel's back. He's quicker."

"Hey. I do my best. It's not my fault I have little legs."

I drop to all fours and drop my head, push it between his thighs, then fling back. He yells, somersaulting through the air. He lands on his stomach with a groan, scurrying around so he doesn't have a view of my ass.

"You could have just asked me to jump on."

"That would have taken too long. Ready?" I ask Louie, wishing it was her on my back. I already miss her touch. The way she runs her fingers through my hair, how she grips it, the way she buries her cheek into the thick of my neck– she reminds me I have something to protect.

"You better hold on," I warn him. "If you fall, I'm not

coming back for you."

"Psh, yes you would," he sasses.

Fucking. Brat.

"Let's go." I start running, the weeds of the field coming to life. They nip at my paws, trying to embrace my ankles to bring me down. I'm too strong. Louie has to hop on my back to avoid the wicked blades.

I guess I'm a chauffeur now. Surprisingly, I don't mind. Louie is safe along with her friend. This journey to survive might kill us but at least we will die together.

We'll fight for our existence. We'll get back home. We'll be a family.

Iggy too.

Chapter Eight

ELOUISE

When we finally arrive at Purgatory Pins, I let out a heavy, stressed breath. We're safe here. If there is one thing I know about this place, it's that it's somewhat of a safe haven. Creatures on the outside who mean harm can't enter the doors but if a fight breaks loose inside due to too much Deadly Ale or Between the Life and Death shot, you're on your own.

"If it isn't my favorite fighter!"

Aziel groans. "Fuck. Why is he everywhere?"

"Scorder," I hiss, flashing my fangs at the dragon shifter who profits off death.

I understand why he does it, but I'll never respect it.

"He's kind of cute though," Iggy wiggles his fingers at the guy.

I slap his hand down. "No, we don't like him."

"Oh." He narrows his eyes and lifts a middle finger in the air. "Fuck you, Scorder. Eat a dick."

"Name the time and place, Cutie." Scorder winks and blows a kiss.

I slap Iggy in the chest. "Look. See what you've

done?"

"I didn't think he'd be receptive," he grumbles.

"Scorder is receptive to everything," Aziel explains. "He isn't the trustworthy type. He's a con man. Be careful, Iggy. Especially here. I'm going to go out on a limb and say you're probably the only one of your kind here."

"A bear?"

"An omega," Aziel says with a tone that makes my stomach twist with worry.

Iggy clutches Aziel's fur tighter, then hides behind his neck. Aziel must feel Iggy's unease because he stretches his arm back, grips Iggy's shirt, and lifts my best friend off his back.

I slip to the ground too, patting my holster to make sure I have my daggers. I'm so glad Iggy had them when I ran into him in the field. Granted, we were then surrounded by wolves. Nevertheless, they come in handy in the worst times.

"I won't let anything happen to you, Iggy. You're safe here. They might stare and make comments, but for the most part, Purgatory Pins is a safe place. Everyone has an understanding this is a place to unwind, not fight," Aziel explains.

Scorder has a giant grin on his face as he skips over to us. "Tell me, Cutie, how do you feel about placing a bet?"

Faster than Scorder could blow smoke from his nose, I have a dagger against his throat and Aziel has Uri pressed against his nape. The scheming dragon freezes, raising his hands in surrender.

I apply a bit more pressure, leaning forward to get close to his face. I curl my lip and warn, "You'll stay away from him, or I swear, you'll never place a bet again. "

"Oh, feisty thing, aren't you?"

I flash my fangs. My vision turns red, and I hiss, "You have no fucking clue."

He tries to lean away from me only to stop when he

feels the sharpness of Uri against the back of his neck.

"I wouldn't move another muscle unless you want me to decapitate you, Scorder."

The dragon begins to sweat. Beads form over his top lip and his tongue wipes them away. "I thought we were friends, Ripper. Come on, we make a good team."

"We aren't a team. You don't care if I live or die. You only care about making money. If you don't want to be at the end of my wrath, you'll leave Iggy alone. Forever. When the next fog hits, I'll see you at The Graveyard. I'll do my job. Am I clear?"

"As a crystal," he says.

I ease my dagger from his throat and Aziel pushes Scorder away. He doesn't holster Uri. He keeps that weapon in hand, tightening his grip until the handle creaks. "You still owe me the clue from my last win."

Scorder rubs his hands down his shirt, smoothing out the wrinkles while gaining his composure. He bows, waving his hand in a circle as if he is a gentleman.

"A days travel up Dread Mountain, to the west. Now, I bid you farewell. Until next time." His eyes slide to Iggy before grinning, sending me a wink.

Losing my patience, I snag a dagger and throw it at the infuriating man. He wiggles his fingers before disappearing into thin air, my blade cutting through the air he used to breathe. The silver embeds itself into a nearby tree.

"Ugh, I can't stand him." I stomp my way to the tree, yanking my dagger free. "I'm going to kill him just because I can't stand his face."

"I didn't mean to cause any issues. I'm sorry."

Aziel and I turn to Iggy who is making himself smaller by slouching, toying with the hem of his dirty shirt.

"Don't apologize. Scorder is a piece of work, just be careful who you challenge. Even if it is all fun and games. Some take everything seriously to use to their advantage, like Scorder. He knows you're an omega and if he gets his hands on you, I have no doubt you'll be another bet for him to rake in eeries. Stay by our side, okay?"

Iggy nods in agreement, still gripping the hem of his shirt like a kid in trouble. It doesn't take a paranormal to notice his unease and fear. I can't imagine how he must feel, the guilt, blaming himself for being born how he is.

"Don't think like that." I pry his hands from his shirt, holding them in mine. He's shaking. "Iggy, look at me."

He shakes his head, a tear falling onto my arm from his jaw.

Aziel's immense shadow falls over us, his presence bringing protection and comfort. Iggy snaps his head up with wide, scared eyes, blowing out a breath with inflated cheeks to see it's only my werewolf.

"Don't think like that, okay?" I repeat, wiping his tears away.

"I didn't say anything," he says, lifting his shoulder to dry his tears.

"You don't need to. Your thoughts are painted all over your face."

"Well, if I was different, if I would have been born normal, none of this would have happened. I'd be alive. And even in Purgatory, I'm not welcome."

"That's where you're wrong," Aziel's deep voice booms, the baritone slithering down my spine and enticing a memory of him whispering filthy things into my ear. "You are *too* wanted here. The problem is you'd get used, but we won't let that happen, Iggy. Okay? Let's go inside, get cleaned up, and get a good meal. You're safe."

Iggy's gaze jumps around to take in our new surroundings. Looping my arm through his, I guide us to head to the entrance, wanting to see what Iggy sees. A few motorcycles– larger than any bike I've ever seen— are parked in front of the building. They are made of skulls and other bones, including the kickstand.

A few creatures are outside, smoking Purgatory Pure by the smell of it. The stench is terrible but it's one of the only plants in Purgatory that's safe to smoke and gives the smoker a high. It reeks of decay, and I can't help but wonder if the smoke is slowly decomposing their insides.

A centaur and a lion shifter stand outside the door, passing Purgatory Pure back and forth while watching us.

The centaur slaps Aziel's chest, my werewolf glancing down at the unwelcome hand touching him.

Aziel slowly lifts his head, cocking it toward the centaur and Iggy gulps from the soon-to-be confrontation.

"Get your fucking hand off me," Aziel snarls, placing the sharp edge of Uri against the centaur's wrist. "Or you won't have a hand to fuck yourself with."

"You have something that smells good—" the centaur stares directly at Iggy. "How about we allow you in if you give us the little bear shifter?" He inhales the Pure only to exhale green smoke into Aziel's face.

What an idiot.

I slip a dagger free, hiding it with my arm, assessing the situation. My arm stays looped with Iggy's, not wanting to let him go when there are too many who want him. Aziel can handle this.

Aziel tosses his head back, and a boom of laughter explodes from him. I take a step back, forcing Iggy to do the same.

Uri twists over Aziel's fingers, spinning in circles across his knuckles before he clutches the handle, swings Uri to the left, and the centaur's eyes stay wide. His mouth opens. He tries to speak but it comes out as a croak. Slowly, the centaur's head slides from his body, thumping on the ground while his body remains upright.

Blood spills from his neck, flowing fast like a rushing river.

Eventually, his body sways before collapsing against his lion friend.

"How about–" Aziel slings Uri against the lion shifter's throat next, still wet with his friend's blood "–Fucking no."

The lion's pupils are blown wide from smoking, but he isn't too far gone not to surrender.

"I don't want him, man. I wouldn't say anything like that about someone."

Aziel takes a step closer to the shifter, towering over the lion by a good foot, and looks down upon him as if he is nothing but a mouse waiting to be crushed.

"You better mean that because I'll skin the mane right off, kitty cat, and I'll wrap it around my weapon as a fucking cape every time I kill someone who speaks that way about my friend. You might want to spread the word that I kill first and don't ask questions. Got it?"

"Got it. You don't have to worry about that from me, man." The lion takes another hit of Purgatory Pure before offering it to Aziel. "You want some? I'm the sharing type. Not like that– I'm not asking to share, you know, them– just the Pure. You feel me?"

My beloved curls his lip to show his fang. "No, I don't 'feel' you. And I don't care to. Get out of our way before I make you," he warns.

Aziel's authority is a ripple through my body. All I want to do is get on all fours and present myself to him like he deserves.

The lion takes a step to the right, away from the centaur's body.

"Good choice." He twirls Uri around before stashing it in its holster.

Aziel opens the door, gesturing us to walk inside. "My mate goes first but keep that dagger out just in case." He kisses my forehead, not minding the grime of blood and dirt caked onto my skin.

"What dagger?" I bat my eyelashes at him, feigning

innocence.

"My Light," he laughs, sliding a claw down my inner arm before it clinks against my dagger. "That one. You can't hide anything from me. I love that you were at the ready, but as soon as you walk through the door, be ready."

"I always am, Beloved." I cross the threshold, dropping my arm from Iggy to take his hand instead while wielding the dagger in the other.

This place is run down. The lighting is dim and what's terrifying is the floor is translucent. We're able to see the fire depths of hell, souls pressing their faces against the barrier screaming to get out.

"I'm going to have nightmares from this, aren't I?" Iggy asks, trying to step over the empty faces begging to be set free.

To the right is a bar with a long counter that has different types of creatures sitting on stools. One hiccups, leans to the left, then right, before gravity takes hold and he falls to the floor.

There are bowling lanes stretching from each end of the building. The bowling balls are different-sized skulls with a variety of eye sockets and mouth sizes for everyone's fingers. The pins at the end of the lane are made of spines. Whose spine? I don't know and don't want to know.

Ribcage lights hang from the ceiling, twinkling as if they have been freshly polished.

Odd.

I look behind me to see Aziel right there, his chest nearly hitting my nose with how close he is. Iggy tightens his grip on my hand as he looks around, the fear wafting from him in intense waves.

"Iggy, they will eat you alive if they smell fear. You need to take a few deep breaths," Aziel says, thumping his fist on the counter.

"Someone will be right with you!" The bartender with two arms and even more tentacles shouts, slinging beers and shots.

"No problem," Aziel replies.

While we wait, I give the counter my back so no one else can take advantage of it. I swing my dagger in my hand, back and forth, in circles, flips, anything to pass the time. A few creatures side-eye me as they leave, but nothing too serious that makes me react.

"Damn, you three have seen better days, haven't ya?"

I spin around to see a massive bull shifter wiping down the countertop we are leaning against. He has short-cropped black hair and a septum piercing in his nose. He is intimidating but his kindness is off-putting in a place like this.

"Sorry for the delay. Someone died on lane four because they got a strike and someone else really didn't like that."

"I'm going to die here," Iggy yelps, huddling between me and Aziel.

"No, you'll be fine. I promise." He holds out a hand to Aziel. "I'm Trelo, the manager of Purgatory Pins. How can I help you?" He tosses the bar rag on his shoulder, waiting for Aziel to greet him. "I'm thinking of a place to stay, some food, fresh clothes, and a shower?"

My wolf slaps his hand into Trelo's. "Yes, to all that. And add one game to that, will you?"

"Sure. No problem. Everything is a flat fee so once you pay, you can walk into the room where we keep all the supplies. Want to put in an order for food? I can have it delivered to your rooms."

"Rooms?" Iggy clutches me tight. "By myself? I don't want to be alone here. Please, Elouise."

"Your room is a suite. So same place, two rooms. You won't be alone, Little One, I wouldn't do that to you due to what you are."

Iggy hides behind Aziel and in a burst of rage, I jump onto the counter, holding a dagger to the bull's throat. "Why? Do you have a plan for him? I will fucking cut you from ear to ear if you even think about touching him."

"Omegas are cherished by most shifters. I have no plan other than protecting him. That's it. I promise."

I inhale his scent to try to detect any lies and unfortunately, I smell nothing but honesty. I was looking forward to a fight.

"So, can you lower your weapon before you draw attention? We don't need a bar fight."

I nod, sheathing my knife. "Fine." I jump off the bar. "For now."

"What's the total?" Aziel asks. "I need to shower. This blood is starting to itch." He proceeds to scratch the dried blood on his chest.

"Sixty eeries. All-access to all the food, drink, and games. Arcade is right behind you too."

"Excellent." Aziel unzips his pouch, counting out sixty eeries. "Here's an extra ten you can keep for yourself." He flips the coin in the air and Trelo catches it.

The bull quirks a brow. "Thank you. You must make your eeries at the fights to have so much at once. Be careful with that here. We have master pickpockets, and you'll never know who took it."

Aziel plops the pouch in his bag where he keeps his skull mask— which I want to *explore*.

"Here are your keys."

"Why aren't I surprised to see they are made of bone?" I pick up the key, a little grossed out that I'm holding someone's skeleton, someone who died and is now being used to unlock doors.

That's sad.

"With all the bones in Purgatory, we do our best to use them so they don't clutter the forest floor. We also use them to feed the hellhounds. They love bones."

"Hellhounds?" Iggy squeaks. "Like the one with three heads? You have them here? I thought they were only in Hell."

Trelo shakes his head. "They like to explore Purgatory."

"You mean, hunt," Aziel corrects him, wrapping his arm around my waist. "We're going to go get cleaned up. Thanks for your help, Trelo."

"No problem. When you get to your room, the Purgatory menu is on the nightstand next to the bed. "

"Thanks again," Aziel says, ushering me and Iggy to the open door next to the bar.

There's a red neon sign with blood-dripped font that says, 'Purga-Mart.' In the corner, there is a skeletal figure dressed in black, licking his finger as he flips the pages of a magazine. He frowns before acting impressed as he turns the magazine so he can see the full spread.

"Nice," he compliments, and I can't help but roll my eyes.

Aziel's loud footsteps cause him to glance up from the magazine. He grins, tossing the magazine in a dramatic gesture before hopping to his feet.

"Welcome to Purga-Mart. The only place in this hell hole that can maybe, kind of, sometimes, give you what you need." He straightens his nametag, straightening his spine. "I'm Lorcan." He salutes.

"Hi, Lorcan," I greet him with a smile. His energy is infectious.

Iggy waves and Aziel doesn't bother to give him the time of day. Lorcan seems to latch onto Aziel, vanishing in smoke before appearing right in front of him.

"I think I know you," Lorcan says.

"No, you don't." Aziel snags a few shirts for me off the shelf that says, 'Purgatory Pins' while the only other shirt they have states, 'I love Purgatory.'

That's a stretch.

Lorcan hums, tapping his finger against his mouth. "No... I think I do know you."

"I have never seen you before in my life." Aziel exhales with annoyance.

Iggy and I snicker which causes Aziel to narrow his eyes at us.

Aziel walks around Lorcan but he cuts my mate off again. "Wait a minute. Do you have a brother?"

Aziel freezes, a low deadly growl is loud in this room from the acoustics. Iggy gasps, inching closer to me. My wolf grips Lorcan by his shirt and lifts him off the ground.

"How the fuck do you know my brother?" Aziel tilts his head, the thunder rolling in his chest never wavering.

Lorcan kicks his feet like a child before vanishing again, only to reappear to the left of Aziel.

"Woah, let's play nice, okay? No need to get grabby." He brushes off his shirt. "I've met Anwyll. You two look alike. You're more 'Grrrrr and roar' and he's more 'Aw and cute.' No offense, I prefer your brother. You're kind of an ass."

Aziel snarls, whipping his arm out to grab him again.

Lorcan gives him the slip.

"You mother fucker." Aziel glances around the mart, searching for the irritating skeletal figure.

I'm loving this.

Lorcan pops up behind Aziel, crossing his arms. "I find that rude as I have not fucked your mother. I have met her though. Lovely woman. You came from her? That's interesting."

"You have met her?" Aziel yells, slinging Uri free and pressing it against Lorcan's throat. "Fucking vanish and this will slit your... bones. Or whatever you have."

Lorcan raises his hands. "Okay, okay. Let's not get testy, Roofus. Mmmkay, pumpkin? I can explain."

"You are annoying."

Lorcan's hand flies to his chest. "Oh my gosh, thank you. You're so nice. We're making so much progress. Aziel, isn't it?"

"How do you know my name?"

"I talked to your brother. Did you not hear that

part? Are you listening to me? I don't like it when people don't listen. Repeating myself is a pet peeve."

"You have five seconds before your head is on the floor."

"Okay? I'll just pick it up. There is one thing in this entire universe that can kill me and that isn't you, Roofus."

"My name isn't Roofus."

"Yeah, but you're kind of cute like one. I just want to scratch behind your ear." Lorcan reaches for Aziel's ear, daring to irritate him further.

"Enough!" Aziel throws Lorcan across the room, expecting him to smash against the wall.

Lorcan glides onto his feet, sighing. "Okay, let's talk. All this anger. You need therapy. I can recommend a good blob. They are great listeners. They don't really talk back though, but, I mean, do they need to reply?"

"Will you please–" Aziel gripes through clenched teeth "–Shut up and tell us who you are? Before I lose my patience."

"Before? Yikes, someone didn't hug you enough as a child and it shows."

I dash to Aziel's side, taking his hand to calm him. His patience is non-existent. "Listen, Lorcan, we are very tired. We have had a hell of a day. How do you know his brother?"

"I'm a Void. I work for Death. You know when someone dies, I take them to where they belong. I can travel through different dimensions with ease because of what I am. I talked to your brother on his journey to get your treatment, you know. He nearly died and so did his mate trying to save you."

"I thought Death was the ultimate reaper?"

Lorcan scoffs, taking offense. "He is the ultimate reaper. He is my boss. The boss. He can't do it all himself. Too many die at the same time."

"Why are you here? Aren't people dying?" Aziel asks. "I think I hear them dying now. You should go."

I nudge Aziel's side, giving him *the* look to be kind. "Are you trying to get rid of me?"

"Nooo. I'd never." Aziel's voice is flat with no emotion, staring at Lorcan unamused.

"Oookay, I think that's enough. So, why are you here?"

"I'm being punished. Death stationed me here because I– mighthaveeatenasoulortwowithoutpermission– but it was just a misunderstanding."

"Say that one more time? I didn't catch it," I question him with a tilt of my head.

"I ate a few souls. No big deal, okay? Jeez. They weren't good ones. They were pedophiles and I didn't think they deserved the warmth of Hell. Death didn't like that I made that decision, so I'm serving time here. It isn't too bad. I like it."

"You make my head hurt."

"Stop saying all those sweet things." Lorcan pats Aziel's arm. "I might start getting the wrong idea."

"Okay, I'm going to leave you guys to it while I browse because I want to shower and your bickering is stopping me from doing that. Lorcan, it was nice to meet you."

"Madame, you are nothing but lovely." He takes my hand and kisses the top of my knuckles. "Until we meet again."

"Get your lips off my fucking mate!" Aziel punches Lorcan in the face, sending him soaring through the air once more.

I give them my back, snag a basket, and start grabbing things.

"I don't think Aziel likes Lorcan."

"Yeah, be thankful he likes you, Iggy, or this entire situation would be a nightmare."

"He doesn't like anyone, does he?"

"Mmm," I think about his question, placing a few beef jerky sticks for Aziel and Iggy in the basket so they have snacks before we order dinner. "He has always felt everyone expects a lot from him. He's had to be a certain way to survive. He was supposed to be the Alpha of his pack, but they were massacred. I think he carries that with him. He is a good soul. He'd protect Lorcan with his life because that's who he is but then he'd complain about it later."

Iggy snickers, grabbing a few bottles of water from the fridge. "How do they get all these supplies?"

Something shatters from behind us, the commotion makes us turn around to see Lorcan being slammed against a shelf.

"We bring items back from different— fuck!" Aziel punches him in the gut. "—Different dimensions." Lorcan giggles as he flies through the air. "Faster. Faster!" Which only pisses Aziel off more.

"That's really cool," Iggy says, placing the water in the basket.

Glass breaks. Grunts sound. I catch a flying bottle before it can hit Iggy.

"Woah, thanks."

"No problem." We start walking down the hygiene aisle and much to my disappointment, there aren't many options. I pass a locked glass case, barely getting a glimpse of what is inside, and it hits me what it is. "Oh my God." I backtrack. "No way are these real. They can't be. Holy shit, Iggy. I need these."

Dooming footsteps quickening toward me after a final loud crash has Lorcan moaning for his mom.

"What is it, Louie? Are you okay?" Aziel asks.

"Yes! Oh my God, Aziel. Please, can I get these? I know they are expensive, but I haven't seen them in so long."

"What are they?" he quizzes, tapping the glass with his claw.

"Blood Cloudberries. They are perfect for my hair. They clean it so well and they can be used as a conditioner. Nothing works better. I never—" I whisper before swallowing, unexpectedly emotional. "—I never thought I'd see them again. I never thought I'd be able to take care of my hair the way I want."

"Well, let's get all of them then. My mate gets the products she wants. Lorcan, come unlock this."

"Ugh, you're so—" he twists his head back into place "— Demanding." He wiggles his jaw back and forth before it pops. Lorcan unlocks the case and grabs a silken pouch from the drawer under it to place the berries in, so they don't get damaged. "How many?"

"All of them."

"That's thirty eeries. These berries aren't included in the inclusive price at the bar because they are so rare to find. Do you have that kind of change on you?"

"I do."

"Good. Since you're buying them all, don't say you have them. There are plenty of people who want these berries. Okay?"

"Okay. No problem. They are only for me anyway." I bounce on my heels, waiting for Lorcan to give them to me.

"My Lady," he bows, holding out his palms to give me the pouch.

I squeal, jump up and down, dirt dusting from my hair at the motion. "Thank you. Thank you. Thank you!" I jump as high as I can and still can't kiss Aziel, so he bends down to meet me. "I love you."

He smiles, the soft kind, the one where his eyes almost change shape, a serene expression melting my heart. "I love you too, Louie. I always have. I always will."

Sniffles have me twisting my head to the right.

"Holy shit. You two are so cute. That was beautiful. Death would lose his mind." Lorcan dabs under his eyes. I'm guessing to dry them, but I can't see tears. He stops crying instantly, digging out a device that he points right at us. "Can you do that again? Death would like to see this, and it might spring me from this place."

Aziel snaps his fangs together, pretending to bite

Lorcan, and the Void yelps. "Let's get out of here before I take Lorcan to Hell myself."

"I'm telling your mother about this, Aziel," Lorcan warns.

Aziel snorts. "Doubt it. She wouldn't be able to stand you either."

We leave the mart and the way to the room is a blur because all I can focus on is the small bag in my palms. They are just berries, but to me, it's a form of self-care I haven't been allowed to do in many years.

I ignore all the shouting. The pins hitting the lane after a strike fades. The lights flicker. I think. Perhaps that's just me blinking. I'm not sure.

All that matters right now are these berries.

And to shower.

With Aziel.

Chapter Nine

AZIEL

I couldn't wait to get away from that maddening Lorcan. I've never met a creature more persistent and annoying. Louie is all too happy about her berries.

I know about them only because of Louie. I remember now. When we were kids, sneaking off to those cliffs, she'd teach me which berries she liked to use on her hair, but the Blood Cloudberries are rare. They typically only grow where blood has been spilled.

She's entranced with happiness, and I don't want to ruin that for her, so I guide us to our room on the third floor. What's odd about Purgatory Pins is on the outside it looks small but, on the inside, it's huge. No one can see the upper floors from the outside.

I'm assuming it's a protection spell and I'm thankful for that tonight. I need to shower, not because I care about being clean, I don't. I could be crusted in mud for weeks if it weren't for Louie.

I want to bathe Louie. I want to take care of her. I want us under that hot spray of water and to roam my hands down her beautiful curves, revealing that gorgeous flesh under that blood and dirt.

Then, I want to wash her hair. I've dreamed of running my fingers through her curls since we were teens. Then, I want to braid it. She never knew but I learned how to braid for her. I never wanted her to stress about her hair. Since I love touching her, caring for her, watching her relax into my embrace, learning how to braid her thick tresses was the easiest choice I've ever made.

I keep my hand on her lower back, needing to touch her at all times so every creature glaring at us right now knows she is mine. They can scent me on her but that means nothing to a lot of paranormals. The claim hasn't been bound by the moon yet, so others with no moral compass, would make a move.

"Shit." Louie trips over her own feet, the small pouch flying from her hand.

I catch her before she has the chance to hit the ground, but she's faster when it comes to snagging those berries. She's a blur when she dives for the floor, opening her palms just in time for the bag to plop down.

"She must really like those berries," Iggy says, crossing his arms and staring at her as if she's insane.

"They mean a lot to her. We wouldn't be able to get more," I inform him.

A burning sensation in my eyes reminds me how exhausted I am. I don't think I'm going to be able to last much longer. I need to sleep.

"Are you okay, Louie?" I help her to her feet, checking her over for any injuries.

Not that it would matter. She would probably heal before I saw anything.

She tugs on the small strings of the pouch and blows out a breath. "We're good. Berries are safe."

I bop her nose with my finger, loving how it scrunches. "But are you?"

"I'm fine. I would have been more upset if something happened to these. Thank you for getting them for me."

"I'd get everything for you, Louie." I kiss the middle of her forehead and wrap an arm around her shoulders.

She rolls her lips together to hide a smile, rocking on her feet. "I think I might have hurt my ankle when I dove for the berries though." My Light pouts her bottom lip as she leans down to rub her ankle.

Iggy chimes in, "You're a vampire, Elouise. Your ankle is fine. Duh."

I give him a slight slap on the back of his head, never breaking eye contact with my mate. My heart skips, a butterfly must be soaring through the chambers. The longer we stare at one another, the more hopelessly fucking in love I become.

I knew I loved her then, all those years ago, but now? Love isn't a strong enough word.

"Is that so?"

She nods, placing her hands on my chest while lifting her 'injured' foot. "Yeah, I must have tweaked it."

I rub my hands down her arms, slip my arms around her waist, then throw her over my shoulder.

"Aziel!" she keens, laughing as I slap her ass for good measure.

"Can't have you walking on that injured foot now, can we?"

She giggles again, a beautiful sound I didn't think I'd ever hear again. "No, we can't. I might have to end up losing my leg."

"Oh. Okay. I see what's going on here. You're flirting."

I give Iggy a dumbfounded look, lifting my brows in question at the lack of common sense.

"Obviously," I mouth so Elouise can't hear me.

"Makes me sick, but go off. Snaps for you two." Iggy proceeds to snap his fingers, pretending to gag.

I'm sure love does make him sick with everything he has gone through, but that doesn't mean I'm going to stop showing love to my mate.

And he can stay uncomfortable for that matter because I don't give a fuck.

"Cute tush." Louie pinches my ass then tugs on my tail.

I jump, completely startled. "Don't do that. Not here."

Louie snorts, giggling to herself and patting each cheek with every step I take to the elevator. A few creatures laugh as we walk by and all I do is growl, flashing my fangs to shut them up. They are jealous they don't have a mate to play their ass like bongos.

She can slap my cheeks all day, I don't care.

I hit the button on the screeching elevator. As it descends, the souls in Hell scream as they use their energy to power the machine. When the door opens, blood sticks to the edges. It's used as oil to keep the elevator moving.

"Up or down?" the demon in the corner asks before laughing to himself.

Down is Hell. No, thanks.

His eyes are black, his arms are crossed, and he is wearing a cloak to cover most of himself except for his mouth. Flames make his teeth and the entire area reeks of sulfur.

I go to step on and an invisible wall stops me in my tracks when he lifts his hand.

"Pay The Ferryman," he warns, turning over his boney palm.

"I have a few eeries left."

He shakes his head, a puff of smoke causing me to cough. "Don't want eeries. I want something that matters, or you can't go to your room."

Louie wiggles to get free. "Put me down," she whispers. "I have something."

"I'm not putting you down." Not with this demon in the elevator who would probably take her to the depths of the fiery basement under us. "Just give me what you have to give."

A few seconds go by before her arm bends back. "Here." The annoyance in her voice has me wondering if I'm going to be sleeping on the ground.

She hands me one of the berries. They are soft with a swollen appearance because they are full of liquid. Their coloring is gorgeous, a deep burgundy that's almost black.

"Absolutely not," I tell her.

"Blood Cloudberries?" The Ferryman is in awe, snatching it from my hand. "That will do. Come in." The moment he pops it into his mouth, we are able to see the juice drip down his throat and innards. "What a delicious snack."

The invisible wall fades away. The pressure I didn't realize was there fades allowing me to inhale until my lungs can't expand further. Iggy gulps but he is the first one to step inside the elevator.

Brave little bear.

I follow behind him, tightening my arm around my mate's legs while side-eyeing the demon.

"Floor?" he asks, his deep voice villainous.

"Three, please," I reply, clearing my throat when I feel the heat under my paws from the flames licking the metal of the elevator.

The Ferryman presses the button with his decomposed finger. Blood splashes onto my feet when the doors close, adding to my filth.

Jazz music drifts through the speakers and The Ferryman whistles along. The ride to the third floor is unexpected with slight tension. Who wouldn't be stressed? A fucking Ferryman is in the same space as us. He could take us to Hell right now.

The screams from the underworld remind me just how close we are to being trapped. Sweat beads on my forehead from the heat. This box is fucking hot. I glance over to Iggy to see he has his head resting against the wall. His hair is damp from sweat, his cheeks flushed, and he fans himself.

"Not even my own heats feel like this," the words breathless and broken as he speaks.

"Get off or die," Ferryman warns, the doors opening to our floor.

"Your bedside manner could really use some work," Iggy advises.

I push him out of the elevator. "Don't mind him. We've had a long day."

The Ferryman sneers, the doors closing just as the demon stands, glaring daggers at Iggy.

"What the actual fuck?" Louie hisses at him, dangling from my shoulder. "You're challenging a demon?"

"He was rude. People who have bad behavior need to know so they can learn and grow."

I feel a headache coming on.

"He is a demon. Bad behavior is literally given in the title, Iggy."

"Well, he doesn't have to fall into the stereotype," he utters.

Yes, the headache is definitely there. All I want is water, food, a shower, and to run my hands down Elouise's wet body.

"Here we are."

"You can put me down."

"Over my dead body," I scoff at Louie, then flip her into a wedding-style hold.

"Hi," she greets me with a smile. "Long time no see."

"It has been too long since I've gifted my eyes with your beauty."

"Can we please go inside before you fuck her against the skull door?" Iggy, once again, ruins the fucking moment.

"Skulls?" Louie and I say in unison, our attention moving from one another to the door.

My brows raise to my hairline when I see dozens of empty eyes and mouths. Some of the skulls have teeth, some don't. All are a variety of different colors too, ranging from white to a grungy yellow.

"Holy shit," I breathe.

"I think you put the key there." Louie points to the door handle.

The mouth is wide open showing a small keyhole. The jaw is the handle. I press my hand down, twisting the key, and all the skulls move into different spots and directions.

"Woah." Iggy is astonished and reaches out a hand to touch one of the skulls, then yanks it back just before touching a cheekbone. "Nope. Never mind. I'd probably get cursed."

"So dramatic," I grumble before applying more pressure on the jaw.

Hinges release a murderous screech, probably the screams of the people those skulls belong to.

I wasn't sure what I expected of the room. Blood walls? Hellhounds waiting for us? A cemetery for a living room– I don't know– but I did not expect luxury.

"Woah," Iggy says again. "This is gorgeous!"

"Everything probably bites." I narrow my eyes at the ribcage chandelier gleaming with bright light bulbs.

I set Louie down, her eyes stopping at every wall, the ceiling, the kitchen, and the living room. Squatting down, I press my hand against the floor. It's cool to the touch.

"This is Igneous rock," I tell them, noticing the kitchen counter is made of it too.

"What's that?" Iggy questions, following my lead to touch the ground.

"It's a type of rock formed from the cooling and solidification of magma or lava. It makes sense considering where we are."

"That's absolutely terrifying." Iggy slaps his thighs before standing. "Okay, as much as I'd love a tour of this death trap, I'm going to take a hot steamy shower, cry, and contemplate my life choices." He saunters away, taking the room to the left before closing the door.

"Come on," Louie urges, slipping her touch across my wide back. "Let's go order food and shower, Beloved."

My eyes travel the length of her, taking her in, and appreciating every fucking curve. My cock begins to fill, wanting her in ways that not even Purgatory could handle.

"Aziel." Her irises churn a brilliant shade of ruby gleaming in the low light. "Shower. Right. Fucking. Now."

I stand, marching over to take her hand. "We aren't going to leave this room unless it's for food." My finger slips under the torn section of her top. "I'm going to make you wish for the flames beneath us to swallow you whole."

Her claws trace the scars on my chest. "Well, make me see stars then, *Wolf.*"

I clutch her dainty wrist, practically dragging her to the other room. The moment we slam the door, Louie slithers away from me, sneaking into the bathroom.

"Order food. I'll be right back." She blows me a kiss, leaving me alone in the bedroom.

While she's in there, I take the time to check out the space. The bed is huge with black silk sheets. The frame is made out of the same Igneous rock with gorgeous carved angels and devils.

A sculpted statue of a hellhound is in the corner, the three heads caught in a permanent smile. There's a box telephone hanging on the wall only the box is a ribcage, the bell is where the heart would be, and the piece you bring to your ear is an open jaw, the microphone you speak into is made of mocking horned goat.

I pick up the horn and turn the arm on the side to make a call while I look at the menu.

"Kitchen," a high-pitched voice answers.

"Hi, I need room service. I'd like five gallons of water, a cow, cooked please because I have company and a few bottles of red wine. Also, five salmon."

"Is that all?"

I cover the horn with my hand, so I don't hurt his ears. "My Light!" I shout. "Want anything special?"

"I could really go for chocolate cake!"

"And chocolate cake."

"That all?"

"Uh—" I whisper, glancing over my shoulder. "You wouldn't happen to have any fresh hearts, would you? Dragon, if you could."

"I do. Give me twenty minutes." He hangs up on me before I can say goodbye, but I don't mind. I'm ready for this day to be over.

The bathroom door swings open, and Elouise is standing naked in the doorway, leaning against the frame.

"Come take care of me."

Well, I'm not *that* ready for the day to be over.

Aziel marches over to me in his beast form, towering over me like a skyscraper. I tilt my head all the way back to be able to look at the hunger on his face.

Directed toward me.

I'm so lucky.

He shifts into his human form and it's always amazing to see the bones adjust, his fur recedes, and his sunkissed skin takes the place of slate grey. He is filthy. His hair is crusted with blood, sweat, and dirt. Even the silver strip that's framing his face is discolored.

The scars riddle his body from years of fighting for his life. I walk my fingers up his chest to my mating mark, the small twin pinpricks on his neck. A deep growl resonates in his chest and tickles my fingers.

His cock thickens, filling until it's heavy and hard. "Your touch awakens every single one of my nerve endings." His voice is soft but it echoes as if we are on top of a mountain, screaming at the top of his lungs.

The bathroom's acoustics are amazing.

Steam fogs the mirror before swirling around us,

heating our bare skin. I take Aziel's hand, leading him toward the shower. There's no curtain. It's just a stall without a tub with a wide showerhead in the middle of the ceiling.

The water hits us at the same time and both of us groan, standing under the hot waterfall. We do nothing else but enjoy the warmth. We don't move. I feel the exhaustion in the bond coming from Aziel, the kind that has me wondering how the hell he is still standing. He hangs his head, catching himself on the wall with his hand, and allows the water to cascade from head to toe.

His muscles ripple as he stretches his neck left to right. I can't help but look my fill. Aziel's body is a work of art. His shoulders are wide with a strong back. Every defined rope of strength is more pronounced as the water catches the shadows. I suck my bottom lip into my mouth, following the river flowing down his spine.

His ass is round, bubbly, and firm. I want to sink my fangs into each cheek.

"See something you like?"

I rip my gaze away and his chin is tucked on his shoulder, his searing gold eyes peeking at me through the curtain of water.

"I see something I love," I reply, taking a rag and the bar of soap from the shelf. "Stay just like that. Let me bathe you."

"I'd never say no to your hands on me." His hair hangs on either side of his face, blocking my view of his square jaw.

Brown and red-tinted water circles down the drain as I rub the rag and bar of soap together. When there's enough suds, I fold the cloth over the chunky white bar and start scrubbing his back.

The scent of pine is a refreshing smell after scenting the stench of death. From shoulder to shoulder, I wash the grime from his body. Even on his back, there are small scars but there is one to the right of his spine that is raised and bigger than the rest.

"What happened here?" I ask him, wishing the soap could wash away the bad memories he carries.

"I had a human fight me back. He was a hunter, so he carried silver blades. He fought well but it wasn't enough. I killed him."

"Do you remember everyone you killed when you were cursed?"

He sighs, leaving us in silence for a few seconds. The hiss of the water splashing against us is white noise, a filler for the truth he is about to spill.

"I remember every single face," he admits. "Every single scream. I remember it all. I remember trying to fight the curse. Every day I'd tell my wolf to listen to me, to stop, that Brenden isn't our Alpha, that he can't control us. My efforts didn't matter." He rubs a hand down his face, spitting out water that slid into his mouth.

I stay quiet, not knowing what to say. I continue cleaning him, squatting down to clean his legs. The cloth slides over the large curve of his ass and I know it isn't the time to get aroused but the way it does a slight jiggle from my touch has my fangs lengthening.

"Turn around," I order him, trying my best to be good while he pours his heart out to me.

He does as he is asked, and if I thought his backside was impressive, it is nothing compared to his front. Aziel leans his shoulders against the wall, his eyes tracking me when I step closer.

Naturally, I glance down to see his cock.

Forcing myself to look away, I start washing his chest, but it does nothing to help sate the growing desire inside me. Now, I can't stop staring at how his pecs curve with muscle definition.

My tongue becomes dry as I lower the cloth down his abs. No one should be this defined or in shape. He is a work of art, a masterpiece, sculpted and created to be appreciated.

"I can't take back what I've done. All I can do is move forward and hope I can survive the healing process."

Unable to stop myself, I kiss the middle of his chest. "You won't be alone." I can't risk taking a peek at his facial expression. I'll lean in for a kiss and this shower will go from needing to get clean to staying filthy.

His hands fall to my hips, and he tugs me closer as I wash every inch of him.

"Lift."

He raises his arms for me to get the nook of his armpits. Tracing the indent of the V leading to his cock, I kneel, focusing on his thighs, calves, and feet.

"It isn't going to wash itself, Louie." He gives his cock a good stroke. "The quicker you wash me, the sooner I can bathe you, and the faster I can have you flat on your back."

I unwrap the soap from the rag and let it fall to the shower floor, using what's left on the cloth to clean him. Gripping the base of his extra-large shaft, I take my time getting every spot of skin. His cock jerks in my grip with every twist and tug I give him.

He grunts, the scent of his lust is too much. I'm not sure how much longer I can control myself.

Reaching between his legs, he spreads his stance wider to allow me in. I fondle his sack before slipping up his dick again, massaging the head. The water washes all the suds away, revealing a clean cock waiting to get extra attention.

We don't have time to play. I still have to shower too.

"What is it, Louie?" His thumb brushes over my cheek.

"I'm starved," I whisper, my tongue rubbing against my left fang.

My mouth waters from the thought of feeding and I use it to my advantage. I spit on the head before swallowing as much as I can whole. I choke, taking too much at first.

"Fuck. Fuck, Louie. I'm not going to last. I'm too worked up. You have to stop."

Oh, I didn't plan on this lasting at all.

I fondle his balls in one palm, circling the base where his knot will be with the other.

"Elouise," he moans, his head dropping against the wall.

My hunger wins. I bite down, my fangs slicing into his girth.

"Louie!" he roars to the point my ears ring again, filling my mouth with his come. It tingles, nearly numbing my mouth to accommodate his size and the amount of seed he pours into me.

Between his blood and come mixing down my throat, my own orgasm invigorates me. I hum, taking more long drags of his blood as he continues to tense with every stream shooting into my mouth.

When I'm done, I groan, uncaring how the concoction of him drips down my chin. He forces me to my feet by gripping my biceps and surprises me by licking my face clean.

"I can't wait for you to do that again."

I chuckle, giving him a messy kiss. "Come on, let's get cleaned up, and get you some food."

"You aren't hungry?" He washes his own hair with the two-in-one shampoo I got him.

It's all the Purga-Mart had.

I suds the rag to wash my body, but Aziel knocks it out of my hand. "What was that for?"

"I want to wash you. I'm only washing my hair because you can't reach and squatting in this space is not going to happen." He rinses his hair once, twice, and only the third time does the water run clean.

The way he stares me down feels like I'm being hunted. "Your turn."

We switch spots so I can have most of the water. I soak my hair, then squeeze it to get some of the grime out. I expect Aziel to wash my body first, but to my surprise, he opens the pouch I have on the shelf and takes out a Blood Cloudberry.

"You could have used one for your own hair. They are ours."

"They are yours," he corrects me. "I only want you to have these. I know how important they are. Turn around, My Light. I can't wait to do something I've been dreaming about doing."

I'm confused. Nevertheless, I do as he says because I trust him.

"Um, how do I use these again? I squish them, right?"

"Yes and then you'll rub your hands together until it becomes foamy."

I hear a soft pop before he curses, "Shit. It's bright red. I don't think this is right. Am I doing it right?"

I spin around, my hands an echo on his. The red juice from the berry is everywhere and Aziel is frozen. His brows crinkle together, and the outer corner of his eyes turn downward.

"I ruined it, didn't I? I'm sorry. I didn't mean to waste anything."

"You didn't," I say quickly so he doesn't dare feel bad. "So far you're doing everything right. Now, bring your hands together." I apply pressure, pushing his palms together. "Rub like you're starting a fire with a stick."

Back and forth our hands work together. There's something very intimate about this, showing him how to wash my hair and it has me falling in love with him even more. Tears burn my eyes, but I hold them back. I'm not sad. I'm happy. I'm so incredibly happy.

"It's working! Look, Louie. It's working!" He is in awe watching the red foam begin to pile high in his hands. "Okay, okay, okay, turn around."

I can't hide my smile as I give him my back. I'm not sure what to expect but the moment his fingers hit my scalp, my eyes close. I'm sent to a place of relaxation and peace. He rubs my scalp for a few minutes before starting on the body of my hair.

"Let's rinse and wash again." Gathering the curls, he tugs my head back, using his hand to run the water over my head. "You have so much hair."

"I know. It's a lot of work."

"I love it. It's gorgeous. Your hair has always been one of my favorite things about you."

"Really? What's the first?" I'm prepared to hear something about my appearance, my lips, anything along those lines.

"Your bravery." He kisses the side of my temple and inhales. "You know what this berry smells like?" The question is a whisper in the spray of the water as his lips dance upon the shell of my ear.

Slightly turning my head to the right, I reply, "What?"

He massages the back of my head, working his way through the curls. "The flowers that grew on the side of the cliff and the air just as it was about to rain." He groans when he takes another deep breath. "It's my favorite scent in the world. Your scent."

Aziel begins round two on my hair, only this time, he sections every piece. He divides my hair down the middle, then across my crown to have four large chunks separated.

He is meticulous. We would have run out of hot water if we weren't so close to Hell. My Beloved takes care of my hair like he takes care of me, with all of him.

"Does that feel good? Am I doing okay? Do you need me to change anything?"

I shake my head, my eyes hooding with exhaustion. "You've relaxed me. I'm sleepy. You're doing amazing. I never want to wash my own hair again," I laugh so he knows it's a joke.

"Like I'd ever let you wash your own hair again," he huffs, moving to another section. "Absolutely not. It's my job to take care of you. Plus, I love this. I feel closer to you."

I know what he means. I feel it too. Our bodies even come closer. It's beyond sex. It's intimacy.

"You know what else I love?"

"Hmm?" I ask in a tired hum, barely lifting my brows in interest.

"Seeing our skin against one another. It's one of my other favorite things. I dreamed of the day to see you next to me again. If I was going blind and someone asked what I wanted to see one last time, it would be you against me, reminding me how beautiful the world was."

A tear drips free, lost in the sea of water traveling to the drain.

"Rinse." He tugs on my curls, signaling me to tilt my head back, and who am I to deny him?

He takes his time, getting every section he has scrubbed clean. My eyes are still closed. I'm soaking in every second of this.

"Now, when you squish the berry, don't rub your hands together to create the foam. The liquid is also a great replacement for hydrating oil."

"I'll need to find this plant so we can have it at home when we get out of here. Then, you can have these berries whenever you want."

"They can only grow where blood is spilled," I remind him. "I don't think they can grow in a garden, but it's very sweet of you to say."

"So I'll spill my own blood so you can have your berries. I'll water the plant every day with a cut on my wrist."

Heat warms my cheeks, and my heart does a somersault. I've never felt more love than I do right now.

"We will have to save a berry for planting, so let's not use all of them so I can give you your favorite hair product, My Light."

I nod fast like a bobblehead. I'm too excited thinking about his plan.

We fall into a comfortable silence. Instead of focusing on words, I'm focusing on his touch, his breaths, every time he kisses my shoulder while he massages my scalp. I never want this shower to end. He's showing me how much he loves me and that's something I never want to escape from.

Aziel continues to rub my scalp, working from the back of my head to the front. I fall into peace. Even the dead would be jealous of how still and safe my soul is.

"Will we rinse this out too?"

I shake my head. "No, the red tint of it eventually goes away and will leave my hair nice and soft."

"Okay, when we are done, I'll brush it."

"Do we have a comb?"

He ponders then growls in frustration. "No, but don't worry about it. I'll make one." Aziel snags a clean rag from the shelf, adds the soap, and starts washing.

He focuses on my back. "I can't bend down to get your legs. There isn't enough room." I hate how upset he sounds about something so unimportant.

"That's okay." I spin around to give him my front. "You can still wash my upper body, right?"

His nostrils flare partnered with a snarl that has my clit pulsing with need. "I would need to be dead not to, My Light." His eyes lock onto mine, dragging the cloth across my collarbone. Dipping between the valley of my breasts, he closes the distance between us.

My back hits the wall, trapped with nowhere to go. I inhale a sharp breath when his claw slides over my nipple, the bubbles hiding the beaded peak.

"It's a good thing you accepted me as your mate, Louie, or I'd tear you to pieces just like the legend says I would. I have an urge to feel your bones on mine, your blood warming my fur, and if you even tried to run from me, you'd become my prey."

He cleans the rest of my chest, slipping the rag

down until I'm forced to spread my legs.

"Aziel," I gasp when his thumb circles my clit before slipping the rag between my lips.

"Such a waste of soap when you and I both know I'm just going to dirty this cunt all over again with my come."

My vision becomes red with want.

A dark chuckle annoys me as he continues to kiss my clit with his fingers. "Oh, you like the sound of that, don't you? You're going to have to wait. I want you on the bed, legs spread, and my face buried so deep, you'll be able to feel my tongue in your womb."

"Oh, Aziel. Please." I rock against his hand, wanting more, needing more, and he allows me to take it.

Good. I'd force him to give it to me if he didn't.

"You're close already, aren't you? You came while feeding from my cock, but it wasn't enough, was it? You need more from me. Be a good girl and tell me just what you need."

"Faster. I'm— I'm so close." My mouth parts as a silent moan gets caught in my throat.

"You'll need to fuck my hand harder then, because the only thing I want to do is watch you fall apart."

I grip his wrist, pressing his fingers against me harder while I push down to rock.

"Look at those fangs." He leans down, licking the left cuspid with his tongue and an unexpected whimper pours from me. "Oh, you liked that?" He moves to the other fang, flattening his tongue under the point until I taste blood.

A throaty growl announces just how much of a predator I am. "You taste so fucking good. I want more. Give me more."

"No."

"Yes," I hiss, snapping my fangs at him.

He wraps a hand around my throat to keep me in place, to still me, to control me. "I said no." Aziel has the audacity to smirk.

"That's too bad, isn't it?" In a blur, I have his neck bent, and my fangs embedded in his neck. I moan, gulping down the rich blood of my werewolf. His blood invigorates my body unlike any other. It's more than him being my beloved. It's also because he is a werewolf. I *feel* more powerful and I'm waiting for the time when someone tries to challenge me.

I have werewolf blood in my veins. There's nothing more powerful than that.

My orgasm tenses every muscle in my body. My hips stutter on his hand as I moan against his neck while his blood fills my mouth.

Aziel growls with his own orgasm, his come warming my skin.

I clean his neck, sucking the skin until every drop is gone.

"You didn't seem to mind that much." I nibble his earlobe.

"You better be glad I love it when you use me." Capturing the back of my head, he pulls me to his lips, planting a rough kiss on me. "Finish up. I'm going to go make your comb."

"Okay," I slur, a little drunk from his kiss.

With a smug smirk, he steps out of the stall, leaving me with a view of his delicious backside. He dries off with one of the white towels, then wraps it around his waist, covering the bubbly, succulent cheeks I want to kiss and bite.

"I think you have a thing for my ass, Louie." He stares at me in the broken mirror.

"I can't help it," I pout, scrubbing my legs with soap. "It's a peach and I love peaches."

He grins at me before giving his teeth a quick brush. He pivots, leaning against the counter, crosses his arms, and now all I can stare at is his cock pressing against the towel. I can see the outline, how thick he is, the crown of his head threatening to break through the cotton, and it would take the weakest gust of wind to blow the towel away.

Part of me wants to blow on it and see if it will just drift away.

"My Light." He snaps his fingers. "My eyes are up here."

"Yes, yes, but your marvelous cock is down there."

He pushes the towel lower on his hips, the 'V' more pronounced. A small dark bush teases me. "You'll get me soon enough." A sly grin takes over his face before he heads out the door.

I hurry, wanting to spend time with him. To be safe, I wash my body three times until the water runs clear. By the time I turn off the shower, I'm exhausted. I can barely keep my eyes open.

Done drying off, I toss the towel on the floor and walk into the bedroom naked. There is a shirt for me on the bed with a pair of actual underwear. Real panties instead of the makeshift ones I've had to piece together on my own.

I slip on the shirt, then the panties, and it's ridiculous, but I sigh from the comfort.

"That good?" Aziel asks from behind me.

"So good," I sigh. "I forgot what normal felt like."

"When we get out of here, I'll give you all the normal you want."

"Good because I am tired of fighting to survive. I'm ready to sit on my ass all day and do nothing."

"Let's start now. Sit."

Quirking a brow at him, I sit on the bed and don't ask questions. Aziel rolls in a cart filled with food.

"Two things. I gave Iggy his salmon and I also might have broken the table in the living room." He holds up a piece of bone. "I'm not sure what monster they made the table out of, but damn the bones are huge. I tried to make it small and compact to mimic the one you had when we were teens."

"You really made me a comb?"

He nods, walking over to me in that towel. "And I

want you to eat your food while I comb your hair."

"But you need to eat," I argue, tilting my head at him when his stomach rumbles.

He crawls onto the bed, settling behind me. "I'll be fine. I want to take care of you first."

I snag a plate from the cart that has a steak on it, grab it as if it's a sandwich, and bite into it. Blood spurts into my mouth as I chew.

A gentle tug begins to pull on my curls while Aziel attempts to comb my hair.

"Is this okay?" he questions, sectioning my hair again.

"It's perfect. I love this so much."

"Good. I do too." He kisses the back of my head and gets back to work, dragging the bone comb he made for me through the knots.

It's hard to keep my emotions in check when I'm overwhelmed with so much love.

When he is done, he places the comb next to me. I lean forward to grab him a plate when he stops me.

"What are you doing? I'm not done. I sectioned your hair for a reason." He pulls me back and to my shock, he begins to braid every section. "I've been dying to braid your hair since we were kids. Let me."

"You— You learned how to braid for me?"

"When will you get it, Louie? There isn't anything I wouldn't do for you. You're my mate. You before anything and anyone else. And when we have kids, now I'll know how to do their hair."

If I could give him a child right now, if I could get pregnant at this moment, I would. I would give him all the kids he wants because this proves not only is he an amazing Beloved, but he will be an amazing father.

Purgatory is terrible. I truly thought I'd die here. Aziel being put in my path gives me the haven I've been searching for.

Living has been brutal, but the love has been easy.

"How are you going to tie the braids at the end?"

"Um, so– ow."

He reaches around to show me a long piece of werewolf hair.

"Aziel! You didn't just pluck that from your head."

"It will grow back. Plus, the hair is strong. It will last."

"But it's your hair," I raise my voice. "And you don't need to tie the ends. My hair won't unravel."

"I know, but I want to be everywhere you are. I want to be with you at all times. I want to be on your body. I want more than my bite mark on you. I want to integrate myself into every aspect of you. That means, wrapping the ends of your hair with mine so you know my love is bound to you. I'll find other ways to place my claim too." He kisses the side of my neck. "You just wait and see."

I lick my fingers when I finish the steak and reach for another piece. "Take a bite before I start crying because you love me so fucking much."

"Fine."

I lift the steak over my shoulder. He tugs, pulls, and growls before he rips off a giant piece. Every time he chews, he snarls, and it's adorable.

I take my own bite before offering him more. "More?"

Licking the blood from his lips, he makes eye contact with me before tearing the steak in two.

His hunger for food reminds me of the hunger he has for me.

Never sated and always waiting to fill me.

Chapter Eleven

AZIEL

There are four days until the full moon. Four days until blood rains down and we are trapped here forever. I'm not sure how to bring that up to Louie. If I'm lucky, she already knows.

I haven't found the avisseus yet and it's been months. The chances of me finding the creature in four days are slim to none.

My exhale is so loud, it disrupts Louie while she's sleeping. She mumbles, readjusting her position. My mate scoots closer to me, rolling over until her head is on my chest. Wrapping my arm around her, my fingers draw small circles on her back to keep her relaxed.

I think about Scorder's clue.

Dread Mountain.

Getting up the mountain will be exhausting. It isn't because of paranormals. No one likes to go up the mountain because of its wild weather.

"You're thinking so loud, Beloved," she grumbles into my shoulder. "Shhh." Her finger presses against my forehead to keep my mind quiet.

"I'm sorry, My Light." I bring her hand to my mouth

and kiss every finger. "I'll think quietly."

"No, it's okay. It's best if we get up. We need to make our way to Dread Mountain. It felt so good to sleep in a real bed. Now, I understand why eeries are so important." She stretches, yawning before it turns into a yip.

"We could stay here," I say out of nowhere, without a real thought. "I can fight in The Graveyard, win, and we can live in this room. We could live a good life in Purgatory."

She lifts herself up on her elbow, sleep still hooding her eyes. "Aziel, you could die in The Graveyard. Every fight I would wonder if I'd be living without you. I can't do that. We have to get out of here."

The world's largest sigh leaves me. "I know, but we might not have a choice if we can't find the avisseus."

"What do you mean?"

I sit up, popping my neck left to right, then lean against the bedframe. "I mean if we don't get out of here by the time the blood rain falls, we are trapped here."

"What!" Louie's eyes are round in shock and disbelief. "No, that can't be right. Who told you that? That has to be a rumor."

"Death told me."

She slouches, rubbing a hand down her face before rolling out of bed. "Well, that means there's no time to waste. We need to get ready. I'll go wake Iggy. Order breakfast. We need a plan, Aziel."

"I don't know what kind of plan we could have. There isn't anything we can do except go up that mountain."

"We need to find Scorder again. He might have new information. We can start there because if he gave you an old clue and we head up that mountain for no reason, I'm going to kill him."

I'm able to snag her hand before she reaches the bathroom. My thumb rubs back and forth across the top of her hand but I can feel the anger in our bond.

"And the full moon is that night, is it not? How can we complete the bond?"

"I don't know, but we will. Okay? We will figure it out because I refuse not to have *us*. I'll do anything and everything I can. I won't have blood rain or our souls being trapped here when there is an entire life waiting for us on the other side. I will fight tooth and nail. I will kill who I need to kill. We will figure it out."

She shuts her eyes and nods, falling into my arms and burying her face in the crook of my neck. I rub her back, not wanting to express the same fears she has. I also have the fear that when we mate under the full moon and my werewolf won't stop breeding her until she's pregnant, I'm wondering how the hell she can get pregnant in Purgatory. What would that mean for us? What would that mean for my werewolf? The more questions I think of, the less confident I feel about getting out of here.

"Let's take one more shower before starting our journey," I tell her. "I'll let Iggy know what the plan is."

"Okay."

Defeat weighs down her tone, and I slip my finger under her chin, forcing her to look at me.

"Everything will be fine, Louie. I promise. Go shower before I spank you." Those fucking eyes become tinted with red, and I growl. "Louie," I warn, slapping her ass so hard she yelps.

She runs to the bathroom, and I follow after her, tickling her sides, making her scream and giggle.

"Oh my God! Stop!" She wails in laughter, trying her best to get away from me.

I don't stop. I continue my tickle attack, moving up and down her sides. Louie tries to push away from me and her leg makes contact between my legs.

Everything inside me freezes. Louie stops and gasps.

I grunt in pain, cupping my balls, and fall to my

knees.

"Oh my God. Aziel!" She lowers herself to the ground to check on me, her palm over her mouth. "I'm so sorry. I didn't mean to. I wasn't trying to kick you. I'm so sorry."

I have officially forgotten how to breathe. "It's okay," I croak. "I'm fine." I succumb to the pain and decide to lie down to accept my fate. Maybe this is how I die.

"Aziel. I feel so terrible. I'm so sorry. What can I do? Maybe I can try to find ice?"

"I don't think they have ice so close to Hell, My Light. It's okay." I finally let out a breath. "I'll be fine. I just need a minute."

"Want me to see if you're still intact?" She scrunches her nose.

"Please. I don't have the heart to look."

She tucks my hair behind my ear. "My Wolf will fight and kill but he won't check to see if his balls are okay."

"That's different," I argue. "What if we can't have kids?"

She rolls her eyes, pushing my hands out of the way. "Let me see."

I toss an arm over my eyes, her hands sliding up my inner thigh.

"Well, you don't seem to be in that much pain if you can still get an erection."

"Your hands are on me. I'll always get hard for you, no matter the pain."

"So romantic." She cups my sack and the pain quickly turns into pleasure. "You're fine. They are in the same place they were yesterday."

"Oh, thank fuck." I laugh in relief, but then groan when Louie wraps her hand around my cock. I hiss, dropping my arm from over my eyes to look at her. "Is my mate in need?"

She nods in a slow steady beat. "And since you're already on your back. I don't think you'll mind if I just–"

Louie climbs on top of me wearing the shirt she slept in and her new underwear. "–Take advantage? Unless, you're in too much pain for me to fuck you, Beloved."

She pushes her panties to the side, sliding her lips up and down my shaft to force me to feel how fucking wet she is.

"Fuck." My hands find her hips, my nails digging into her flesh to have her press against me harder. "Louie, you're so wet. If you want me so bad, take me, mate. Use the fuck out of me. Make. Me. Come. Your pussy is hungry for it, isn't it?" We are getting closer to the moon. She might already be experiencing signs of the intense heat she'll have that night.

"Shift into your hybrid form."

"Filthy little vampire wanting to fuck me in my beast form," I growl as I shift.

"You won't be in the form I really want you in, but it will be close." She bends down, her braids tickling my chest as she sucks my bottom lip into her mouth. "Come on, Wolf. Give me what I want and maybe I won't hurt you to get it."

"Hurt me? What could you possibly do?" I know tempting her isn't the right choice. I love seeing that split second of fire in her eyes from a challenge.

She reaches behind her, pulling out one of her daggers that she must have tucked in the waistband of her underwear. "Maybe I'll do more than you think I will."

Her daggers are made of silver. She drags her tongue across the blade and her flesh begins to sizzle. "I've built a tolerance to the pain silver brings. I actually think it feels good. Plus, I heal. But what about you, Beloved?" She hovers the tip of the blade of my chest. "How high is your pain tolerance?"

"Find out," I dare her, lifting my head from the ground until our noses touch.

She grins, easing the dagger onto my skin at the same time she lowers herself onto my cock. The array of sensations has me roaring so fucking loud, the mirror shatters.

"Oh you like that, don't you? I love your hybrid. Gives me the best of both worlds when it comes to your body." She yanks my head back by my hair, placing the dagger against my throat. "Lie here like a good fucking boy until I come. You aren't allowed to do anything but take what I give you."

She slices my jugular before diving in; biting the wound with her fangs to get her breakfast. Her bite alone is enough to make my orgasm slam through me and fill her until it drips down my shaft, then the floor.

Louie licks the blood clean. "I love that my bite does that to you. And I love how your come tingles." She sits up, her panties still bunched and pushed to the side to take my cock. "And I want to feel it again."

From my view, she's stretched so wide, I'm afraid if she takes any more of me, she might tear.

Not that I think she would care. I bet my pain slut would love that.

She rides me fast and hard, placing one hand on my chest for support to increase her speed. "Yes, God, you feel so good, so fucking big, Aziel. I love it when you give me this cock."

I moan. "I love it when you take it. Fuck, Louie. Your pussy is so fucking tight." I glance down to see where we are connected, noticing how wet she is. I'm able to see the slick shining against the grey of my shaft.

Louie drags the knife across my chest, splitting the skin open. Blood tickles my skin as it drips down the valley of my sternum. She leans down, flattening her tongue against my abs, and peers up at me through her lashes while my blood gathers against her taste buds.

"Fuck, fuck, fuck," I chant, clenching my teeth together to stop myself from coming again. "Goddamn, do it again."

A dark chuckle breezes across my flesh. "What? This?" The tip of the dagger is carved into my chest.

The pain is unbearable. My skin burns and the scent is even worse.

"What if I carve my name into your chest? What would you do?" she asks, twisting and scrapping the knife in different directions as if she's already cutting her name into my skin.

It's a brand.

It's a claim.

It's ownership.

And I fucking love the sound of it.

"Do it. I want you on me for all eternity. Fucking scar me to your liking, My Light, and I will show everyone who owns me."

"One day, I'll tie you up and have my way with you *with* my dagger. I'll bring you to the edge so many times." She's careful not to lick the wounds that make her name or they would heal. Unlike her mating mark, it's as if our bodies know she's submitting her claim, so those won't ever heal.

Her name carved with a silver dagger? That won't heal fully and I'm more than okay with that.

She gathers the excess blood that drips down my left pec, sucking on my nipple which has me arching my back. The move causes me to bury my cock deeper and she tosses the dagger somewhere to the right. It clatters against the wall, forgotten.

Louie's hands slap on my chest, her fingers pressing against where she carved her name, and I growl from the pain. Her mouth is drenched in red from my blood, her beautiful full lips painted in a forbidden red.

Her body moves like a wave, curling, rocking back and forth. Elouise stretches, moaning, tilting her head back as she picks up the pace.

"Elouise," I pant her name, gripping her hips for dear life.

My claws pinch into her hips, the scent of her blood causing me to become hungry and feral.

Needing more, needing to bury myself as far as

I can, I change our position quicker than she can say no. I have her against the counter, staring at us in the mirror.

"I didn't say I was done." Her eyes are bright red with hunger and lust. Elouise's fangs flash at me, promising violence and power.

I grab the back of her neck and pull her against my chest. My cock drives into her as hard as I can. Our skin slaps. I feel my earlier orgasms drip down me, and when I look down, I see my cock draped in white come.

"Look at us." I slip my hybrid hand around her neck. "Look at me fucking you. Look what you've done to my chest."

Her eyes fall to the spot where she carved her name and her nostrils flare. The scent of lust is so powerful, that I become dizzy.

"You're so proud of yourself, aren't you? Marking me like that. You just wait until it's my turn. You just wait until I hunt you down, catch you, and fuck you until you beg me to stop."

"I would never beg you to stop."

"You will," I snarl. "I don't think you understand how far gone I will be. The Aziel you know won't exist. When I tell you I won't be able to stop, I mean it. You need to be okay with that or the full moon night—" I nip at her shoulder "— will be more difficult for you."

"I'm more than okay with it. I can't wait. The thought— Oh, god— I'm close. I'm so close."

"You are. You are so wet. You're making it so easy to give you every inch of me. You're such a slut for this werewolf cock." I tighten my grip on her throat until she gasps, her eyes widening in the mirror before they roll to the back of her head. "Only *my* cock. No one else will have you. No other werewolf will take you. This pussy is mine," I sneer, slapping the round curve of her ass before gripping on to each cheek to bring her down faster onto my dick.

"Ah, oh, holy fuck! Aziel!" Her fist slams against the

counter, cracking the igneous rock until a large chunk falls off from the edge. "Yes, God, give it to me, Aziel. So fucking good. Harder. Harder!"

Growling, I slap my hand in the middle of her back, forcing her down. Her tits press against the counter, her ass up and in the air for me. Elouise's head is turned to the side and she's crying out at the top of her lungs.

Iggy has to hear us.

And for some reason, that fuels me more. I hope he does hear us. I want everyone in Purgatory to hear what I do to my mate. She's mine. She belongs to me.

I ram into Elouise, wishing I could give her my knot. I grip the edge of the counter, then clutch her shoulder, wanting leverage to fuck her how I want.

"Yes! Yes, fuck, I'm going to— I'm going to—" She can't finish her warning before she moans, her pussy pulsing on my cock. Hot slick squirts onto my cock, soaking my shaft, and drips down my legs.

"Fuck yes, Louie. Give me another." I don't stop the momentum. I curl over her, sweat dripping down my temple, my muscles burning as I give her every ounce of strength and endurance I have.

Something cracks.

She cries in agony just as one more orgasm rips through her, more of her come drenching my cock.

Picking her up by her neck, our bodies align. Her back against my front. That's when I notice how limp her arm is. I must have pulled her arm from her socket somehow.

"Kiss me."

"I can't, the angle—" She whines. "I'm close again. I can't. I can't again."

"You will give me what I want." I force her head to turn, the bones breaking until her head is turned around and her lips are finally near mine. "Just like you'll give me another kiss." I capture her lips, filling her once, twice, three times before I plant deep inside.

I bit her lip so hard it bleeds, and I eagerly lap it up like a fucking dog dying of thirst.

We collapse onto the counter, gasping for air. Her head cracks as it heals, turning into its rightful spot.

"Fuck," I groan, kissing from one shoulder to the other.

The counter moans. Our eyes catch in the reflection before the entire thing crumbles under us, sending us to the ground in rubble.

"I guess—" Elouise pauses to breathe "— I guess we will be needing that shower now."

I grunt in reply, not having the energy to say another word.

A knock sounds on our bedroom door. "Can you two keep it down? I'm trying to sleep before we go off and save ourselves or whatever. Jeez. It's like living in a brothel with you two."

Elouise slaps her hands over her mouth to stifle her laugh.

I roll on top of my mate, bracing my hands on either side of her head, and I tuck one of the braids behind her ear. "I love you, Louie. I don't care what it takes, but we're going home."

"Aziel." She sits up, placing her forehead against mine. "You are my home. Even if it means we are here, at least we are here together. You are and have always been my home."

I want to give her more than me, though.

I want to give her my world.

Chapter Twelve

ELOUISE/AZIEL

The elevator doors open to reveal The Ferryman again. He holds out his hand, the bones cracking as he unfolds his fingers.

"Pay The Ferryman," he orders. "And I will take you where you need to go. Perhaps, Hell? I hear it's warm this time of year."

"Uh," I mumble, glancing at Iggy and Aziel. "I smell what you two have been up to. It's Hell worthy. Congratulations," The Ferryman attempts to grin but all that's there is an abyss.

"Oh my God." I bury my face in Aziel's furry arm, wanting to hide and possibly disappear from the face of this dimension.

Aziel snarls at him, taking a step forward to invade The Ferryman's space. "Keep your mouth shut when you're talking about my mate. You don't have the right to talk about what we do behind closed doors—"

"—And even then," Iggy blows a raspberry and his lips vibrate together. "—sometimes the door being closed isn't enough."

"You aren't helping," I bite.

"What? It isn't a bad thing. I hope someone fucks me like that."

"Iggy!"

"I also wish that," The Ferryman sighs. "It's a long immortal life doing this job. I meant no harm, but I will need something of value for you to continue on your way." He wiggles his boney fingers. "Anything but money."

Aziel tilts his head back, completely defeated. "I don't have anything."

I untie the wolf hair keeping one of my braids together. "I can tie the end with another piece of your hair," I tell Aziel with a comforting smile. "It will be fine, but here you go." I hand the long strand to the demon.

"What am I going to do with a piece of hair?" The Ferryman is unimpressed, holding the long werewolf hair up to get a better look at it before shivering in disgust.

"It's my Beloved's hair. He plucked each hair from his body, piece by piece, to tie my braids at the ends. That singular piece of hair is full of more love, devotion, loyalty, kindness, and commitment than you might see in your entire immortal life. That piece of hair might mean nothing to you–" The familiar burn behind my eyes has me trying to swallow the emotion building. "–but it means everything to me."

Aziel wraps his arm around my shoulders. In his werewolf form, I only stand at his abdomen, and yet, his arm around me, bringing me comfort, makes me feel as tall as he is.

"This one little hair holds so much?" The Ferryman asks, bringing it closer to his face, and inspecting it as if it is a rare object he has never seen before.

"And so much more," I add, hoping it is enough.

"Interesting." He wraps the long strands around his giant wooden staff, right under the onyx stone at the top. "I like it. I accept your token. You may enter," he says.

I blow out a breath, taking Aziel's hand as we step onto the elevator. The doors close and blood splashes onto our shoes, again. Jazz music trumpets through the speakers and The Ferryman whistles, bobbing his head to the horrible tune while hitting his staff on the floor to make his own beat.

So. Awkward.

I look down, the fire and souls screaming as they press their faces against the floor to be set free.

"Don't mind them. They are always complaining." The Ferryman hits his staff on the ground. "Shut up. No one wants to hear your screams."

To my surprise, the souls shut their mouths and drift somewhere else.

"They do it for attention. They know they deserve to be in Hell," he explains.

"Who is in Hell? If you don't mind me asking."

"A lot of people think the smallest things will send them down south, but that's not the case. Lucy doesn't care if you steal food to eat because you're hungry and are having a tight month financially. He doesn't give a fuck if you have sex before marriage, he encourages it, and he really doesn't care if you curse, or kill in self-defense. You really need to be the worst of the worst to land yourself in the flames."

"That's a relief," Iggy's voice is sullen. "I've stolen food before."

"I know. It's why I used it as an example." The Ferryman gives a slow nod of his head as the elevator screams when we reach the main floor.

"Thank you," I tell him.

"I hope you're sinned with the darkest of days!" He smiles again and waves as the elevator doors close.

Iggy scratches the back of his head. "I think he meant that in a nice way."

"I do too." Aziel scans the room, the bowling alley thriving with other creatures.

Pins clash and balls roll in the gutter. Cheers fill

the air along with sounds of disappointment.

"Before we head out, I did buy us one game. You two up for it?" My Beloved crosses his arms, his muscles becoming more pronounced, and I'm taken back to when we broke the counter in the hotel room.

"Will you keep it in your pants for five minutes?" Iggy teases, nudging my arm with his elbow.

"Yes, mate," Aziel bites in a warning. "I can't take you here for all to see. That's too many to kill for witnessing what belongs to me."

"Though, I can understand why you'd get hot and bothered so quickly." Iggy pinches the neckline of his shirt which reads, 'I love Purgatory' and fans himself. "I want someone to talk to me like that."

"Come on. Let's take lane three. It's the only one that's open." Aziel points to the lane directly in front of us.

I clap, jumping up and down with excitement like when my parents would give me a blood popsicle.

"Not to brag, but I'm pretty good at bowling."

"And when was the last time you bowled, My Light?" He lifts a brow at me, sitting down in the seat to input our names on the screen.

"It's been a while but it's all up here baby." I tap my head, giving him a little dance to show my confidence.

A catcall from beside us has Aziel unsheathing Uri, slicing him through the air, and taking the head off an orc.

He wipes Uri off on the body belonging to the head. "If anyone else wants to disrespect my mate, please try. I am in the killing kind of mood." He scans the lanes next to us, flashing his fangs as he snarls. "No one?"

The orc disappears, leaving nothing but his bones where he used to sit.

"If you kill again, I'm going to have to force you to leave." Trelo, the bull shifter stands beside us, arms crossed with a stern expression on his face.

"I won't kill anymore if everyone decides to leave

my mate alone." Aziel slides Uri in its place behind his back.

Trelo narrows his eyes before uncrossing his arms and pointing a finger. "Fine, but any other violence, you're out of here, Aziel. This is the only peaceful place in Purgatory. Don't fuck that up."

Aziel gives him a two-finger salute. "I'll be an angel."

Trelo rolls his eyes with disbelief. "Right. Do you all need shoes?"

"Yep. I'm afraid I don't know my size in this form." Aziel stares at his giant werewolf feet, wiggling his toes.

"That's okay. I'm bringing venlilly. It's a plant we use. You put them on the bottom of your feet and they will do the rest. I'll be back with six of them." Trelo pats the seat Aziel is sitting in.

And that's when I notice the seats for what they are.

Giant skeletal troll hands and we sit in the palms.

"I'll go grab us some drinks," Iggy says, hopping down from one of the hands. His feet don't even touch the ground when he is sitting down. It's cute.

I stand behind Aziel and rub his shoulders.

"Mmm, that feels good, My Light."

"You're so tense. It's probably from carrying Uri around."

"I'll deal. Uri has saved me far too many times. I'll deal with tight shoulders."

I bring my lips to his ear, the fur at the tips tickling my nose. "I guess that means I'm going to have to massage you more."

"Mmm, I like the sound of that." He reaches behind him, grabs my shirt, and yanks me over.

I flip into his lap, staring up into his handsome werewolf face. He has more of a mane in this form, fur lining his cheeks, and his nose is black. His eyes have changed to the same color as mine, proving our bond.

He is vicious. His features are defined and cut. When he looks at me, all of his features soften.

"Holy shit, you guys." Iggy returns, carefully placing the purmugs on the table. Seems the purmugs are made from igneous rock too. The foam sloshes over the rim. "There is a guy at the bar, cute, but has gnarly scars on his face. It looks like he got scratched by a werewolf."

Aziel sits up, his energy shifting, and he sets me on the ground. "What did you just say?"

"There's a guy at the bar with scars on his face." Iggy shrugs like it's no big deal. He picks up his drink, takes a sip, and has a foam mustache. He licks it off the top of his lip. "He is grouchy, and he hated to know a werewolf was here. I didn't gather all he said, but I heard the statement, 'All werewolves should die' and that's when I made my escape because he started to scare me."

"That's impossible. It can't be," he whispers, staring in the direction of the bar. "Why don't you two look for balls? I'll be right back."

I grab Aziel by the arm, stopping him before he takes a step. "You aren't going up to him, are you? You heard what Iggy said."

"I think I know of this guy. I think– I think he might be my Alpha's brother."

I rear back, staring at my Beloved as if he is crazy. "The chances of that, Aziel. Come on. It probably isn't him. Don't risk your life for someone you don't know."

"But if it is him, I can tell Alpha Monreaux," I whisper, not wanting to say it too loud. "Maybe we can figure out a way to get him out. Maybe he can come with us to Dread Mountain."

"I'm coming with you."

"No. You stay with Iggy. He can't be left alone. We don't want anything happening to him. I promise I'll be back with a ball, and I'll kick your ass in bowling."

"Fine," I huff. "But if he attacks you, don't say I didn't

warn you."

"When I come back and I'm bleeding, you're going to tell me, 'I told you so.'"

I swallow a big gulp of Deadly Ale. "Don't act like you know me."

"I know you better than you know yourself." He kisses my forehead. "You guys get started without me. I'm last anyway."

"I love you. Don't get wiped out of existence when I just got you back."

Aziel

I bend down to whisper in her ear. "I'm the Ripper, My Light. I'm the best fighter in Purgatory. It's going to take more than him to kill me." With that, I give her a confident smirk before turning around and heading toward the bar. It's packed.

The bartender with eight tentacles is pouring drinks at a record speed, sliding them down the bar top for people to catch. A few Purgstitues are hanging over a few guys, hoping to earn a couple eeries.

At the end of the bar, near the wall, is the guy Iggy was talking about. From here, I can only see the marred side of his face. Claw marks. Five thick lines ruin his face and as I glance down at my own nails, I have no doubts that those wounds came from a werewolf.

"Excuse me. Sorry. Excuse me." I push my way through the crowd.

"Hey, big boy. Looking for a good time? I'm Holly, at least that's what my killers called me." A succubus cuts me off and stands in front of me in her red lingerie and light purple skin, holding out her hand in a dainty way for me to take. She frowns, immediately removing her hand from my reach. "Shit. You're mated. My seduction doesn't work on you."

I give her an eerie anyway. "I hope you find what you're looking for." I walk around her, bumping my shoulder against someone else.

"Thanks!" she yells over the crowd.

The guy I bumped turns around. "Watch it," he sneers, showcasing pointed teeth.

I pick him up easily and set him behind me. "How about you get mouthy with someone who can't kill you so easily?" I growl, turning around to head towards my target.

"Excuse me. Sorry." I swear if I get bumped one more time, I'm bringing Uri out.

I finally reached the end of the bar and Iggy was right, this man's energy is keeping everyone away. There are three empty stools beside him, and he is sitting in the one closest to the wall.

Risking my life, I take a seat, leaving a spot open between us.

"Werewolves aren't welcome around me. You need to go." He is calm and collected, staring at a picture of Lucifer on the wall as he drinks his beer.

"I know. I just need to know something first. I am not here to hurt you. I'm sorry for whoever did."

He slams his purmug down and twists in his bar stool, giving me a clear view of his face. The scars must have been deep to cause so much damage. One eye is milky, a side of his mouth doesn't move, and his skin seems tight to the point that it must cause him so much pain.

I know what that's like.

I'm in pain now and it's hard to fight through.

"You're Alexander's twin," I say, completely shocked I'm staring at Atreyu.

"How the fuck do you know him? Is he here? What the fuck did you do to him?" His voice trembles with barely controlled rage.

"He's my Alpha, my Master, I suppose."

He flinches. "He has werewolves in the coven?" he spits. "He would never. Not after they bit us and did what they did to our family."

"Atreyu—"

"—Don't say my name as if you know me, Wolf. I haven't killed you yet because Trelo would throw me out for killing someone again. I like it here. Don't talk to me like you know me. It's insulting."

"I didn't do that to you." I point to his face. "But I killed many others and so did my brother. Our werewolves were spelled. We were trapped in our beasts and forced to be killing machines. My brother and I were cursed for fifteen years before your brother and his Beloved saved us."

His mouth twitches in an attempt to smile. "He found his Beloved?"

I nod. "Her name is Maven Wildes."

"I've heard of her. She opened the portals to other dimensions. I had no idea she belonged to my brother. I'm happy for him. Now, leave me the fuck alone. I'm not good company to keep and I do not want *your* company."

"Is there anything you want me to tell him? Or your father?"

"My father?" Atreyu drops his purmug on the counter and it splits in half, the beer spreading across the surface.

I have to lift my arms, so it doesn't stick to my fur.

"My father is alive?"

"Your father, your sister, the ones you thought you lost. They are alive."

"You're lying!" he shouts, grabbing a broken piece of the mug and placing it against my throat. "Give me a reason not to end your existence." He is trembling with so many emotions and yet the one I scent the most is sorrow.

Not rage. Not guilt. Not disbelief.

But pure, unfiltered sadness. It's so profound, so strong, it almost has me falling from my seat.

"I promise they are alive. Your father and your brother talk to your tomb in the catacombs. The tomb that's spelled by Sarah Wildes herself." I stretch my neck, trying to get space between me and the piece of sharp rock. "We're going up Dread Mountain soon. We're going to get out of here. I was going to ask if you would come with us, but you said you were bitten—"

"Only my beloved can get me out. I know. I think I'm better off here." He drops the broken piece of rock on the counter. "I'm too damaged for anyone to love me like your mate loves you."

"You know I have a mate?"

"I see her mark, plus, she hasn't stopped staring me down with a dagger in her hand." He turns to me again and the similarities between him and Alexander are uncanny. The only difference is Atreyu isn't as pale as Alexander. My Alpha's personality isn't as... grumpy either. "Leave me be, Wolf. If you find a way out, which I don't think you will, but if you do, tell my brother I'm fine."

"Is that all?"

"And that I'm pissed he allowed werewolves in the coven."

I flinch when he spits my species name with so much venom. "There are other creatures too if that makes it any better."

"Don't care. Just don't want you or your brother there. I've run out of time to give you, along with my give a damn. I don't trust a word you say. You're a werewolf. Too much has been done to me, too much has been taken from me to trust anything you say. I don't know you. I don't want to know you. Please, leave me the fuck alone and have a safe journey to wherever the fuck you're going that doesn't involve being around me."

I stand, knowing my welcome has run its course. "Your family misses you. Your father sits next to you and reads your favorite book. Alexander has kids now. He talks to you about them all the time. Don't... Don't settle in Purgatory when you have an entire life, a family, on the other side wanting you home."

"I can't go home with you there. It's no longer my home." The bartender brings Atreyu another round of beer. He snags it, chugging half in a few gulps. Without looking at me, he stares at the wall again. "Leave."

Taking one last look at the vampire who is so different from my Alpha, I give him what he wants. I'm far from giving up on him though. I'm going to find a way to bring Atreyu home one day.

And he'll thank me.

Chapter Thirteen

ELOUISE

It's the last frame. I'm winning. Iggy is in second place, and Aziel is in last. My Beloved is amazing at so many things. He's a strong fighter, an amazing lover, and a protector, but he cannot bowl.

He's rolled a gutter ball every single frame. His score is currently a zero. I'm not sure how that's possible.

I think his mind is elsewhere. Ever since he came back from talking with Atreyu, he's been quiet.

He's sitting in a giant troll's hand, tapping his leg as he watches Iggy get another strike.

"Oh, come on. No one can be this good at bowling." Aziel huffs, crosses his arms, and slouches.

"You're such a sore loser." I head over to him, wrapping my arms around his shoulders. "It's just a game."

He points to the scoreboard. "I have zero points."

"I guess I'll just need to give you one-on-one les-sons." I nip at the shell of his ear.

He perks up, sitting straighter. "It definitely sounds like I need lessons. What's your charge?"

I slink around him, sliding my fingers across his chest before I take a seat on his lap. "I don't know if you'll be able to keep up with my demands. You'll need a lot of stamina."

He growls, his claws digging into my thighs. "I have plenty of that." He licks his lips, his eyes dropping to my mouth, then my breasts.

I tease him, dragging my fingers across my collarbone, then down, and up. Aziel is practically panting.

"I don't know if you'll be able to keep up with everything I want to show you." My voice becomes husky, my own lust heating my body from the far-from-innocent flirtations.

"Or, I hate to say it Aziel, maybe you found the one thing you aren't good at," Iggy chimes in with his two cents before cracking his knuckles, sitting down, and stretching as if he has had the hardest day. "I'm leaving here with a perfect three hundred score."

"I'm leaving here with a perfect three hundred score," Aziel mocks him.

"Childish, Beloved. Just childish." I pat his hand, scolding him while trying not to laugh at how much losing bothers him.

The pins are reset. Ten standing and waiting to get smashed by a bowling ball skull.

"You haven't said how your talk with Atreyu went. I mean, you told me who he was when you came back, but you've been quiet." I play with his long grey mane, hoping it eases his frustrations.

"He is a cranky bastard for good reason. He isn't pleasant to talk to. I'm lucky I walked away with my life. He hates my kind. He is scarred because of the cursed werewolves."

"But did you scar him?" Iggy asks.

"No, but I can understand his unease."

"He needs to understand that you aren't to blame for his pain."

"He has too much to work through to see that. I'm

hoping his beloved finds him soon. He doesn't have much time left before the coma turns to death."

I stand, grab my seven-pound skull ball, and line up my feet with the arrows. The venlillies under my shoes took some getting used to. The plant is sticky and the leaves hug around my boots to stay in place.

Releasing a breath, I step forward, bring my arm back, and sling the ball forward. Ten spine pins fall with ease giving me another strike to add to my record.

Aziel is up next. His feet pound on the floor. The vibrations tickle my feet as he snags a twenty-pound skull ball.

"You can do it, Beloved. I have faith in you." I clap for him, grinning with encouragement.

"Makes one of us," Iggy grumbles under his breath, and I elbow him in the ribs. "Ow. What? I can't fight to save my damn life, literally, and Aziel can. I would have to say, when it comes to skills, bowling isn't one he needs."

"That actually makes me feel a lot better, Iggy." Aziel gives him a very toothy smile that looks more like a snarl with all the sharp teeth.

Iggy leans toward me and whispers. "Is he smiling? Or is he about to eat me? I can't tell. It's creeping me out. Tell him to stop. Oh God, the smile is going on too long. Elouise!" Iggy pats my arm faster and faster, the stench of sweat breaking out over his skin.

I giggle, pointing at the pins. "Let's finish this game and get on the road."

"Does Purgatory have roads?" Iggy questions.

"No, but you know what I mean." I shove his head away and he falls from the chair. "Oops. Sorry."

"I'm nervous guys. I don't think I want to roll." Aziel's tail tucks between his legs.

I need to get him into a fight. He'll be in his element. Once I do that, he'll be reset.

Iggy crawls up the hand, wrapping his arms

around the fingers to swing his legs up. "That was rude, and I won't forget it."

"Aw." I place my hand on my chest, pretending to be sad. Getting up, I bring my fists to my face, twisting them to imitate that I'm crying. I stick out my tongue at Iggy before spinning around to give Aziel my attention. "How can I help you, Beloved?"

"I don't know."

"Can I show you?"

"Please."

I scoot him over a bit. "You want to stand here. Don't aim for the middle pin. You want to aim between the middle and the second. Look at the pins, not the arrows. Keep your arm straight when you release." I guide his arm back and then forward. "You don't want to release the ball too late or you will throw it too far left. It will curl and go into the gutter which is what you have been doing."

I give him a demonstration, showing how my back leg crosses and I tend to bend low when I release the ball. It has me in control of the ball more. He practices too. He is so large, that every motion is awkward.

"You can do it," I whisper. "It's just a game. Pretend those spines are someone you hate and you want to kill."

"Brenden," he growls, holding the ball to his chin.

"Perfect and pretend this ball is your weapon. You're going to aim it at his stupid fucking face."

"I can do that."

"I know you can." I tug on his tail. "Now show yourself you can. No one else." I step away, giving him space, but My Beloved turns to see where I'm at. "I'm right here. I won't go anywhere."

"That's so fucking cute," Iggy sighs with hearts in his eyes. "He's so lethal and needs support just to go bowling. How adorable. No wonder you love him."

Aziel exhales, his tail swooshing back and forth in confidence. He steps forward. Iggy and I hold our breath. Aziel's arm swings back, then he releases. I inhale, standing up on the chair so I can see over Aziel's shoulder to watch the ball.

"Come on. Come on," I urge it, wishing I could control the direction the ball is going in. "It's going to hit! It's going to hit them, Beloved!" I squeal, jumping up and down when the ball curves at the last second, taking down six pins.

But that's better than none.

"Holy shit, I hit them. I got six!" Aziel laughs, tugging on his hair next to his eyes, and sprints up to me, snagging me in a tight hug. He spins me around in circles. "Thank you. Thank you for showing me." He peppers kisses all over my face and sets me down, my head swirling with dizziness.

He cups my face and stares into my eyes, happiness shining so bright in his pupils.

"Don't ever be afraid to teach me something new. I love it when you teach me."

My knees become weak, my entire body softening, my heart falling deeper in love with him.

"Fog! Fog is rolling in!" Trelo announces over the speakers. The lights flicker on and off. The siren blasts through the bowling alley. "Those that don't want to fight, you are more than welcome to stay here. Those that do fight, good luck. I hope to see you again. If I don't, it was nice knowing you."

The sweet expression on Aziel's face disappears. The fighter, the killer inside possesses his bones and hardens every surface of his body. He stands up straight, chest out, chin high, and the adorable werewolf who didn't know how to bowl has vanished.

"That's our cue." Aziel rips the venlilly from his feet, tossing the sticky green plant in the trash. "One more fight."

"Why not just cut out the middle man? Let's just threaten Scorder." Iggy laces up his shoes.

"Because we have a dangerous journey ahead."

Aziel double-checks the straps on Uri to secure it to his back. "He knows everyone, and we do not want to get on his bad side or Dread Mountain will be worse than we could ever imagine. Scorder isn't a trustworthy dragon, but he is someone you want on your side. Keep your enemies close, keep Purgatory enemies closer."

Iggy contemplates, intertwining his fingers through the trolls' that make the seat he is sitting in, not that they fit together, and kicks his feet in a small tantrum. "I can't stay here with my new friends?" He lifts the orc's skull from the floor, the one that Aziel killed for whistling at me. "He means well."

I snort, knowing Iggy is joking, but his humor doesn't land with Aziel.

"You'll be someone's bitch if you stay. Knock yourself out."

"Aziel!" I scold him.

Iggy gasps, hand to chest, then wiggles his brows. "You think? I don't think any of them could handle me."

Aziel rolls his eyes and takes my hand. "I'm sick of him. Give him to The Ferryman."

I slap Aziel on the shoulder, turning to Iggy. "He didn't mean it."

"I meant it. Let's go." Aziel walks ahead, the only one leaving the building to go fight.

And I follow him because I'd follow him anywhere.

Of course, I drag Iggy with me.

Atreyu— if I remember correctly— steps in front of Aziel right as we reach the door. Trelo is behind the counter, staring at us with worried pinched brows.

"What the fuck do you think you're doing?" Atreyu blocks the doors, his eyes the color of freshly spilled blood.

"I'm going to fight to get a clue about where the avisseus is. I'm taking my mate and her headache of a friend back home with me. You know, home? Where your brother is, where your family is, or don't you care anymore?"

Atreyu lifts his fist to hit Aziel. I blur to him, dagger to his neck, the silver burning his skin.

"Try it and you'll be forgotten by those you love," I threaten, our gazes locking.

"You'd kill your own kind?"

"I'd kill anyone who dares to harm my beloved. I don't give a fuck if you're a vampire. If you're a threat to him, to me, you're done."

Aziel tugs me back by grabbing the neckline of my shirt, then loops his fingers in the belt loop of my pants to keep me there.

"It's okay, My Light. He was just getting out of the way."

Atreyu's jaw ticks as it clenches, his fists balling at his sides. "Fine, go get yourself killed. It's one less thing for me to do." He walks away, bumping into Atreyu on purpose. He pauses, turning slightly so we can only see his scars. "Try not to die, not that I care, but my brother would. And if he cares, I guess I'll have to give a fucking shit too. Tell my family I miss them if you live and I'm better off here."

"If I don't get myself killed?"

Atreyu huffs with impatience. "Yes, not that I care, remember?"

"How could I ever forget?" Aziel drawls.

We watch Atreyu disappear to the bar, to the same corner, to the same seat, and pick up his mug. He doesn't give us another glance.

"Be careful, Aziel. It was good meeting you." Trelo holds out his hand. "I hope you live and find a way out."

Aziel slaps his palm into the bull shifter's. "What about you? Ever plan on leaving?"

Trelo dries off a clean glass. "No, that time has passed for me. Plus, I'm happy here."

"You're happy here? In Purgatory?" I step in front of Aziel, completely dumbfounded by Trelo's answer. Who in their right mind would want to stay here? "We are talking about the same place, right? The one with weird, wicked creatures that want to kill you? The one with thick fog and deadly fights? The one with acidic rain?"

"Sometimes it's acidic. Not all the time."

I tilt my head, putting my hands on my hips. "Really? Don't try to find a rainbow in darkness, Trelo. You'll be disappointed."

He grins, stealing a quick glance at someone. I spin around to see who he is looking at but no one is there.

"It isn't so bad. I like it, here as weird as it sounds. I like my job. I have freedom here that I didn't have on the other side."

"That's..." My shoulders slump. "That's really sad."

"Don't be sad for me. I'm fine. It's your mate you have to worry about. He's about to go to The Graveyard. Every fight there has me holding my breath. I hope you live to see another day, Aziel."

Aziel puts on his skull mask. It sits perfectly on his snout and the sides wrap around his temple, so it stays in place.

"Don't worry about me, Trelo. I have more experience killing than I do truly living. If there's anyone you need to worry about, it's my opponent." Aziel slips his hand across my lower back. "We need to go," he whispers into my ear.

My heart pounds with anxiety. My palms begin to sweat. I realize talking to Trelo was just a distraction. The longer we talk to the bull shifter, the longer Aziel has to go without risking his existence.

"Best of luck, Trelo." Aziel waves before turning me to the door.

"Same to you, Friend."

The silence hanging in the air is heavy when we leave. People watch us as if we are walking the plank to our deaths.

"I don't know Aziel. Please, let's just take the information we have and go to Dread Mountain. Please," I beg, taking his hand and stopping directly in front of him. "Please."

"If we go to Dread Mountain with no new informa-tion, what then, My Light? The journey will be wasted if the avisseus isn't there."

"But you'll be alive."

"Yeah, I don't think this is necessary," Iggy states, rubbing the back of his neck. "It's too risky."

"No risk. No reward. I'll be fine. I've been fine all the other times I've fought."

"It only takes one time." I lift a finger, my middle finger to be exact because I'm not too happy with him right now.

Aziel tries to hide his smile, kissing the pad of my finger. "It will be okay, I promise." He drops to all fours when we are outside, the bones of the centaur he killed are still there. "Come on. It's faster this way. Climb on."

I jump onto his back first, furious and afraid, grip-ping the hair on the back of his neck a little hard. He turns his head, narrows his eyes, and huffs.

I lift a shoulder, acting innocent.

He scoffs again, and I roll my eyes at his attitude. If anyone has a right to an attitude, it's me. He is the one risking his life. Again.

Holding out my hand for Iggy, he grabs it, and I yank him up. He settles behind me, wrapping his arms around my waist so tight, I can't breathe.

"Iggy," I croak, slapping his arms. "Can't. Breathe."

"Sorry. Sorry. Makes me nervous getting up here. It's so high off the ground."

Without warning, Aziel takes off sprinting. Iggy screams, embracing me in a deadly hold again. I clutch onto Aziel's mane, hunching low to avoid the wind in my eyes.

Aziel's head snaps to the left and I follow his gaze, gasping when I see a suffogrim.

And it screeches when it sees us, flying to get to us. Aziel growls, picking up the pace of his strides. The suffogrim gets close enough that I can smell the rotting flesh it has hanging on its bones. I gag.

Iggy groans from the retched scent, burying his face in my back. I do the same, only I bury my nose in Aziel's fur. I'm bombarded by his scent. He still smells of the shower we took together. Peace settles over me and my hand drops to his neck, rubbing the tough hide. I think about him combing my hair and taking the time to braid it. I hear his small grunts when he plucks a hair out of his scalp just so he can tie the braid off at the ends.

My eyes water and fear replaces the happiness I feel. I can't lose him to this fight. I can't. I'll die anyway because he is my beloved but the difference is that I'd want to die. I wouldn't wait to wither away. I'd go ahead and take my dagger, place it against my heart, and sink it into my chest until the silver steals my last breath.

The screeching becomes so close, I feel the breath of the suffogrim against my cheek. I turn my head to look at the creature just as it opens its mouth. Its tongue is black, blood dripping from its sewed-on lips. I'm caught staring at it too long and he inhales, stealing the air right from my lungs.

"Elouise!" Iggy screams, snatching one of my daggers.

My best friend attacks, stabbing the suffogrim in the arm. Blood splatters onto my arm and I scream in agony, unable to move, barely able to breathe. Aziel comes to a hard stop, sliding a few feet before shaking us off his back.

Iggy and I fly into the air, away from the suffogrim, landing hard on the ground.

"Elouise!" Iggy scurries over to me as I gasp for air, holding my hand against my chest. "It's okay. Breathe. I have you. Breathe."

I'm on all fours, digging my fingers into the black dirt, spit dripping from my mouth, tears streaming down my face as I desperately try to get air. Iggy rubs my back which helps me relax.

Tears fall from my cheeks and onto the cold soil. I'm finally able to see. I glance up when I hear a roar and Aziel has Uri out. He leaps through the air and brings Uri above his head before planting Uri in the skull of the suffogrim.

It releases a murderous cry that makes my ears ring.

Aziel lands on his hind legs, blood dripping from the mandible of Uri. The suffogrim screeches again, the stitched skin dropping from his bones as it dies.

Aziel grips the sardonic creature by the back of the head, its blood coating Aziel's hand. I can smell the scent of flesh burning, his flesh.

"Aziel!"

I know he can hear me. He chooses not to. He doesn't act like he is in pain and that's concerning. My Beloved is too used to agony. Every now and then, he has pain from when he was sick. It reminds me of phantom pain. The sickness is gone but the ghost of it remains inside him.

"You dare try and steal the air out of my mate's lungs? You dare try to kill her? Her air is not yours. It is hers." He rips the suffogrim's head back, placing Uri at the creature's throat. "And it is mine for when I want to swallow her moans," he snarls, slicing Uri through the suffogrim's neck.

Aziel tosses the head in the forest; the branches stretch out to grab the head. The trees fight for it, leaves falling onto Purgatory's floor, and one of the trunks engulfs the head, swallowing it whole.

Aziel doesn't holster Uri. He runs to me, dropping onto his knees to gather me into his arms.

"Feed, My Light. You need blood." He pushes my face against his neck, and I don't hesitate, I sink my fangs into his throat, sucking long drags of his delicious red life source.

The panic flees my body. It becomes easier to

breathe with every swallow. The burns on my arm begin to heal.

He moans, cupping the back of my head. "That's it, Elouise. Take all you need."

"I'm going to... turn this way so I'm not intruding." Iggy spins around in a circle a few times before finally finding a direction he wants to look in.

I close my eyes, tasting Aziel, the relief, and the way he is holding himself back from fucking me right here. Vampire bites with their mates are extremely pleasurable. Aziel is barely holding on by a thread not to orgasm. It isn't the time or the place.

I find the will to stop before it becomes too much for the both of us. I ache between my legs and his cock is hard, stretching across his stomach. Precome leaks out onto his abs. All I want to do is bend down to clean him up, but we are already behind in getting to The Graveyard.

I lift his hand, eyeing the burn marks that are taking too long to heal. I bite my wrist, shoving it into his mouth. Aziel grabs my arm so tight; I think he is about to break the bone. His eyes flash gold, my blood powering his system in the same way his does to mine.

I have to roll my lips together to keep myself silent. The way he is feeding from me strengthens our bond. Our souls intertwine, his emotions sink into me, giving me a breath of fresh life I had no idea I was missing.

He removes my wrist from his mouth, his lips tinted in red, and now he seems to be the one breathless. His chest rises and falls, that's when I notice the ropes of white on his chest.

"I couldn't stop. I tried not to, but you tasted so good, and it reminded me how the full moon night will go. My imagination took hold."

I giggle, loving that he reacts to me in such a way. I rip the lower section of my new shirt off and wipe him clean before tossing the cloth onto the ground.

"I can't wait until we have time to explore one another," I say, my fingers playing with the thick patch of hair nestled above his werewolf cock.

God, it's huge in this form.

I can't wait to take it.

"Come on. We need to go." Iggy shuffles on his feet. "You guys make traveling awkward."

Aziel stands, holstering Uri. "Yeah, I won't apologize for that. We're close. Is everyone good walking?"

"I'm fine," I reply, patting my body to double check my daggers are there.

"I will be fine if you two manage to keep it in your pants."

"That's not what happened, and you know it," Aziel gripes. "I can't help my body's reaction. She helped me heal. It's not as if I planned on coming all over my chest. It isn't something I tend to share with people, Iggy." Aziel walks forward, staying a few steps ahead of Iggy.

"I don't think he likes me," Iggy whispers.

Aziel overhears.

"I like you just fine. Sometimes, I find you insufferable, but I'll get over it."

"Ouch," Iggy mumbles, a frown taking over his face.

"Don't listen to him. It's the entire circumstance, Iggy. Nothing seems to be convenient anymore, and we just have to keep that in mind."

He nods, still looking down. I forget how submissive he naturally is due to his omega nature. I loop my arm through his and bend down to press my cheek against his shoulder.

"Aziel is ornery. Don't mind him. He likes you or he probably would have killed you by now," I try to reassure my best friend.

"She's right," Aziel sings from in front of us.

Iggy whips his head up and smiles. Just as quick as his happiness arrived, it leaves when we hear the murmuring from the crowd.

The Graveyard.

"We're here," Aziel announces.

The three of us stand just outside the tree line, taking in the huge ribcage that lies on the ground. Inside the bones is where everyone fights.

"I always wonder what creature existed to leave such a skeleton behind," Iggy says, impressed and terrified by how his words are broken between breaths.

"Don't know. Don't care. All that matters is what happens inside the cage." Aziel charges forward, walking straight to Scorder who is currently taking bets.

He is in an extravagant outfit. The coat is longer in the back, and he isn't wearing a shirt underneath so everyone can see his body. He's wearing a top hat that has seen better days. The rim is jagged, the material fraying, and there's a big red stain on the front.

He probably killed whoever that hat belonged to.

"Scorder." Aziel cuts in front of everyone to speak to him.

"Ah, Ripper! You all better bet on this guy! He's the champion." Scorder continues to take money from the patrons, his pockets brimming with eeries. "You want in on the fight?"

"Only if there is updated information on where the avisseus is."

"There always is." Scorder's grin is off-putting, a deceitful twinkle in his eye.

I step into his space, my hand itching to dig my dagger into his neck. "And you won't just tell us? Since you already know he will win."

Scorder tsks, counting the eeries. "That's not how it works, Love."

Aziel is quick with Uri, placing it against Scorder's throat. "I just killed a suffogrim with this and I will kill you too if you think you can call my mate that."

Scorder's fingers press against Uri to push him away. "Alright. Alright. Don't get your soul in a twist. I meant no harm." He tugs at the lapels of his jacket. "In order to get information, you have to fight. That's the deal."

"So break the deal!" I shout at him.

The dragon actually seems regretful. "I can't break the deal. My life is on the line too. I have to keep the show going or it's my existence. Okay?"

"Who are you working for? I thought you ran the show."

"I'm the manager, so to speak, but the idea?" He gestures at us to come forward.

Scorder glances left and right. "This show has been around for a while but not the same people have been running it. It's a new guy, one with connections, power, and experience with shows. He killed the previous owner."

Aziel straightens, a storm brewing in his chest. "I think I know who you're talking about."

"You know Azazel?" Scorder questions in a whisper.

"Know him?" Aziel scans the crows to see if Azazel, whoever he is, is here. "I was captured on the other side by him, but the Horsemen caught him and brought him here. He specialized in carnivals and freak shows," Aziel informs. "And it really pisses me off I'm somehow trapped by him again. This will be my last fight, Scorder. Understood?"

"Understood." Scorder opens the cage for Aziel to enter. "You know the deal, no weapons."

"Like I ever need them." He unhooks Uri and hands the weapon to me. "If anything happens to me, promise you'll still try to get out of here."

"Nothing is going to happen to you. You can't talk like that." I do my best to keep my emotions in check and it's the hardest thing I've ever had to do.

Scorder closes Aziel into the cage. I press myself against it, my nose and lips peeking through the holes so I can be as near to Aziel as possible. His fingers grip the chained fence as he leans down, giving me a deep, passionate kiss.

"Everything will be okay. Keep Iggy safe. I'll be out soon. It's only one fight. I can do this. And then we can go home."

"Aziel." I drop my forehead against the cage door. "How many times do I have to tell you? You're my home."

He doesn't say anything. He just lifts my chin, rubs his thumb over my bottom lip, and gives me a thoughtful smile.

"Even if I didn't exist, the memory of your lips would be strong enough to keep my spirit alive."

And just like that, he backs away, sinking into the dark. I can only see the outline of his frame and the mask he covers his face with.

"Creatures and Creaturettes! Welcome to the show!" Scorder blows fire into the air, the crowd cheering for more. "If you're new here, please let me introduce you to Ripper, our reigning champion. He hasn't lost a fight yet!"

And he better not start now.

"He is one of the largest werewolves you'll ever see. Standing ten feet tall and over eleven hundred pounds, please shine the light on our very own, Ripper!" He sings Aziel's nickname and right on cue, Aziel roars so loud, it shakes the bones under my feet.

The crowd loves him, standing, clapping, and screaming for more.

"Our other opponent has been in Purgatory for a while but has decided to come out and play with us." The crowd roars. Scorder scans everyone with his wicked, charming smile. His gaze lands on me and he tips his hat in my direction.

I sneer. "Keep looking at me and I'll carve your fucking eyes out."

"Maybe I should take the weapons that are..." Iggy waves his hands up and down my body. "—On your person. You seem a little murdery."

"I'm fine. I just hate Scorder."

Scorder spreads out his arm, pointing in the direction of the other opponent. "He is also a werewolf, standing at nine feet tall, and one thousand pounds. Please welcome, Ghost, as he hasn't ever been seen until now. You know what they have to do! Tell me." Scorder cups his hand by his ear.

"Fight for your existence!" The crowd yells, rattling the cage with their hands.

"You heard them fellas. Fight for your existence." Scorder runs out of the arena. The crowd dies down and silence falls.

The cage doors on either side open, allowing the fighters to enter the ring. Aziel walks out first, spreads his arms, and roars to the moon. Bones beneath our feet tremble from the power.

On the other side, another werewolf steps out. He's nearly equal in size to Aziel, granted Aziel is a foot taller but his opponent is wider.

"They kind of look alike, right? Or is it just me?" Iggy asks.

The bond shakes like an earthquake, complete shock, fear, and sorrow filter through into my heart. I gasp, clutching my chest from the pain.

"What? What is it?"

And for the first time, I can hear Aziel's voice in my mind. It's distant since our bond isn't complete, but it's there.

"It's my dad."

Chapter Fourteen

AZIEL

I stand completely frozen. That can't be who I think it is. He died so long ago. That's impossible. He couldn't have been here all this time.

"Dad?"

He doesn't seem surprised to see me at all. His eyes show warmth, but he doesn't smile. His body is wide, his arm barely touching his sides as he circles me.

"I want nothing more than to hug you," he mumbles, a hitch in his voice. "I knew I'd be able to find you here. I've been searching for you ever since I heard a werewolf named Aziel entered Purgatory. Slash me," he says.

"What?"

"Slash me!" He shoves my back, and I sneer, kicking out my leg to trip him.

He falls onto his back. The air is knocked out of his lungs. I use his position to my advantage. I wrap my hands around his throat, but I don't squeeze.

"What are you doing here? I can't kill you. I won't. I can't. You can't be here. Why are you here?" I'm too dumbfounded to say anything else.

"I want to die," he croaks. "What better way than to see my

son one last time?"

"We have to fight. We have to put on a show. It's Scorder's rules." One. Just one tear falls from my lash line onto the ground. I have to get myself together. Neither the crowd nor Scorder can see this.

"I know. I know. We will but I won't be the one killing you." He tucks his knees to his chest, plants his feet on me, and shoves.

I fly backward, slamming against the side of the ribcage.

"Oh my God, Aziel!" Elouise rushes to me. "Are you okay? Is he really…"

"He is. I had no idea he was here."

"What are you going to do?"

I'm lost when it comes to that question. "I have no idea. I… I don't know, Elouise." I clutch the ribcage, staring at my mate for answers. "What do I do? I don't know what to do. I don't… I can't. I can't." I shake my head, my breath catching in my throat when the memories of my parent's howls filling the night as they were killed play in my head. "I can't do this."

"You can," Elouise says, looping her fingers through mine. "You can do this because if you don't, you're dead anyway. You have to, Beloved. I'm so sorry, but you have to."

I open my mouth to speak when my leg is grabbed. My chin hits the ground so hard that my teeth clank together. My dad swings me in the air, spinning me in a circle until the arena is nothing but a blur.

He lets me go and I soar, crashing against the

ribcage again.

"Ooo," the crowd cringes in unison.

The killer lurking beneath my skin swallows the pain to feed its own violence. I flip from my back to all fours, snarling at my dad.

"Come on, Son. I know you have more in you than that," he whispers as we circle one another.

I snarl, rearing back on my hind legs, howling in warning.

"That's it. Come on. Kill me. What are you waiting for?"

"Why are you doing this?" Spit flies from my mouth as I ask the burning question through my clenched teeth.

"I wanted to see you. This place, it plays tricks. I wanted you to know I was here and not an entity using me against you."

"What do you call this? You're being used against me now!" I shout at him, throwing my fist directly into his face. "Why bother! Why not stay a ghost, then?"

He tackles me to the ground, slamming me onto my back with force. "Because I wanted to see you one last time before I decided to be wiped from existence."

I flip over him, wrapping an arm around his throat, then constricting him until he can't breathe. "If you do that, I won't be able to remember you," I remind him, squeezing harder for the hell of it. "You want to take that away from me? From Anwyll?"

"You barely remember me now," he replies in a crushed whisper. "It's okay to let me go."

I shake my head, unable to do such a thing. I can't. I've lost too much. I've done too much. Why can't I have one fucking thing? Why can't I live my life without so much strife and fucking chaos? I've killed hundreds, probably thousands, and now the fucking universe wants me to kill my father?

No.

No, I can't do that. I might have been made into a

killing machine and I might be really fucking great at it, but it isn't who I am. I am not the blood-thirsty out-of-control monster I used to be.

"No," I simply croak as tears hit my cheek. "Don't ask this of me. Please. Please, don't."

He elbows me in the ribs, one snapping in half, and I release the hold I have on him to try to inhale some air. Every attempt hurts.

Dad wraps his hands around my neck, choking me but not hard enough to kill me. His own eyes water. The pain, the sadness, the grief, it all swims in the dull irises that used to shine a brilliant blue.

"I am so proud of you," he says. "And your brother. I know whatever happened with that warlock couldn't have been easy. Now you're fighting to get out of here." He smiles fondly, as if remembering a time when we were all together. "You've always been a fighter. It's okay to let me go. Bring me peace, Son. I love you. It's okay to let me go."

"But I won't remember you," I argue, grasping his arm for dear life. "I don't want you to go. Come back with me. With us."

"I have no bones waiting for me. I can't go back. I am already dust. This fight is between you and me. Why would I want to live if it meant my son would die? Kill me, Aziel. Put me out of my misery."

"No!" I roar.

"Do it!"

"I won't." I try to get out of his grasp, but he tightens his grip.

"I said to kill me. Your Alpha commands it."

"You aren't my Alpha anymore. I do not have to obey you," I seethe.

His face softens. "But I am your father."

I slam my elbow on his arm, hearing the bone break in two. He falls to his knees, and I follow him. Cupping the back of his head, I pull him to me, hugging him one last time.

"Dad. I'm so sorry. I'm so sorry," I sob, missing him more every second that he is here because I know I have to live without him again.

Only this time, I won't remember who he is.

He hugs me in return. My ribs ache from how hard he is holding me. I don't care.

"Don't apologize. It's okay. This is what I want. Make it brutal. They like that here."

"Dad—"

"—Do it."

"I can't."

"You can and you will." He takes a deep breath. "I hope your mate whom you have loved since you were a pup can remind you of me," he says more for her than me. I won't remember this conversation. "I love you and your brother. Get the hell out of here and make a good life. Do it. Now."

I don't.

"Do it. Now! Do it!" he roars and with an agonizing roar, I plunge my fist into his chest and rip out his heart, a werewolf's favorite way to kill.

"My son," he rasps on his last breath before falling limp against me.

I toss my head back and howl in mourning, holding him as his body fades. He becomes lighter, fading away from me, from my mind, my heart, and everywhere else he used to live inside me.

He's gone and all that's left are bones.

I lift his skull, staring into the blank sockets, and have no memory of why I am feeling so much grief for this skeleton.

"Our winner once more! Everyone give a round of applause for Ripper!" Scorder announces, and then I'm drowned in the crowd's cheers.

I've never been more confused.

"Oh my God, Aziel." Elouise dashes to me through the cage gate, Uri still in her hands. "Are you okay? Talk to me, My Beloved." Her hands slide across my cheeks, my neck, my shoulders, everywhere she can touch, she does.

"What happened? Who did I fight? Why do I feel so sad?"

"Oh God." Iggy covers his mouth with his palm before squeezing my shoulder.

"What? What is it? Louie, tell me," I beg of her. "Who do these bones belong to? Why do I miss the person who made them?"

Louie's bottom lip trembles.

"Don't cry. Don't let the crowd see you cry, My Light. Those tears belong to you and me." I wipe them away before anyone can see.

"You fought your dad, My Beloved. I heard him beg you to kill him. He said he wanted to see you one last time, which is why he wanted to fight you. He wanted to die. He was so tired and the only way he would go was if you killed him. I'm so sorry. God, Aziel. I'm sorry."

"My dad?"

"You know how it works. You remember, right? Any blood relative won't remember the person who is wiped from existence. I'll tell you about him. I didn't know much, but I know a few stories you told me. I'll happily tell them to you again so you can have something to remember him by." She presses her hand against my heart.

"Anwyll. Holy shit, Anwyll. He must be so confused right now. I have to get home. We have to get home. Maybe we can take my dad's bones back? And give him a proper werewolf burial?" My brows bend together as I stare at the heap of my bones in my hands. "You're sure it's him?"

"I'm sure, Beloved."

"I didn't know, Aziel."

Louie, Iggy, and I turn to Scorder who must have overheard our conversation. His face has lost its color. He runs his fingers through his hair. He genuinely seems stressed.

"Aziel, I had no idea he was your father. I swear, I wouldn't have allowed that fight. Azazel must have set it up. I promise." He runs his hands down his face. "I can give you a bag for the bones. If you want to travel with them."

I tighten my jaw, my teeth groaning from how much pressure I'm applying to them. "You never allow bones to be removed from The Graveyard," I remind him.

"I know, but this is the exception. Aziel, fuck. I'm so fucking sorry. I don't just consider you a fighter, but a friend. And I know I'm not the greatest example of friendship because of what I do here, but Aziel, I wouldn't have you kill your father. I might be a fucking asshole but I'm not heartless. I'll get you a bottomless bag. It's small and easy to carry but anything can fit inside."

"Those are very rare. How did you get one?" Louie asks, suspicious.

"It's The Graveyard, Aziel's Mate. Thousands have come and gone. They trade what they can for eeries."

"And you'll just give us one?" Iggy kicks Scorder in the shin. "As if we are supposed to believe you!"

"Get'em, Iggy!" Louie cheers him on, swirling her dagger in her hand. "Because I'm debating skinning his scales from his body."

"Woah, woah. Let's not get hasty. I'll bring the bag to you. It's right over there in the ticket booth for the busier season. You know, when it snows on the other side? All the accidents and... stuff, you guys don't care. Got it. I'll go."

"I'll go with you," Iggy says, shifting into his bear to be more intimidating.

It doesn't work.

He looks like a stuffed animal.

Scorder reaches out a hand to pet him behind the ear. Iggy bellows a warning not to touch and Scorder rips his hand back.

"Okay. Looks cute. Sounds horrifying. Got it. Let's go." Scorder walks to the cage door. Iggy is on his heels, swiping at the dragon's ankles.

"Oh." Scorder snaps his fingers. "The clue. I wasn't lying when I said that. Apparently, the avisseus is still on Dread Mountain. As of this morning. It's the newest information I have. If I had more, I promise, I'd give it to you."

"Thanks," I force myself to say.

Scorder gives me a small nod before walking away with Iggy.

When I'm left alone with Elouise, the air is heavy with sorrow, and I begin to pick up the bones that belong to my father. Elouise helps, not allowing me to carry the weight of someone I used to know by myself.

"How are you, Beloved? I know you aren't well but talk to me."

I blow out a breath, stacking my dad's bones in my arms, and the pain of losing him, the pain from the treatment, it all hits me at once. The bones fall out of my arms, and I punch the ground, breaking the skulls of other strangers.

"What is it?" Her hand lands on my elbow. She leans forward, trying to catch my gaze.

The broken rib finally heals but it only takes away a very minimal amount of pain.

"Pain," I state in a simple, short baritone.

"You're used to it though, from the treatment, right?"

"That is easier to deal with. It's the pain of losing my dad." I hold up his skull. "It's wild to me that every memory I have of him is gone. I have to trust you to tell me anything and that shouldn't be on you. That's not fair. You know what doesn't vanish? The emotion. The emotion is there acting as its own memory but I remember nothing about his face, his voice, nothing. I only remember how I felt about him. And holy fuck, Louie. I'd rather live through sickness all over again." I rub my chest, massaging the area where my heart beats the strongest.

Louie takes my hand and rubs her thumb back and forth over my knuckles. "Want to know something about him?"

I nod eagerly, feeling like a little kid at bedtime wanting to hear a story.

"You told me once that he helped you shift for the first time. Apparently, you were caught between your hybrid and your wolf form. You couldn't seem to shift all the way. You told me he took you deep into the forest and he roared so loud, that you had no choice but to shift into your wolf. And when you shifted, you two kept practicing again and again. He celebrated you. He put you on top of his shoulders, announced your shift to the pack, and he threw you a party."

"I don't remember that." I shut my eyes to try to bring up the memory.

All I see is black. Nothing is there.

"Focus here." She touches my heart. "It's all here like you said. Emotions don't die, Beloved. They stay with us forever. They are the only thing in this entire universe that can truly live forever. Emotions will never die, and they can carry on. Either like a disease or a cure. It's how you choose to heal that will determine that."

I gather her in my arms and hold her tight, wrapping myself around her so she can't go anywhere. This is what I need to regulate myself.

Louie. In my arms. Her heartbeat against mine. Her breath brushing across my skin.

She's the treatment.

Chapter Fifteen

ELOUISE

We're finally on our way up Dread Mountain. Aziel is carrying Uri and his dad's bones. The bag is tied to the harness along with his mask. Ever since the fight ended, Aziel has been different. Leaving The Graveyard took time. Aziel grieved. He sat in the same spot for hours before he finally stood. He left Scorder without saying goodbye. My werewolf put The Graveyard behind him and is more determined than ever to get home.

Especially to see Anwyll.

Aziel has been quiet and focused. The death of his father is weighing hard on him, accompanied by the knowledge he only has emotions now, and no memories of his dad. I can't imagine how hard that is. It's like crying over an empty space, missing what was there, but nothing ever was.

Aziel stops in his tracks. My gaze falls to his hand on his weapon, his fingers tightening around the handle. He growls surveying the area.

I stop beside him, spinning around to analyze

the area around us. Twigs snap, echoing in the shadows of the living forest.

"What do you sense, Beloved?" I ask, twisting my daggers in my palms. I'm just dying to toss them and hope they land between someone's eyes.

"Yeah, what do you sense? Because I hear nothing."

"Bears don't have great hearing." Aziel twists his stance, staring into another portion of the forest.

"There's no need to be rude about it. It's not like I go around saying you smell like dog, which you don't, but I could. Kindness is free, Aziel," Iggy sasses.

Aziel doesn't reply. He stands there, eyeing Iggy, grunts, and gives his attention back to the night of the woods. "Someone is following us. I don't know who. I could be wrong, but I sense it."

"Always trust your instincts. They are never wrong. I feel it too," I say, scanning the abyss of the forest for movement. "I don't see anything."

"Let's keep going. We can't afford to lose any more time. The blood rain is in a few days along with the full moon. I already feel it, the need, for you."

"I do too," I admit in a low whisper. I haven't brought it up but ever since we left The Graveyard, I've had warmth in my stomach.

"I know." He inhales, growling. "I smell it."

"Well, I don't want to get caught up in that, so let's keep walking so I'm not a third wheel. Again," Iggy begins stomping ahead without a care in the world that he could get caught by something inhumane.

Aziel sneers at Iggy's back, stretches Uri behind his head, and lets Uri fly. The weapon made of bone cuts through the air. I gasp, thinking it is going to hit Iggy when it skims right by his head, thudding into the tree in front of him.

"You took off a piece of my hair! Cutting it a little close with that damn thing, don't you think?" Iggy picks up the small strand of hair from the ground. "It's not like I can glue it back! Damn it, Aziel."

"No, fucking enough with the sass, Iggy. You better be glad it wasn't your head." Aziel marches over to Iggy, yanking Uri from the tree where it is embedded. "Stop complaining. You didn't just kill your father and have no memory of him. You're only alive because of us. We keep you alive. We will be why you get out of here. I won't apologize for wanting my mate when it is my fucking instinct. Stay behind me, keep your fucking mouth shut, and maybe you'll survive if you listen to me and stop acting like a know-it-all brat."

"Aziel Monreaux!" I push between him and Iggy, noticing Iggy's eyes water. "That was unnecessary and rude. Iggy doesn't have a mate so imagine how he must feel having to be around us. Nothing about this is easy, for anyone. And coming down on him for your feelings that you are having a hard time being in control of isn't the way you treat friends."

"It's okay, Elouise. He is right. I'm just scared. I tend to get this way when I don't know what's going on. I'm sorry."

"Don't apologize," Aziel sighs, running his paw hand down his face. "She's right. I'm the one who is sorry. I shouldn't have treated you that way."

"That's better. Now, we have a lot of ground to cover to get to the top of Dread Mountain. Do you know anything about where the avisseus lives up there?"

"No. For all I know, Death lied to me. Maybe the avisseus is a trap. I don't know. All I know is, there shouldn't be a lot getting in our way. Souls tend to ignore this part of Purgatory due to the weather. They don't want to risk being put out of their existence. It's dangerous. No one has ever made it to the top."

"Wait." Iggy stands in front of Aziel and me with his hands in the air. He stressfully runs his fingers through the strands until they stand up. I can see where Uri cut a piece too short as well.

Hopefully, that grows back in quickly.

"No one, that you know of, has ever made it to the top? No stories have been told? No rumors? There's nothing we can go off here?"

"Just our will to live."

"Well, since my will to live is on the fucking floor, that's going to be difficult."

"You really aren't talking about your hair again, Iggy. I'll glue it back if you say it's that piece of fucking hair on the ground."

I look between the two men. Yes, men, as they stare each other down.

"I won't confirm or deny anything." Iggy stands tall-ish. He doesn't break eye contact with Aziel. He keeps his head tilted all the way back just to look at Aziel.

"You are…"

I cough, interrupting Aziel's mouth so he chooses his words better.

"You are something," Aziel mumbles, side-eyeing me while speaking to Iggy.

Iggy grins. "Thanks, I get that a lot."

I lift a finger to Aziel, warning him not to say another word because I know he wants to. I see it all over his face.

"Great." He gives a bitchy smile to Iggy, one that means nothing, with eyes narrowed.

God. I need this journey to be over with.

The dead leaves hanging on the slim branches rustle together as the wind picks up. Somehow, the sky becomes darker. Instead of being able to see like someone would walking alone at night, it's pitch black.

"I can't see anything," I whisper. "Aziel? Iggy?"

"Me either," Aziel sneers.

"Thank God I'm not the only one. I thought Aziel knocked me out with Uri and this was me seeing nothing but an empty void of death."

I snicker when Aziel lets out the biggest sigh ever. He does that a lot with Iggy and always will. Iggy and I will always be a package deal.

"Please tell me that is you holding my hand?" I ask, noticing my breath is a frozen cloud when I speak.

It's freezing.

"It's not me," Iggy says.

"It's not me either," Aziel snarls as a thousand wicked cackles fill the air. "Louie, I need you to step to me slowly. Follow my voice. Let go of the hand holding you."

I try to remain calm. My teeth begin to chatter from how cold the temperature is. My hand almost becomes frozen. I can't seem to move.

"I can't." I tug to try and get my hand free. "I can't move, Aziel. I thought you said creatures didn't come up the mountain?"

Lightning strikes, illuminating the area around us, and for a brief moment, all I see are hundreds of glowing skeletons. It's the one in front of me that scares me the most. Its hand is in mine but nothing else is happening.

"Dread walkers," Iggy informs us, sounding as if he is enthralled by their presence. "I've heard stories about them, but I didn't think they were real."

"You asked me about stories, and you didn't think to bring up the mountain had a fucking army of dead people?"

"They were a myth. I didn't think they existed."

"What can you tell us? Why is this one holding my hand?" The wind roars and the hold on my hand becomes tighter.

When the lightning cracks and breaks through the darkness, the skeleton that is in front of me begins to say something.

Aziel lifts Uri, but another dread walker snags his weapon. I'm only able to see as the lightning flashes.

"What can you tell us about them, Iggy?" I yell over the howl of the wind.

"They are rumored to be kind. They don't kill. I

hear they only reveal themselves to those in need. The dread walkers become your army."

I hiss when my palm begins to burn. "Ah, fuck! It's hurting me." When the light illuminates the dark, I risk staring at the dread walker, its jaw is still moving but no sound is coming out.

"Let her go!" Aziel roars louder than the wind, louder than the lightning crashing all around us.

One of the dread walkers lifts its hand and aims it at Aziel, and a blue ball of electric light slams into Aziel's chest.

"Aziel!" I scream when I see him fly into the darkest part of the forest. "Aziel!" I cry for him before staring at the dread walker who has its hold on me. "You better not have hurt him. I will... find a way to kill you."

Another cackle sings.

My hand continues to burn to the point my knees buckle. I fall to the ground, shouting in pain, the fury of lightning and wind continue around us, faster, quicker, to the point where it becomes impossible to see the dread walkers.

And then everything stops.

The pitch black of the sky lifts, gifting us with good old regular darkness. The lightning ceases to exist. I glance down at my hand to see nothing is holding it.

"They're gone," Iggy states, helping me to my feet.

"Aziel." I hold my hand to my chest, heading in the direction they cast him into it. "Aziel! Aziel, where are you? Aziel!" I keep shouting, my panic rising by the second when he doesn't answer me. "Aziel," I shout his name as loud as I can, my own voice echoing to me.

"He isn't answering. Why isn't he answering? Iggy."

"Don't cry. Remember where we are. Keep it together, okay? Aziel would want you to."

I know Iggy is trying to be reassuring but it isn't helping. He is talking about my Beloved as if he is dead. He isn't. I can feel him in my soul. His heartbeat is strong, he is alive. I only need to find out where he is.

"Aziel! Please," I beg him to make any amount of noise.

Iggy and I stand on soggy dirt. Insects and worms begin to crawl on our shoes.

"Gross. Yuck. Now, I'm going to feel like they are crawling all over me." Iggy kicks them off.

I jump away. "Don't kick them to me!"

"I'm fine!" Aziel finally announces through the dark. "I need you to come to me."

Iggy and I don't move. Purgatory can mock anyone. This place will make you think you're heading straight toward your friend when really, it's a demon wanting to kill you.

"I'm not a fucking demon!" Aziel yells from the stomach of the forest. "I'm stuck in muddy water and something keeps biting me. It's freaking me the fuck out."

"It's him. I can hear the asshole in his tone."

I bark out a laugh, then wince when my hand continues to burn. "Let's go before he gets his tail bit off."

"Maybe that's what he needs," Iggy grumbles.

I slap him with my good hand while we hurry to Aziel.

"What? I can't thank karma?"

"You two are so annoying." I open my injured hand to see how bad the burn is on my palm. Words are branded into my skin.

"Woah." Iggy clutches my hand. "I can't read it though. It's too... blegh." He shivers, dropping my hand as if the burn is contagious. "Gross. I'm sorry." He covers his mouth and nose with his hands, folding them together in a praying position. "I'm sorry. I don't like when flesh is... fleshing." He points to my grotesque palm.

"I get the picture." I continue to try to read it, but I can't seem to figure out the words, so I decide to let it go. "Aziel!" I shout for him again, stepping over a fallen log with devil beetles all over it. They are bright red with black horns, and they even have little red tails. Apparently, their bite makes you feel like you're on fire.

"I'm over here." Aziel's voice is louder which means we are getting close.

We zig-zag our way through the maze of fallen trees.

"I think these trees that are on the ground are from Aziel zipping through the air like a fly." Iggy whistles, gesturing his finger in the air to mimic a fly.

I wince. "That had to hurt."

"About. Fucking. Time."

Iggy and I stop at the edge of a pond of some sort. It has a steep edge that reminds me of a crater and below, sitting off to the side, is Aziel.

He plucks something from his tail and throws it back in the water. "Can you two please come help me? I have these odd skeletal panda-like fish everywhere. They have a strong fucking grip." He plucks another, tossing it in the bright purple pond.

"Are they poisonous?" Iggy asks.

Aziel flicks another fish into the water, staring at Iggy like he's an idiot for asking that question. "I don't know. I hope fucking not. That would suck for me."

"It really would," Iggy agrees, then climbs down the crater. "Since you've been keeping me alive, the least I could do is help."

"Thank you."

I snicker when I hear how annoyed Aziel is.

Instead of climbing down, I jump, keeping my hand against my chest. I'm surprised the burns haven't begun healing yet. I'm worried the dread walkers did something horrible to me. What if this is the start of being one of them?

My boots sink into the mud, the squish reminding me of the soft ground near the cliffs where I first fell in love with Aziel.

"Little fuckers are everywhere," Aziel bitches, plucking another odd skeletal panda fish from his shoulder. "I swear to Fate, when I see those dread walkers again, I'm going to pluck all the bones from their stupid skeletal bodies."

Iggy squats next to Aziel. "If you can get close enough. They seem to have a lot of power. They hurt Elouise too." The bear shifter yanks one of the tiny fish from Aziel's nipple.

"They hurt you?" Aziel growls, rubbing his chest. "Ow, Iggy. You could warn a guy."

Iggy holds up the small aquatic vertebrates. "You're complaining about this little guy? It is the size of my pinky."

"Well—" Aziel scoffs, frowning. "—Maybe you have big pinkies because their bite is uncomfortable. Especially when there are hundreds on your body, Iggy!" My Beloved slowly raises his voice to make his point.

Iggy eyes widen before taking another fish from Aziel's body. "Okay, jeez. No need to get so testy. Are you always like this?"

"No."

"Yes." I roll my lips together to keep from smiling when we answer at the same time. "I mean, just a little, Beloved. You're a little ornery but that's okay. I love it." I kiss his cheek and use the moment to tug a fish from under his chin.

"Do you really think they are venomous?"

I bring the little creature to my nose and inhale, seeing if I can scent anything putrid. "I don't think so. I think they were shocked you crashed into their pond and defended themselves. They are kind of cute. You don't think so?" I put the fish side by side to my face and smile. "See? Not so scary."

"I guess they aren't so bad when they have someone as pretty as you next to them," Aziel charms, hissing when Iggy removes another from the werewolf's toe. "Iggy!"

"Stop being such a damn baby. My God. You carry a weapon made of bone, you were a fighter at The Graveyard, and you can't handle a tiny little fish that you could squish from probably narrowing your eyes at it. Stop it."

Aziel huffs, crossing his arms to pout. "Elouise, back to what Iggy said. Did the dread walkers hurt you?"

"Kind of?" I hold out my palm, showing him the burn marks. "It says something, but I can't figure it out. The skin is too puckered."

Aziel slips his hand under mine, keeping his hold soft and gentle to not hurt me. He brings it closer to his face, his thumb bending mine back to stretch out the words. I hiss.

"I'm sorry, My Light. I'm trying to see what it says." His brows raise. "No wonder you couldn't read it. This isn't a message for you. It's for me. It's written in a dead werewolf language. I learned some growing up, but I didn't get to finish my classes because I got cursed."

"What? What's it say?" I ask, looming over his shoulder to see if I can try reading it again.

"Last one," Iggy warns, tossing the last fish into the pond. "Maybe let's not go swimming again in that pond."

"Yes, Iggy, because I so badly wanted to swim in it the first time," Aziel's sarcasm is thick. He doesn't lose focus on my palm.

"Rawr." Iggy motions his hand in the air like he has claws.

"I think it says, "In a cave—" his finger follows the words "—You will find what you seek. Give the blood of the werewolf at the peak.""

Once the message is read, I gasp when my skin begins to heal, the message disappearing.

"Woah." I flex my fingers and rub my palm to see if I'm pain-free. "It's gone."

"They really didn't want anyone else to see that message. I wonder why they helped us," Aziel says, finally getting to his feet. He brushes the dirt from his fur, flinging a fish we didn't see attached to his tail back into the water.

"Legend has it the dread walkers only appear when someone needs them, which isn't often. They protect the mountain, from what I've been told."

"Protect it from what?" I ask, snagging Uri from the mud to hand back to Aziel.

"From others who want to hurt the avisseus, if I had to make an educated guess," Aziel answers, tilting his head back to inhale. "We're going to want to go that way." He points a finger to the west.

"How do you know?"

Aziel jumps out of the crater pond, stretching his arm down for me to grab. "It doesn't smell like death like most of Purgatory does."

I snake my hand in his and he lifts me up. He knows I don't need the help. I can easily jump to the top myself. Truth bc told, I love having him treat me so well. I love that he wants to help me even if he knows I have the ability to take care of myself.

Aziel wants to take care of me and after so many years of taking care of myself, I'm going to soak up his affection.

"What makes you think Dread Mountain is that way though?" Iggy runs up the side of the edge to join us. "I mean, we are still in Purgatory."

"Yeah, but creatures don't come here, like you said. You don't smell the difference? I'm assuming it's because the mountain is cleaner."

"Makes sense." Iggy places his hands on his hips and looks around. "It's still so eerie on this side of Purgatory. It's so quiet."

"Let's use it to our advantage. The quieter we are, the more we will be able to hear," Aziel states, shaking off his fur. Mud flies in all directions.

I don't say anything because I don't want to worry Aziel. . I pretend to smooth out his holster, double-checking to see if the bag that holds his dad's bones is still there, along with his skull.

Whew.

They are.

"Then, let's go. The more time we waste standing here, the more time we lose before the blood rain."

Aziel is the first one to take a step in the direction we need to go in. I follow him, staying by his side in quick strides since his steps are so large. Iggy is beside me and he is constantly darting his head in all directions to be aware of our surroundings.

I hand him a dagger, clutching the blade with the handle pointed in his direction.

"What's this for?"

"I want you to have a weapon to protect yourself. I don't want anything to happen to you. You need to protect yourself. Just in case Aziel and I can't. We don't know what we will walk into."

"It should be easy to get to the top if no creatures will bother us. That's only if it's true." Aziel slips his fingers into mine, taking my hand as we walk side by side. He lowers his voice, "I still feel like we are being followed. My instincts tell me we are."

"I feel it too," Iggy says, glancing over his shoulder. "But I can't see anyone."

"Me either." Aziel takes a peek to the left. "All we can do is stay on alert. To do that, it's best if from here on out, we don't speak, and if we need to, just tap the person's shoulder. We walk side by side. Always. So we can see one another. No one falls behind. No one walks ahead. Okay? We make it out together."

"Together." I squeeze his hand, wanting him to know I agree.

"Like you could get rid of me." Iggy slips his arm through mine.

"I love you, Louie."

I peer up at Aziel, giving him a soft smile, one filled with warmth. "I love you too."

"I can't wait to finally have a future with you. It's all I've ever wanted. I'll do anything to make sure we have it." Thunder booms in his chest. "Anything."

"Anything," I repeat, wanting him to know I'll sacrifice myself if it means he will get one more second of breath.

As we continue on our journey, nothing suggests we are heading in the right direction. Everything looks the same. From the leaves on the ground to the slim talons of the trees hanging over us, I can't tell if we are going in circles or actually making progress with our journey.

I tilt my head back to look at the sky. The red is brighter against the night, filling with the blood of the ones who have died on the other side.

We really are running out of time. The last thing I want is for us to be stuck here forever, especially if Aziel is waiting to get back to his body. I start daydreaming about life with his pack. I wonder what they are like. Will they like me?

What if they don't? Will Aziel still want me?

I scoff to my inner voice. Of course he will. We've loved each other for far too long to let anyone get in the way of our future.

A future. A real chance at happiness with the werewolf I've needed more than I've needed blood to survive. I smile to myself, imagining myself pregnant with his children. Will there only be one? Two? I know werewolves usually always have more than one child.

What will their names be?

It will feel so good lying in bed with him, wrapped in his safety, knowing we won't have to fight for our existence. We will be able to exist without any strings attached.

Oh my God, we will be able to feel the warmth of the sun on our skin. Maybe we can just lay out in the front yard, have the blades of grass under us, the sun beaming down onto us. We'd be quiet, I think. There would be no need to say anything because everything that needed to be said, was said here in Purgatory.

The birds would sing us a song as we soaked up

the sun. Bees would buzz to the nearby flowers, flowers that smelled like fresh rain, and then when the wind rustles, the branches would just sway to cast cooling shadows onto our overheated bodies.

A butterfly would land on my fingers, reminding me of life instead of death. Oh, and the sky! How could I forget? I hope it's so blue with clouds in the sky that look like various shapes or animals. Aziel and I could try to guess them.

And then, I'd roll over onto him, disrupting his peace, and kiss him. I'd want to kiss him for hours, getting lost in the feel of his tongue, losing myself with every glide our lips take together. We'd kiss without worry and without the haunting realization, that death could happen at any second. We'd kiss without thinking it was goodbye because we would no longer be wandering souls but bodies that had finally met.

We'd undress each other, not wanting to break the kiss, but we'd want body-to-body contact. Under the sun with a bright blue sky, he'd slide into me, fucking me on the grass we were just appreciating. He'd knot me, stretch me, make me gasp, beg, scream his name to the sky, and groan.

I want that life. I want the one in the sun with Aziel. I no longer want to live in the dark where our souls are lost. We don't deserve to be forgotten when we have barely had a chance to live.

The snapping of fingers yanks me from my trance. I blink away the haze, staring at Aziel. His claw slips under my chin, his bright golden eyes swirling.

"Where did you go?" he asks, his hand sliding across my cheek.

I lean into his touch. "Somewhere really beautiful," I whisper.

"I can't wait to hear about it," he says, kissing my lips. "But we are here and it's time to climb, so when we make it to the top, maybe you can tell me about it."

"Maybe or maybe I'll keep my dream to myself."

"Then how am I supposed to make it come true if I don't know about it?"

"Ugh, God. Can you two stop? We are finally at the damn mountain. Focus." Iggy snaps, slipping his arm between us to disrupt our flirting. "You can do it. Whenever we get out of here, you can get lost in each other's eyes and forget the damn year for all I care. Focus. Please."

Our eyes slide to him.

"Thank you. See? Now, I don't know if you have noticed but the welcome sign isn't welcoming." Iggy points to the entrance.

"How is there a trail when no one comes up here?"

Aziel sets Uri on his shoulder. "Maybe that's why we don't hear stories. No one ever lives to tell the tales. Over the years, perhaps they made the trail."

"That's not reassuring at all." Iggy takes a step back.

"It's made of igneous rock," Aziel notices, flatting his palm against the ground. "I think this is a volcano."

Iggy leans forward. "I'm sorry, what?"

"A volcano. It makes sense why I saw so much of it. What if this isn't any volcano? What if it's the entrance to Hell? Wouldn't that make sense?"

"It would because it would be easier for creatures to go from Hell to Purgatory if they want," I say.

I step in front of the welcome sign, keeping the handle of the dagger tight in my hand just in case.

The sign itself is made up of skulls. Dozens of them. If we didn't need to find the avisseus, I'd want to turn around.

"Ready?" Aziel steps onto the worn dirt that makes the trail and holds out his hand for me to take.

"Ready." And I clutch his hand as he tugs me forward.

I look up to try to see the top of Dread Mountain. I can't. The top gets lost in the heavy onyx clouds. Lightning veins between each of them, sparking with heat. It's ominous and wary.

"I still feel like someone is watching us, but I can't tell if it's paranoia now. Maybe it's always been paranoia. If someone meant harm, the dread walkers would have stopped whoever was following us, right?" Aziel waits for an answer from me.

"That makes sense," Iggy says.

I kick a rock while walking, not liking how quiet it is. I'm so used to battle, to war, to blood and screams. Everything about this has been too easy.

"Unless they don't mean harm," I toss in my own thoughts. "I don't know. I still feel them lurking and while they might not mean the mountain harm, that doesn't mean they don't mean us harm."

"Way to be a complete buzzkill, Elouise. You could have let me have some hope."

"Hope? You want hope on Dread Mountain? In Purgatory?"

He narrows his eyes at me. "Well, when you say it like that hope doesn't make a lot of sense."

Lightning hits the tree in front of us, splintering it in half, and the heat, the power of it have us flying back.

"Are you two okay?" Aziel gasps, spitting out dirt he inhaled.

"I'm fine." I lift my arm, showing Iggy and Aziel where I got seared by the lightning. I immediately heal. My skin pulls together, the blood reverts into my veins, and in my next breath, the wound is gone. "Iggy?"

"I think I might have pissed myself but other than that, I'm alive. As alive as I can be in Purgatory." He stands, dusting off his jeans.

Aziel helps me up, only for another crack of lightning to hit close to us again. This time in the middle of the trail. I glance up, noticing the clouds swirling with electric current.

Another round of lightning shoots down, followed by another, and another. The strikes land all around us, the loud cracking causing my ears to ring. The hot bolts keep coming from the swirling clouds up above.

"Guys..." I slap Aziel and Iggy wherever I can reach, then point to the sky. "That can't be normal, right?"

Lightning begins to swirl in a circle, creating a vortex, and the wind shear changes. The rope of lightning is able to form now, twisting down to the ground.

The noise is unlike anything I've ever heard. Constant loud rumbles and snaps whip across the sky as the lightning tornado begins to move.

And it's coming right towards us.

Chapter Sixteen
AZIEL

"Holy shit." I stare at the tornado made of lightning.

The three of us are frozen in place, watching as it barrels towards us. Never in my life have I ever seen anything like this. The bolts constantly build, circling and spinning faster and faster. The more speed it gains, the more bolts of lightning crack out of the funnel.

"We need to go!" Louie yells.

"Go where? There's nowhere to go!" Iggy shouts, trying to raise his voice over the gusts of wind and loud pops of lightning.

The sky veins with electricity. The already dead, burned trees surrounding the mountain catch fire and if we don't start moving, we will be next.

Louie digs her nails into my arm. "This isn't a trail from people. This trail is made from that—" she points to the sardonic twister gaining width and speed. "We need to run. Now. Run!"

We all sprint in the direction where the trail leads.

The path inclines the higher we run up the mountain. A loud violent pop pierces the air, a bright light flashing just as hail begins to fall. We skid to a stop, the hail as large as Elouise's fist. The frozen balls of ice smash against the side of the mountain and break branches off trees.

Iggy screams at the top of his lungs, crumbling to the ground when a piece of hail hits him.

"I can't move. I can't. I– I–" He begins to spasm, his limbs tightening and jerking as if he is being electrocuted.

With no time to waste, I pick him up, throw him over my shoulder, grab Elouise's hand, and motion us to start running again. The screams of the tornado sound like tortured souls. Rain begins to pour, hitting our skin with molten heat. Elouise screams in agony, the rain eating away at her flesh.

I swallow the pain. I can't show any weakness right now. I have to get Elouise and Iggy to safety. I don't care if it means my skin is eaten away and all I have are my bones to carry us to a safe space. I'll do it. I'll crawl if I have to.

I take a risk to look over my shoulder. The tornado is getting closer and a harsh realization hits.

We aren't going to make it. We aren't fast enough.

"I love you," I shout over the wind, the fury of rain, and lightning. "We aren't going to make it. We aren't fast enough."

Louie trips and the wind circulating from the tornado tries to suck her in. She claws at the ground, her nails digging deep into the dirt.

"Louie!" I roar, grabbing her hand as she is lifted into the air.

"Don't let go! Don't let me go!"

"Never. I never will." Rain hits me all over. My skin begins to peel away. Blood drips down my wrist and to the ground. Shouting as I pull her with all my might, Elouise begins to get closer to me.

When she's grounded again, she's filthy with blood and mud.

"I'm taking you two and we're running," she warns, gathering me in her arms as if I'm a bride.

Before I can protest, I have Iggy lying on my front passed out, and Elouise blurs up the trail using her vampiric speed. We finally gain distance between us and the tornado but it's still coming for us.

Lightning strikes right beside us, putting a hole in the side of the mountain, and steam billows from it. Elouise is losing strength and she's slowing down. She cries, pushing herself harder than I've ever seen to get us to safety. I don't think there is anywhere we can go to save us from this beast of a storm.

If we die, it's my fault. It's been my journey to find the avisseus. Elouise and Iggy got dragged into it by me. If Elouise wasn't my mate, her soul would still be safe in Purgatory.

"Just up ahead!" Elouise yells, gesturing with her chin.

I can't see anything. My vision blurs from the acidic rain. Elouise uses her last burst of energy, slinging us inside the cave. I hit the ground first, my shoulder cracking from the force, but I keep Iggy close to my chest in hopes of keeping him safe from more injuries.

My head slams against the side of the cave and stars flash in my eyes. My head throbs. My vision becomes blurry. I groan, lifting my hand to my head only to see blood on my fingers. I force myself to sit up and lean against the wall.

Elouise stumbles in, falls to her hands and knees, and then crawls to me. I hold out my good arm for her, gasping to catch my breath. My entire body has red wounds all over. My muscles tremble from the shock of my injuries. The rain, the hail, it nearly destroyed all of us.

She falls into my lap, whimpering from the pain she is in.

"Come here, My Light. Come on. Crawl onto me, feed. You need it."

She inches her way across my lap. Skin hangs from her arms and face. Blood drips all over me. Elouise collapses onto my chest. I feel her fading in the bond. She's exhausted. She's worn herself out carrying me and Iggy.

My uninjured arm wraps around her to scoot her into the position she needs. "Come on, Louie. Don't give up on me now. You're so fucking brave, so strong. You've made it this far." I grab her by her nape, guiding her to my throat where she has left her mark. "We wouldn't be here without you. Come on. Feed, My Light. Feed from me."

The ghost of her breath puffs against my skin before her tongue dashes out. With a weak whimper, her fangs sink into my jugular, and this time, there's no lust. Our bodies are on the brink of survival and we both know it.

I run my fingers through her braids, careful not to ruin or catch them with my claws. "That's a good girl." I exhale a slow breath, close my eyes, and lean my head against the wall. "Good girl," I keep saying, cupping the back of her head, praising her. "Take what you need, My Light. We're safe because of you."

Her hand presses against my bad shoulder and she slams her fist into it. The force has me yelling at the top of my lungs when the wall pops my shoulder into place.

"That was mean," I groan, the tips of my fingers tingling.

She retracts her fangs and rears back, licking the blood from her lips. "It was better if you weren't expecting it." Her flesh rejuvenates, her wounds healing until she's flawless. "Are you okay?" Louie begins to check every inch of me, my wounds have healed faster than usual, and I'm going to assume it's because of her blood.

"I'm okay. Tired, but okay. We need to check Iggy."

"Oh my God, Iggy." She blurs to where he lies, flipping him onto his stomach, and gasps. "It's one of the pieces of hail. It's embedded in his side, Aziel. It's shocking him."

I get up, shake my blood off my fur, and drag my-self to Iggy's side. "I've never seen anything like this." The inner part of the piece of hail is charged. There's an electric storm sparking and that's what's caus-ing him to be unconscious. "He's being electrocuted. We need to get it out of him. Now." I extend my claws, allowing them to grow longer than usual. "Hold him still."

Elouise presses her hands against either of Iggy's arms and I sit on his legs.

"This is going to hurt." I take one last glance at Iggy. He has drool pooling under his mouth and tears staining his cheeks, yet his eyes are shut. "I'm sorry, friend." I dig my claw above the lightning-filled piece of hail and cut.

Iggy's eyes snap open and the scream he lets out reminds me of the soul-wrenching cries my victims filled the air with when I was killing them. My heart hurts for Iggy and for myself.

"I know, I know, Ig. I promise you'll feel better soon." Louie holds him down harder, blinking away tears.

"No, let them fall! He needs them. The moment I get the ball out, use those tears, okay?"

"Okay," she nods fast with a heavy gulp.

I place one more cut under the ball then use my claws to dig it out. Iggy's screams echo in the small cave and if a heart could cry, mine would pour blood for him.

His skin has deep red and purple lines from where the ball of hail struck him repeatedly with electrical currents. I can't feel anything on my claws but a warm buzz as I lift the ice from his body.

Blood, muscle, and skin stick to it from being melt-ed by the heat it gives off. When it's finally freed from

Iggy, his loud cries turn to soft whines and whimpers of relief. I toss it toward the cave opening to get it away from us when a large skeletal foot lands on top of it.

"You've found me, I see."

Louie and I glance up from Iggy to see a bird-like creature standing in the mouth of the cave as the lightning tornado wipes behind it, creating momentary chaos.

Its voice is soft and feminine. Looking closely, I can see this avisseus is a female. She has wings tucked behind her back, her bones are on the outside of her body, and she has a long silver beak and claws.

The rumors are true.

The avisseus exists.

She picks up the ball of hail and then swallows it. I watch in fascination as it illuminates her from the inside out.

"You've brought me a fertility stone. I thank you for that. No one has been able to make it past the wicked storms to get to me. The lightning hail does horrible damage." She stares at Iggy before kneeling, the storm behind her vanishing as she accepts us. "As you can see." She touches Iggy's shoulder; the wound heals in the next blink of an eye. "Only an avisseus can absorb the hail made of lightning. It's what helps carry the next generation of my kind. It helps fertilize my egg. I cannot thank you enough."

"We are here for selfish reasons, I'm afraid," I begin to say. "I'm happy you got your fertility stone. That was an accident that we had no idea about, but we heard you can get us to the other side. My body is waiting for me. I don't have a lot of time. We don't have a lot of time."

"Mmm yes. Only my claws and beak can cut through time and space to the dimension you need."

"How? They are silver," Elouise states.

"They are made of stardust from the universe that

surrounds us. It is why so many seek me here. I am their only hope. You are the first ones to ever make it so far. You must have sacrificed your blood werewolf. I smelled it while hunting and it brought me home. Werewolf blood is…" She licks her lips. "A favorite treat of mine. If you fill this cup, I will help you."

"I didn't sacrifice—" I turn around where I was sitting, remembering I had hit my head. Blood must have gotten onto the cave walls. "—You live here? This is your home which is why the dread walkers said I had to give my blood."

In a phantomesque motion, she is in front of me, her boney fingers caress my cheek. "You saw the dread walkers? Interesting. Not many can say they have. They only help, they never kill. If they trust you, I do." She puts the cup in my hand. "Werewolf blood helps form my egg. Without it, I will not have my offspring. Please."

Like I have a choice.

I cut my wrist with my claw and hold it over the cup that looks like it is made from an orbital socket. Elouise hisses, inching closer, and disliking another is drinking her mate's blood.

"Easy, vampire. His blood won't bind me to him. The blood will only power the growth of my child. Nothing more."

"He's mine."

"He is, but you are in my home to find a way to your home. These are the rules. If you don't like them, you can go back to fighting for your life. Which you will have to do, I'm afraid," she says to Elouise, grazing my mate's high cheekbones with her knuckles.

"What?" I growl, reaching for the cup of blood. "That was not part of the deal."

The avisseus wraps its wings around itself to protect the blood, gulping it behind the curtain of black feathers.

"She comes with me. They both do," I argue.

"He can go. You can go. She cannot."

"Why?" I stand, grabbing Uri from the ground. "Tell me or you'll be the last of your kind to ever exist."

Her wings fold back, her beak dripping with blood, and she tilts her head to me. Her eyes dart to Louie, confusion warping her unique face. "You know," her tone taking on wonderment. "You know why you cannot leave and you haven't told him. You've been lying."

Elouise shakes her head in denial. "No. No, that's not true. I wouldn't lie to him. I didn't know that was why I couldn't leave. I didn't want him to know the rest."

"Know what?" I sneer.

"Can we keep our voices down?" Iggy grumbles, moaning as he tries to sit up. "My head is killing me."

I ignore Elouise's best friend. "What is she talking about Elouise? We didn't come this far to quit. You're coming home with me."

"She can't go home with you. Only her Beloved can awaken her. She was bitten by a werewolf and put into a coma. You were that werewolf, Aziel. You bit her. When you were cursed and your pack got massacred by the warlock, when you were put under his spell, you ran to Elouise's coven. And you bit her."

The air is stolen from my lungs. Uri falls from my hand. Tears of guilt swim in my eyes and they fall when they meet our mate's. "You knew all this time? You knew and you didn't tell me?"

"I didn't want you to feel like this. That's why. It wasn't your fault. I didn't think anything of it. I didn't know it meant you would have to wake me up. I thought since we could escape together—."

"—I put you in a coma. That was your fear, to begin with. I promised you I would never do that, and I did."

"You weren't you!" she yells through her tears. "You want to know what you did? You found me, you bit me, and I screamed your name looking into your eyes, hoping you'd be able to notice it was me. It was your Louie." She touches my chest. "And do you want to know what happened? You let me go. You stumbled backward in a moment of clarity."

"Impossible. I never had clarity. The spell always won."

"You recognized me in that second. I saw it on your face. And then you ran away from me to protect me. You could have killed me."

"He wouldn't have dared. He was your fated mate. Even his cursed beast could sense that. He remembers every other face from when he was cursed, but he does not remember yours because the trauma from that one bite was too much for him to handle. He buried it deep inside himself."

"I'm so sorry," I croak, pressing my forehead against hers. "I'm so sorry. I didn't mean to. My light–" I fall to my knees and wrap my arms around her thighs. "I'm sorry." I tilt my head back. "I'll find you. I'll bring you home. Where are you? Do you remember where you decided to rest?"

Elouise nods. "Remember the cave we would hide in when it rained?" She gives me a sad smile, drifting her touch across my lips. "I'm there waiting for you. I'm right there."

The avisseus uses her claw, tearing open the fabric of time. It looks like a black hole. What if it doesn't lead home but somewhere else?

"I do not go back on my word. You'll go home but you'll have to find your mate before the blood rain comes in just two days. If not, then not even the power of Fate will be able to rejoin you two."

"I can't leave you. I won't leave you." I drift my hands up her body as I stand. "I'll stay here. We will have a good life. I can't leave you. I won't. I love you, Louie. It's me and you."

"And you'll find me because you and I both know Purgatory isn't the life we deserve." She presses a kiss against my chest, right where my heart beats.

"I'm not leaving without you either." Iggy is finally

able to stand. "I'll stay."

"If you stay, the chances of you being able to leave again are slim to none," the avisseus states.

"You two will go," Louie says, tears staining her cheeks.

"I'm going. You lot are taking too long, and my Beloved knows I'll come for him." Azazel stands at the entrance of the cave, Brenden at his side. He gives Brenden a kiss before leaping into the torn dimension.

"No!" I shout, seething. I fucking knew we were being followed.

"You were so close to thinking we weren't a problem. Jokes on you," Brenden says before giving us a wave, and vanishing down the trail.

I begin to go after him when Elouise snags my arm and Iggy's. "There's no time for that. Find me, Beloved. I'll be waiting."

And she shoves us with every ounce of her paranormal strength, sending us soaring through the air and into the portal that sends us home.

All I see is her face getting further away until she's too far to see at all.

Chapter Seventeen

AZIEL

I wake up with a loud howl that shreds my throat. I taste blood.

"Woah! Woah! Oh my God. Holy fuck, Master Monreaux!" A feminine voice is distant and unrecognizable. She sounds nothing like my mate.

My mate.

"Where is she?" I growl, Uri somehow tight in my hand. I roar again to the werewolf standing in front of me. Spit flies from my mouth. I slam the end of Uri on the ground and begin to pace, not knowing where I am.

I'm in a house. There are windows. The floors are wood. Everything is bright. Too bright. I'm used to the dark.

The werewolf in front of me steps forward, and I snarl in warning.

"It's me, Aziel. It's Anwyll." His eyes become glassy, swimming with tears. "It's your baby brother. You remember me. You're home." His eyes dart all over me. "You're safe. Who are you looking for?"

I gasp for breath when I realize I'm home.

I'm home without my heart. Reality crashes down on me and Uri falls from my hand as I stumble backward. I look all over the room, feeling enclosed. Everything feels like it's closing in. My hand clutches my chest as my heart races.

She shoved me through the portal without her. Me and Iggy but I don't know where Iggy is. I honestly don't care right now.

I have to find her. I have to go to her.

"It's me. Anwyll. You know everyone here. Aziel?"

I rush forward, bringing my brother into a tight hug. "Help me find her. Please. Help me."

Anwyll wraps his arms around me tight and for the first time, I feel like the younger one between us. He's comforting me.

"Whatever you want, Aziel. I'm just glad you've found your way back to your body. I've missed you so much. How is the pain?"

"Unbearable," I whisper, my soul shattered from the agony of not having her by my side.

"Maybe Maven can figure out a spell or potion to help."

"No, my physical pain is gone. I don't have any. I need my mate, Anwyll." I pull away from him, gripping his shoulders instead as I look him in the eye. "I met my mate in Purgatory, and I have to go find her. You never met her, but I fell in love with her when I was seventeen. Her name is Elouise. She's there. Where we grew up. I have to go back. Right now. I only have until the full moon or she's stuck in Purgatory forever," I say everything so fast, I forget to breathe.

"How about you eat, fuel up, and we will get everything for your journey," Alpha Monreaux says from the doorway, leaning against the frame in his expensive suit. "You have a lot to catch us up on."

"I don't have time for fucking gossip. I need marigold powder or I'm going to one of the portals. I need to go now." I take a step forward and Alpha Alexander stands in my way.

"You just woke up from being in Purgatory. You were treated for werewolf sickness. You made painful noises in your coma. While you might feel fine now, your body and soul have been separated for a while. You need to eat. We will leave this afternoon for your mate. You'll find her."

A few more of the people who make the coven/pack crowd the doorway.

"That's enough. Everyone go downstairs. He will see us in a minute." Everyone flees except a strawberry-blonde woman who clings to Anwyll.

My memory is fuzzy but I remember Anwyll telling me about her. "You must be my brother's mate. Ru, I think. It's nice to meet you." Everything I ever said to Anwyll about his mate when I was sick has me ashamed of myself. "I'm so sorry for what I said, Anwyll. I would have never– I'm sorry."

"We aren't mad at you. We don't blame you. We're happy you're safe. You're home."

"It's good to have you back, Big Brother." Anwyll hugs me again. "I've been so fucking worried about you."

I pat his back, burying my face in his shoulder. "Thank you for not listening to me," I whisper, remembering the promise I forced him to make.

"I would have never listened to you. Not without trying to save you first," my baby brother says. "Now, enough of this mushy stuff." He shoves me away, wiping the tears from his eyes, and clears his throat.

He always wore his emotions on his sleeves. I envied him for that. For the majority of my life, I've been angry, just like I am now.

"Let's go get some food and fill us in. You can shift into your human form, by the way. No threats here."

I pick up Uri from the floor, staring at the weapon that helped me survive. "If it's okay, I'll stay in this for-

m. I don't plan on being here long when my mate needs me."

Anwyll nods. "I'll come with you back home. I won't let you go alone."

"No. You have children." I narrow my eyes in thought. "You do, right? I think I remember that."

"Triplets," Ru pipes in.

"You'll stay here with them."

"I'm not a baby, Aziel. I traveled the fucking worlds for your treatment. I can handle going home."

"I won't allow you."

"You don't control my decisions!" he roars at me, shifting into his beast to challenge me.

Something he has never done before.

"I am going with you."

"No. You aren't. Not because I'm worried about you. I know you can handle yourself. This is between me and my mate. I won't let you risk your life when you have your own mate and children waiting for you. I'm not thinking of you. I'm thinking of them. And you should too." I holster Uri, give Anwyll a pat on the shoulder, and walk out of the room.

I wish the moment of finally seeing him was better. I wish there were no obstacles to get in the way of being home with my pack again but there's no time to waste. I'll get Elouise and then I can be happy. Right now, I'm only in a different Purgatory.

A life without Elouise after experiencing what life could be like? That's Hell in itself.

I jump down the steps, landing on the bottom floor with a loud thump. The chandelier crystals above clink together from the vibrations. I follow the scent of Alexander Monreaux, the coven's Master, but he's graciously allowed Anwyll and I to call him Alpha. The coven is now our pack. Since that is what werewolves are used to, he wanted us to feel at home.

He's a thoughtful leader. I'm not sure if I'd be the same, which is why it is best I never become Alpha of my own pack. I'm calm and collected most of the time but my patience wears thin fast.

I step over Whiskey, Pa's familiar and now the pack's family pet. He snores, not even bothering to wake up. When I get to the kitchen I see Alpha along with Greyson, Luca, Alistair, Luna, Maven, Dottie, Drayce, and Severide.

That reminds me of Atreyu. They deserve to know everything that happened in Purgatory.

Raw steak is laid out on a plate. "It's all for you, Aziel. Now, tell us about your mate. Where is she?"

I use Uri as a utensil— oh, how the mighty have fallen— and bite a piece of steak free. My stomach growls as the blood rolls down my tongue. I snarl, ripping the steak to pieces as if I'm feasting on a dead animal.

"Damn," Luca sings. "It ain't going anywhere, dude. You can slow it down. Don't choke." I snarl at him, flashing my fangs. I have no doubt there is meat caught between my teeth.

"He hasn't eaten in this form in ages, Luca. Keep your mouth shut." Greyson smacks the back of Luca's head.

I snag another piece of meat, then another, and another. I feel better now and my irritation eases. I wipe my mouth on my arm and lean against the counter. So many thoughts run through my head, so many moments in Purgatory. I can't figure out what to tell them first.

"My mate. Her name is Elouise Durand."

"Of the Durand Coven? I thought they had all died," Alpha says.

"That would be because of me and Anwyll." A new pain rips through me, one filled with so much guilt. "I bit her. So she's in a coma which is why she wasn't able to come back with me. Her friend Iggy was able to come back too, but I don't know where his bones were."

"You can be dead but if your bones are still in your dimension, you can come out of Purgatory and claim them?" Luca asks, wonderment in his eyes.

"Yes," I nod. "So I'll need sunset magnolia powder to go get her if that's okay. I shouldn't run into any issues. I'd prefer to go alone."

"No, you aren't going alone. Greyson and Luca will go with you."

"I've been fighting for my existence in Purgatory for months," I sneer. "On my own. If I died, Anwyll wouldn't have remembered me. Just like our dad."

"I was wondering why I couldn't remember him. I was telling a story to the triplets and midstory, I forgot," Anwyll explains.

"Because he was there, and he decided to fight me. I don't have time to get into this right now."

"Make time," Alpha orders.

"No!" I slam Uri on the counter and break off a piece. "If it was any of your mates you would feel the same. I'm not getting into everything. I will when I get Elouise back. Atreyu was there. He says he misses everyone, but he has no plan on returning ever."

Everyone shouts as one, Alexander and Severide the loudest.

"I don't know! He doesn't want to come back. That's all I know. He said for me to tell you that he misses you. That's it. Also, Brenden was there, and he met his mate, Azazel."

The room falls quiet.

"Azazel escaped when I did, and he plans on finding Brenden to awaken him. Assume Azazel knows where Brenden is because Elouise told me where she is so that only makes sense. It's time for better defenses here. Azazel and Brenden will come."

"Why didn't you kill Brenden?" Alpha questions through a seethe.

"Because he said you would never walk in sunlight again if I did, so I put the pack ahead of my own wants."

I thud Uri against the ground. "It's wonderful to see everyone but where is the sunset magnolia powder?"

"Here." Luna strolls over to a big wooden box by the door and opens the lid. "This is all Reuel has made. It should last a while. Take as much as you need."

"No one here will get in the way of seeing your mate," Maven enters the room, tossing her red hair up in a high, messy ponytail. "If you want to go alone, fine, but you aren't alone. You don't have to do anything alone again, Aziel. If you insist, let me spell your weapon so you're more protected."

I nod, holding out Uri for her. "This is something I need to do on my own. I found her in Purgatory. I need to find her here. I put her in the coma and it's up to me to get her out."

Maven offers a soft smile as she walks up to me, her stomach round with another pregnancy. She eyes Uri, rubbing her hand down the handle.

The Coven Witch is impressed. "You made this out of a creature you killed in Purgatory."

"I did."

"Impressive. Would you want to be head enforcer here? I think you'd be perfect for it."

"Yes, I would. Thank you, Coven Witch."

"No formalities, Aziel. Just Maven."

"Maven. Thank you."

"Do you know why you could feel your mate in Purgatory? Sense her? Smell her? Even here when you fell sick, you said you smelled her, remember?"

"How do you know all that?"

"As if I'd let one of my own be unwell without getting answers," she rolls her eyes. "I read. I read all the books about Purgatory and it is fascinating. Sometimes time in all the dimensions line up." She holds up her finger. "Sometimes. So when you were here and she was in Purgatory, you two were in the same place at the same time, different dimensions, but that's why you could smell her. That's why you spiraled. She was right there for you, but you wouldn't have been able to reach her."

"And when I was there? Why could I smell her? Purgatory messes with the mind, it was probably nothing."

"Or you were smelling her in the same dimension yet at a different time. What if you smelled her because she was in that exact spot you stood in? It doesn't happen for everyone, but fated mates don't play by the rules. You two were always meant to find each other. Only the time had to be perfect for you to meet. You did. And now, it's time to find her again."

"Why couldn't we go to other dimensions while we were in Purgatory? I heard stories about souls being able to leave."

She nods in understanding. "It's so rare. There has to be a small tear when the dimensions line up perfectly for that split second. It's also dangerous. If you had attempted, the tear could have repaired itself and you could have died. I'm glad you knew better." She winks.

Her hand wraps around the handle and she shuts her eyes. Uri begins to get warm. The bone trembles. A cast of blue engulfs it before it quickly fades.

"Now, you'll be able to use it before an enemy is close. Slam your weapon on the ground, point it, or even if you're cutting someone, it will kill them instantly."

"Wicked," I whisper with awe, staring at Uri in more fascination than I used to. "Thank you."

"It's good to have you back, Aziel. Come back safe so we can get more of your story."

I scoop a giant bag of sunset magnolia powder and tie it to my holster. "If I can survive Purgatory, I can survive this. I'll see you all soon."

"You'll think about where you want to go and the powder will take you there," Maven explains. "That's all you need to do."

The group follows me outside. A few lean against the porch railing and the others stand on the steps. Anwyll has a concerned, sad expression on his face with his arm wrapped around his mate.

"Please come home," he says. "I just got you back."

"I will. I didn't fight for my existence in Purgatory to die now, baby brother. I'll see you soon." I toss a handful of sunset magnolia powder in the air and think of the cliff I fell in love with Elouise on, The Lookout Point. I imagine the cave carved into the side, a place where we would go to escape the rain, or just to be alone to steal touches or even just to nap together.

So much innocence trapped in that cave, and I plan to have it unravel.

Opening my eyes, the portal is in front of me. The woods of what used to be my home beacon me forward. It's all so bright, so green. I'm not used to colors yet when everything has been dark for so long.

Taking one last look at my pack, I step through and transport myself to a place I never thought I'd see again.

Chapter Eighteen

ELOUISE

I yank my daggers out of a skelewolf's throat, its blood pooling onto the ground reminding me of my thirst.

The sky has been drizzling blood, preparing itself to pour, and I'm running out of time.

"Well, don't you look pretty and all alone?"

I scoff, wiping the skelewolf's blood on my pants to clean my daggers. I don't need to turn around to see who it is. I recognize the voice.

"Long time no see, Flynn." I spin around in the field where the avisseus seemed to spit me out.

I'm in Purgatory still. I'm on my own. No Aziel. No Iggy. I've never been more terrified to die until right now. Aziel is coming for me. I only need to survive a little bit longer.

"Looks like you've run out of time. I really don't like that you left the group, Elouise. You took Iggy with you." He rubs his hand over his mouth in frustration. "And that really ruined my plans on getting out of here."

"I knew you were going to use him. He is nowhere near you now. You'll never see him again."

"The entire group has died because you left!" he yells, blurring until he is only a few feet away from me. "You kept us all alive with your fighting skills and now it's just me. I'm going to enjoy taking you and killing you. Rumor has it you met your beloved. He's nowhere to be found. It looks like I have you all to myself."

I'm halfway between dead and fucking feral. I dare him to come at me with nothing but fury because I will slaughter him for so much less than that.

Twirling the dagger in my hands, I laugh, a hint of madness to it. My eyes morph red. "I'd really love to see you try, but I can't wait until I'm on top of you, dagger to your heart while I make you my bitch."

I can't remember the last time I killed a vampire but with how crazed I am right now, I'll kill him by draining his blood. Maybe it's an act of cannibalism, but I call it survival and revenge.

"Come on. What are you waiting for? I can't wait to top you, Flynn. Isn't that what you want?" I taunt, letting my daggers dance over my fingers.

Blurring, he launches himself at me. Luckily, since I'm also a vampire, I can track him. I lunge forward, calculating where he will be next. My dagger gets him right in the side. He stops running and holds a hand to the wound. The smell of his blood is rancid. My stomach revolts at the thought of drinking it, but I need to. I've gone too long without Aziel's blood, especially since we aren't fully mated. I need him more.

And he isn't here. I'm so fucking thirsty that I can hardly think straight. He sweeps out his leg and it slams against my ankles. I hit the ground hard and fast, smashing my head on the ground so hard, I bounce.

I groan but I have no time to think about my injuries. Even the split second of realizing I'm in pain is too long to go without being aware of my surroundings.

"You always were a fucking bitch thinking you were better than everyone else." He holds my arms above my head, straddling my waist.

Flynn grips my wrists so hard, he turns my hands to one another, then pushes them together. The daggers pierce through my palm, the silver burning the wound to keep it from bleeding.

"How does that feel, Elouise? To be stabbed with your own daggers?"

A dark, ironic laugh bubbles up my throat. My eyes turn to slits as I meet his manic gaze. "I guess you missed the part where I'd cut myself with these daggers all the time to up my pain tolerance." I rear my head back, smashing his nose with my forehead.

He falls backward, tilting his head back when blood pours freely. "You fucking bitch."

I giggle, feeling slightly crazed from needing my Beloved's blood. At the same time, I pull my hands free, then yank one dagger out, flinging it at Flynn. It stabs him in the middle of the throat. His eyes widen, gasping for air. His hands fly to the dagger in the middle of his windpipe. He tries to yank it frec but before he can, I pull the other dagger from my hand and launch it between his eyes.

He falls onto his back and when he is pulling one of my blades free, I'm on top of him just like I promised, pushing the dagger back in its place.

"Who is the fucking bitch now?" I sneer, bending down to lick his neck where I'm going to feed. "Feels terrible being so hopeless, doesn't it? Maybe I'm not the issue, Flynn. It isn't my responsibility to keep you or anyone alive. Maybe, you should count on yourself before you count on others. You never know when the person who has been protecting you—" I nibble his ear "— decides to kill you."

Ever so slowly, I tug the dagger from between his eyes. Blood drips down the bridge of his nose, and I fl-

flatten my tongue against his flesh, licking it clean. It tastes terrible. It almost burns my mouth from how rotten his blood is.

I spit it out, doing my best not to gag. "I should have known you would taste like spoiled milk."

"You're—" he gasps as my hand remains on the handle of the dagger pushed into his throat. "—You're insane."

Pressing the edges of the blade against his throat, I shake my head. "No, I'm fucking pissed, and I will bleed everything dry to celebrate my rage." I cut his jugular before sinking my fangs into his neck.

He screams in agony the best he can but his voice is so quiet.

I pull free, gagging when his blood tries to come up my throat, but I refuse to let him see weakness. "Aw, what's wrong, Flynn?" His blood stains my teeth and drips down my chin, splashing against his cheek. "Dagger cut your tongue?" I cackle, dipping my hand in his mouth and slicing his tongue so he can't scream.

"How does it feel to be stripped of your dignity?" I rub my hands across his chest. "I think it feels pretty good." I yank his head to the side, shove my face into his neck, and bite as hard as I can.

Vampires don't feed on other vampires. It's the worst kind of crime to commit against your own kind. If we weren't in Purgatory, I'd likely find myself here if I did this on the other side.

I continue to feed. My eyes burn from keeping his blood down. I've never tasted anything so bad in my entire life, but my hatred for this man runs deep. I didn't realize how far until this very moment. He's a user. He was going to use Iggy for his own gain which has me digging my fangs in further, ripping his vein to shreds.

He gurgles, unable to swallow with the dagger in his throat. His attempts to push me off him slow. His hits become softer. His body loses strength and before

I know it, he is still.

No heartbeat. That will change if I don't kill him. Vampires heal and we can't have that.

Taking my dagger from his throat, I stake his heart, releasing the last breath of air he had from his lungs before his skin fades to ash and all that is left are his bones.

I gag, the blood boiling in my stomach, and I fall onto my hands, spewing the putrid liquid from my system. The blood seeps into the hungry soil, reminding me that even the dirt in Purgatory is a monster.

My veins boil with the betrayal of feeding from another vampire. My hand flies to my stomach, cramping as if my own daggers are twisting in my gut.

I throw up again, painting the ground until I dry heave. I spit the excess blood in my mouth and groan, flopping onto my back.

I'm alone.

"You're running out of time."

I don't need to look at the person talking to realize who it is.

"Not now, Death."

"The downpour is going to happen any moment. The full moon is near and so is your heat."

I sigh, throwing my arm over my eyes. "You don't think I know that? I feel it. I feel crazed and hungry. My body is on fire for Aziel. I'm alone in this place, and I hate hoping he finds me in time."

"I think he will," Death says, taking a seat next to me. "I have faith in that werewolf. He's proven himself over the time he has been here." He places his elbows on his knees. "You're an impressive warrior." He praises the destruction around me.

"Yeah, well," I readjust my position on the ground to get more comfortable. "It isn't like I have a choice. Either kill or be killed."

"What will you do if you're trapped here?"

"I'll kill myself," I whisper the words before I even

truly have a chance to think about it. "If it means I have to live the rest of my days here without Aziel, experience the pain of losing him all over again, knowing I can't be with him, why would I want to live?" I shake my head, glancing up at the reddish black sky as the drizzle of blood mists onto my face as the clouds threaten to unload fifteen year's worth of death onto me. "No, I'm not doing that again. I'm not being teased with his love only for it to be taken away from me. I've done that once and that one time nearly killed me. The moment this blood rain happens and I'm stuck here, I'll be staking myself with my own dagger."

"There's no need to cause yourself pain. If death is what you want, I can give it to you very easily with just a touch," Death offers, lifting his hand and wiggling his fingers. "Honestly, doing that will probably hurt me worse than you."

"Why? Why would it bother you if it did?"

"Taking away a life when it deserved to be lived always hurts me. People think I can simply take souls and move on, that I'm accustomed to taking life away from someone. I am not. Every soul I take hurts me because I feel everything they feel in that split second. I experience their grief of dying. All of their hopes and dreams they left unfinished, I feel. The worst is taking a soul and experiencing a monumental love they felt for another because oftentimes, I also feel the mourning of their loved one too. I get a double dose. I feel everything in someone's death because I am Death. I have yet to feel a greater pain than someone's heart clenching from the agony of knowing any second or minute, the love of their life will not be there. I get to experience the soul I took grieve a life they never got to complete."

"That's terrible. I'm so sorry. I had no idea you felt all those things. That has to be so difficult."

He stares into the forest, nodding in agreement. "I also see the rest of the life they missed. I give them the option if they want to see it or not."

"You see what hasn't happened yet in someone's life?"

"Only when they die. It's why I'm such an emotional guy. You'd think it would get easier over all the millennia, but it doesn't. Every day gets harder and just when I think, 'Wow, no one can love a person as much as that guy loved their spouse.' I'm always proved wrong. Someone always loves someone more and more and it consumes for that split second when I reap their soul."

"It sounds like you're the only being in the universe that could handle such responsibility."

"I am," he frowns, a sadness overtaking his voice. "There will never be anyone else but me."

I take his hand and smile at him. "Well, if you ever need to vent, just know I'm here. I'm your friend. I might not be able to experience what you do, but I'm a great listener."

"A friend? Death doesn't typically have friends."

"It's only because they are afraid of you. I'm not. I've faced you too many times and have won." I wink, hoping to bring up his mood.

The blood rain begins to fall harder, bringing a slight sting to my skin with every drop.

He glances up to the sky and smiles before spreading his wings. "And it looks like you have beat me yet again. I'll be seeing you on the other side, Elouise. I hope you know, I feel the love you and Aziel have for one another. In all my time, I have never felt anyone love one another more. I hope to never have to experience your love in death because I think it would kill me."

I sit up in the field, wanting to ask him what he means when Purgatory begins to fade and drip as if it is melting like a freshly lit candle.

I close my eyes and surrender to the unknown.

Chapter Nineteen

AZIEL

I'm standing on the cliffs where I fell in love with a woman who I had no idea was destined to be my fated mate.

What's wild to me is how everything looks the same after so many years. The trees are the same, the view is the same, but nothing is the same, is it? I stare at the part of the woods I'd have to enter to go to where I grew up. It's probably only run-down homes, old firepits, and collapsed roofs now. The part of the forest we made ours would be overgrown with trees.

There's a part of me that wants to go and explore, but I don't need to see the destruction Brenden made us cause. There's no point in turning back when the past is lost.

Yet there is one part of my past that will always be stitched into my future.

Elouise.

I jump from the cliff, using my claws to dig into the stone as I slide down. I glance out to the night sky while I descend to the cave that I hope no one knows about. Guilt stabs my heart, engulfing it in pain at the knowledge that I am the reason she has been in her coma.

Never did I intend to bite Elouise. I made a promise that I would be in control of my beast, that I would never hurt her, but I did. I'll never forgive myself and I'm not sure how she was so forgiving. All I know is I'm going to spend the rest of eternity making her promises that I will always keep.

I growl when I think I hear someone coming from the left, but it's just a bird creating a nest for its future eggs. Other than animals, this place that once used to be my home is deserted. I hear no heartbeats, no footsteps, no howls, or laughter echoing in the night like I used to.

The place I was born to rule is dead in its own way. The only part of it that I plan to revive is my mate. Then, we are getting out of here and never fucking looking back at the place that wouldn't allow a vampire and a werewolf to be together. I can't wait to go home to my pack. I've never been so accepted so easily before and that's the only life I want to live.

Every choice made has either love or hate waiting at the end of it. I'm lucky to have love even with all the heinous crimes I have committed. Even with the killer I have proved to be, even with the promises I have broken in the past, Elouise doesn't care.

She will always be the first choice I make from here on out.

The more I glide down the cliff, my nails create that horrible grind, but the nearly full moon shines its light on me, powering me with what is to come. Lust begins to brew. The need for Elouise somehow becomes stronger. My humanity clutches onto my heart tight, but I feel the venom of the moon wanting to numb it.

I'm able to resist the urge to give in but tomorrow, there will be no fighting what will happen. I'll finally get to knot and claim Elouise. I'll be able to make her mine, something I should have been able to do years ago if the chance hadn't been taken from me.

And I'm going to make fucking sure it is never taken from me again.

I grip the edge of a protruding rock, the stone warm and rough under my hands. Testing my grip to make sure I won't fall, I lift myself up and down, swing side to side, and I'm satisfied the cliff can hold my weight. Reaching behind me, I whip out Uri, needing more leverage to swing down and into the cave.

"Please work," I grunt, swinging Uri with all my strength, and smashing him below me.

He cuts easily through the rock, and while still keeping a grip on the cliff, I find the handle of Uri. I test the weight with my feet, making sure it can support me. I jump down, squatting onto the handle and gripping it with my palms.

Sweat trickles down my forehead, and I sway when I see what is below me.

Fucking nothing but an abyss of thousands of feet that will lead to my death.

"Don't look down," I mumble to myself, knowing that's impossible given the situation.

The cave is below me. All I have to do is use Uri to swing and I can jump into the cave. It has my memory jogging, wondering how the hell Elouise and I got into the cave so easily on rainy days.

I remember us going another way but as I look around, I don't see a trail of any kind.

Securing my grip on Uri, I have to swing myself down while removing Uri from the cliff with my upper body.

"Should be fine," I say to myself, hoping it brings a little confidence.

I swing once, twice, then lift Uri from its place, backflip, and completely miss the mouth of the cave.

"Fuck!" I roar, slamming Uri down on the edge. I dangle from the cliff, pissed off and out of patience.

I use Uri as rope, climbing up the handle until my

hands hit the mouth of the cave. Extending my claws to get better traction, I inch my way forward, using my hind legs to climb the cliff. I fall flat on the cave's floor, gasping for breath, my muscles trembling.

And then I smell her.

I lift from the ground, standing in the dark void. I follow her scent, hope and panic blooming in my chest.

"Where are you? Where could you be in here?" I can see better at night than I can during the day. From one side of the cave to the other, there's only a dirt floor surrounded by rock.

My growl echoes back to me in the small space. Every second that passes that I don't have her, I become more annoyed. I inhale, sniffing the air in constant beats.

The cave parts in two directions and I hang left. I shift into my human form when the tunnel becomes too narrow for my beast. I had no idea there were tunnels in this cave. We only ever hung out at the mouth of it to watch the rain fall.

Water drips somewhere in the distance. The cave walls are damp and slick against my palm. The air has a bite of cold to it. Small whooshes of wings flap around me.

When I get to the end of the tunnel, it opens to a small round space. The ceilings are high and a small amount of light peeks in through a crack in the cliff's foundation.

The walls are slick with water causing the dark brown color to appear black. Her scent is heavy here. This is where she is at. Following the rounded walls, I continue to trace her scent.

My cock begins to harden, my want and need telling me she's right here. Why can't I see her if I can feel her? Where the fuck is she? I smash my fist against the wall, cracking it more. More sun falls through the crack, and I shuffle my weight when something groans under my feet.

Looking down, I test my weight again, swaying back and forth when wood groans.

Falling to my knees, I brush years of dirt off the trapped door. My eyes water and tears fall with every cup of dirt I push out of the way. I'm frantic, my arms moving faster than they ever have.

A silver handle mocks me but I grab it, uncaring if I burn, and rip the door from the hinges. I jump down and it's cooler instantly, goosebumps arising on my skin.

I sweep the floor with my gaze, searching for any sign of her body.

When there, in the far corner, lying on her back, is Elouise.

"Louie! Louie, I'm here. I'm here. I'm right fucking here, My Light. Can you hear me?" I slide across the ground, skinning my knees, and scoop her into my arms. I brush her hair back, marveling at her beauty.

Her dress is worn and tattered from years of being down here. It's nearly falling off her body. I brush my fingers down her arm, her skin warm against mine, and a sob escapes.

"I finally have you." I extend my claws, using one to cut my jugular open. "Come on, Louie. Drink." I press her lips against my throat, waiting for her to awaken and take all she needs. "Come on, come on," I beg, falling into a seated position while holding her in my arms. "I'm sorry. I'm so sorry you're here because of me. I need you to wake up. I need you to wake up so we can live the life we have dreamed."

I focus on her heartbeat, needing to hear its slow comatose beat.

It's there and I release a breath, waiting for her to have enough of my blood in her system to feast.

Finally, the smallest, quietest whimper slips from her and happiness explodes in my chest. I clutch her to me, squeezing my eyes shut as emotion boils over. After everything, we can finally be together.

Her teeth slice into me and she moans with every drag she takes that I willingly give.

"That's a good girl." With a gentle hold, I cup the back of her head to keep her as close as possible. "You're doing so good. Take all you need, My Light. I'm right here and I'm never going anywhere. I have you." I lean my cheek against her head, relaxing as she feeds for the first time in fifteen years. "I'm so fucking proud of you for bringing yourself someplace safe. I'm so sorry, Louie. I'm so sorry," I repeat, needing her to know how much I regret what I did.

She leans away, her lips and chin soaked in red. Her teeth are coated with my blood. Her eyes are glowing garnet.

"Aziel?" she croaks.

I cup her face, smiling from ear to ear. "I'm here, My Light. I'm here." I watch as her soul rights itself in place. Who she was and what she looked like in Purgatory begins to shine through. Her braids appear, then her daggers.

"Aziel." Her own tears wet her cheeks. "You found me."

"I'll always find you. You hear me? No matter where you are, I will always come to you." I trace her lower lip with my thumb. "Run away with me," I say for the first time since we were seventeen. "Run away with me and never look back."

"I'll go wherever you want to go as long as I'm with you."

Resting my forehead against her, the smell of my blood heavy on her breath, I breathe it in, knowing it means she's alive. She's in my arms and there is no one stopping us from being together.

"We finally get to run away." A laugh breaks free and it's contagious. I can't help but chuckle too. "Where are we going to go?"

I dig into the pouch, grab a handful of sunset magnolia powder, toss it into the air, and say, "We're going home. A place where I can give you the world."

"You are my world."

"Then a place where I can give you so much more than I have ever been able to give." I swing her into my arms so she doesn't have to walk. "I planned my entire life the first time I saw you, remember? That plan is still in motion. It might have changed direction, but it never stopped."

"Let's be together," she says, reminding me of what she said when we were seventeen.

I step through the portal, marking the journey of us finally starting our lives together.

Epilogue

AZIEL/ELOUISE

Full moon night
Aziel

    I can barely catch my breath with how much lust is controlling me right now. Anwyll has the same silver chains binding my wrists that were on me when I was sick.

    "You don't have a lot of time," he informs, checking the moon in the sky. He rolls his head over his shoulders snarling. "And neither do I. It's a good thing we will be on opposite ends of the property. Hundreds of acres. We shouldn't cross paths. Everyone is safe and locked away in the house as promised. Except for our mates. They are in the woods. Everyone has been told to leave us alone."

    Like I'd fucking care if anyone got in my way. I'd just kill them to get to Louie. It's what I've always done and I'll continue to do it.

    With every breath, a low menacing growl escapes. "I know what you're feeling. It does get easier as time goes on with every full moon but every time, I feel like I'm about to burst out of my skin."

I launch myself at Anwyll, the chains stopping me from attacking him. My brother doesn't flinch.

"I'll let that slide because I know what you're going through but come at me again with that, and we will fight."

I roar at him as loud as I can which only causes him to retaliate.

"I just want to et you two know, I find this fascinating and will be watching for as long as I can!" Luca shouts from the cracked window upstairs.

Anwyll and I look up, both of us changing into our beasts as the moonlight hits our skin. We sneer and howl at Luca, warning him that if he comes out of that house, he is dead.

He pops a piece of popcorn in his mouth. "Don't worry. I'll be right here where you can't reach me. The house has been werewolf-proofed."

Someone comes up from behind him, Greyson I think, and slaps him on the back of the head. The curtains get shut, finally giving us our privacy.

Anwyll gives me one last look before dashing away on all fours, sprinting south. I only have a few minutes left of clarity before I'm lost to the moon. Anwyll isn't chained because he has gone through a few full moons. He is more in contro, but this is my first time hunting my mate, and God, I fucking want her.

I fall to my hands and knees, the rut hitting me full force, and I whip my head up, zeroing in on the woods to the north. My cock is already hard and hanging between my legs. Precome drips under me, creating a pool of want.

It's too bad my mate isn't here. I'd shove her face in the dirt and force her to drink it. The power as the moonlight falls on me fuels my beast and my humanity vanishes as the moon orders me to hunt what's mine.

Standing on my hind legs, I spread my arms to open my chest, and throw my head back, releasing a crazed

howl so Louie can hear how her time running is about
to come to an end.

The windows to the house shake, the leaves on the
tree fall around me, and the silver burns into my skin
to keep me in place.

Nothing could keep me in place. Louie is mine. I
deserved to hunt her years ago and I swear, I won't
stop knotting her until I know for a fact I can smell my
child in her womb.

Saliva drips from the thought. My cock jerks from
the memory of experiencing her tight cunt pulsing
around me. I leap forward, desire strengthening me so
much that I break the silver chains that no longer have
a home on my body.

I howl again, following her scent. It's so much
stronger now that she's in heat. Her body aches for the
chase just as much as I need the hunt.

I dash through the pumpkin patch, ripping a
pumpkin from the vine with my mouth. I smash it with
one clamp of my jaws before spitting it out. Every
time my front right paw lands on the ground, I crush a
pumpkin under me.

Breaking through the trees, I gain more ground
as I speed up. I use a tree trunk to leap from, using
my momentum to bound from tree to tree until one
breaks. I follow it down to the ground, the rumble of
the earth vibrating from the fall.

Her scent is heavier.

I bury my nose into the ground, my tongue flicking out to gather her slick from the ground. I moan,
reaching down to stroke my cock.

"I can't wait to bury my face in your cunt and swallow your slick to sate my thirst," I shout, knowing she's
close and can hear me. "You better hope you're ready
for my knot. You're going to be ruined, Louie. You hear
me? I know you do. I'm going to hold you down, break
those fucking bones so you can't move, and I'm going
to take—" I break a branch from the tree "—And take." I

snap another. "—And take. Until you're begging me to stop. You'll cry. And all I'm going to do is lick your tears away while I split you open with my knot."

I come to another tree with her slick wiped on it, laughing at her attempt to confuse me.

"Your games won't work on me. You can't trick me. This isn't Purgatory anymore, My Light." I scan the forest, the trees full and thick creating canopies Louie can hide in.

Closing my eyes, I inhale again, her heat seeping into my system and heading straight for my cock. If I don't fuck her soon, I will go mad again.

I'm crazed for Louie. I always have been, and I always will be.

"You always have me on the brink of absolute insanity," I shout at her, wherever she is. "Mmm," I moan, fisting my cock. "You're my madness. You're my fucking craze."

A strong wave of her heat hits my nose. "Oh, you like this?" I change my stance, using both hands to fuck my cock. "You wish it was you, don't you? It will be. Don't worry. I'll catch you and give us what we both want." Just as I'm about to come, I stop, wanting every fucking drop for my mate.

Why would I waste my come when her womb needs to be filled by it?

I hear a twig snap in the distance. Snapping my head to the right, I sniff the air, grinning the best I can in this form before falling to all fours, and sprinting to her.

I'm carried to her aroma, the sweet scent of her heat and fertility has me almost panting by the time I come to a stop. We're so far in the forest, I hope we never find our way out.

I'll take her so hard, fucking her so relentlessly into the ground, that we will surpass the dirt that makes earth and we will find ourselves back in Purgatory.

I sniff the tree, following the line of slick to another

spot, this time a random plant. Sneering, I rip the green leafy plant from the roots and toss it, roaring in anger.

I'm losing my patience.

She's surrounded this area with her slick and now I can't tell which direction she is in. Rage sets in. My eyes turn red, proving just how far gone I am.

A branch up above shakes and before I can check to see what's going on, Louie has her legs wrapped around my neck. I bellow, clawing at her legs to get her off me, but my mate is a vampire, and she's using her strength against me.

Pain bursts through my sides, and when I look down, a dagger is sticking out of my side on the left and right.

"You thought I was going to make it easy? You thought you were going to hunt me?" She laughs in my ear. "I'm hunting you."

Louie leaps from my shoulders. Mid-air, I grab her ankle and slam her to the ground. I grunt when I yank the daggers from my side and toss them where she can't reach.

She grins as she backs away. Her shorts are soaked with her heat. Sweat glistens on her skin. Her nipples are tight under her white cropped shirt. I can see the hard beads beneath the thin material taunting me.

Louie turns over and tries to use the ground as leverage to launch herself into a sprint, but I catch her again. Snarling, I claw her clothes off, sneering and salivating as more of her skin becomes visible.

She's almost naked. Her shirt is in pieces, hang-ing off her shoulders in shreds. Her shorts are gone, nothing but wasted cloth on the forest floor. Her cunt shines with how much she is aching for me. Her thighs are wet, and I know once I drive my long, thick cock inside her, she will be so welcoming.

"You think you could hunt me?" I lift her off the ground by grabbing her plump cheeks. "You could never," I snarl, licking my tongue up the lips of her pretty little cunt. "Mmm." I gather her slick, drinking it down as if it is water and I'm a werewolf dying of thirst. "You're all mine, Louie." I drive my tongue into her entrance, igniting a passionate cry.

While I feast, she tugs and twists her nipples. Her eyes are shut, completely lost in pleasure. My claw flicks her clit and with that much ease, my mate is orgasming, squirting more slick down my throat.

I growl, wanting more.

She gasps, her chest glistening with beaded sweat, and then she shoves my chest with her foot causing me to fly backwards until I hit a tree. My mate blurs away, and I'm left with nothing but the taste of her on my tongue.

Elouise

I knew challenging him during the hunt would be bad but I couldn't help myself. I can't make this easy for him. So when I had the idea to stab him with my daggers, I couldn't resist.

Now I have to reap the consequences of my actions because there is a livid werewolf behind me. I have two voices in my head. One is telling me to run as far as I can. The other is telling me to stop and present myself to him, have him fuck me like I know I want him to.

I pass one of my daggers and pick it up, losing half a second, and Aziel becomes closer. I swear, he runs faster when he is in a rut. I dare to look over my shoulder. I can see the spit dripping from his mouth, the ferality in his eyes, and I can scent the blood from his wounds.

He's running as if the daggers didn't even nick him.

Aziel growls, his claws sweeping at my feet. I jump,

yelping, picking up the pace when I feel the heat of his breath on my back.

I'm not quick enough and I'm not sure any paranormal could beat a werewolf on a hunt for his mate.

He pounces, locking his jaw around my shoulder while pinning me to the ground. Those sharp teeth sink into me while his claws grind across my back from shoulder to hip, marking me like the wild beast he is.

Aziel explained to me that naturally, they slip into their hybrid form when they finally catch their mates, but I told him I didn't want that.

I wanted him in the form that protected me in Purgatory.

Snarling, he keeps the lock on my shoulder while he pries my legs apart. Without giving me a warning, he presses against my entrance and drives in.

"Aziel! Fuck. Oh God, you're too big in this form. I can't take it."

He ignores me, sneering, blood dripping from where he has his jaw clamped on me. My beast slides out, leaving nothing but the wide tip inside me before slamming into me.

He fucks me without mercy, without a care in the world other than needing to claim me.

"You're mine." He licks the wound on my shoulder, cleaning the blood off. "You're all mine."

"I thought I could take it. I can't. It's too much. I'm going to die, Aziel. You're splitting me in two." I claw at the ground to try and get away from him, something he warned me about was that it didn't matter what I had to say, he wouldn't be able to stop.

I don't want him to but I do at the same time. I'm wound so tight. I feel like I'm about to explode from my skin if he keeps going.

"Good. More of you to fuck." He slaps my ass, pulls out of me, and flips me onto my back, then in one smooth thrust, he's inside me again.

He's so large, so thick, my stomach bulges from his

intrusion. My Beloved spreads my legs, watching his massive shaft somehow glide in and out of me.

"This cunt belongs to me. Doesn't it? You'll be all stretched and ready for my cock whenever I want to claim your pussy." His giant werewolf hand wraps around my throat. His lethal nails dig into me, breaking the skin, and more blood drips out of me.

I moan from the pleasure of being used, being filled too much. I feel the stretch of my pussy, the hint of pain that warns me I might tear.

I'll heal.

"Nothing but a whore for my cock. You've always wanted me in this form and now you get to have me. You can't run away this time. You're my prey." He plants his hind legs firmer against the ground, his free hand raking down my side to grip my hip as he gets closer to my womb.

A tear leaks from my left eye from the intensity. Aziel is there, licking it clean before it has a chance to dry on my cheek.

"Like I said before," he thunders, tightening the grip on my throat. "Your tears are mine." He slams inside me. "Your cunt is mine." He thrusts. "Your body. Your fucking soul. Goddamn it, Louie!" He fucks me so hard, I slide against the ground and off his cock.

He drops to all fours, tilting his head as if he is waiting for me to run. I don't think I can. My thighs tremble. My clit is throbbing, and I cry out as an unexpected orgasm quakes my body from head to toe.

I can't breathe. There's no use. I can't go anywhere. I'm trapped with a beast who is three times my size. His cock dribbles with come onto the forest floor and with every step he takes to get closer to me, the more my insides turn to molten lava.

Wrapping his hand around my throat, he slams me against a nearby tree, keeping me high off the ground. His other hand works its way up my inner thigh, his fingers grazing my pussy before slipping inside, claw and all.

I moan, looking down to see blood trickling down his palm. My gaze locks onto where my name is scarred onto his chest. Knowing my brand is on him, my stamp of ownership, my own claim has another orgasm building in my system.

"You're going to come, again? Like this? Being thrown against a tree and claw fucked? You're my dirty, pain-addicted slut. Tell me."

I shake my head. I don't think I could manage to say a word right now.

"Tell me you're my dirty, pain-addicted slut. Tell me you're a werewolf whore. Tell me…" He drives his finger in deeper, his claw tearing my insides, and I love it. I gasp, doing my best to rock against his hand. Blood is a river flowing down his forearm. "Tell me what I fucking want, and I'll let you come before I throw you on this floor, break your fucking back until you can't feel your legs, and knot you until I split you open."

I moan at the thought of him tearing me to pieces and the orgasm is waiting on the edge, just waiting for My Beloved to show me mercy.

"Please," I beg him. "Please."

"I don't give a fuck about your pleas."

I know he means it. I see it in his eyes. He always had the kind of eyes that I could see right through into his soul. Right now, there's nothing there but the overwhelming urge to stamp his claim all over me.

"I'm your werewolf whore." His nostrils flare and the pace increases as he finger fucks me. "I'm your dirty, pain-addicted slut."

The classic, deep, dark, eerie growl a werewolf creates leaves him and the power of the alpha he keeps on a tight leash has shivers blasting across my body. I tremble as if it is below zero.

"Oh—" he exhales, his shoulders relaxing. "I do love it when you tell me what I want to hear, My Light." His thumb presses against my clit and that's enough to send me tumbling over the edge, pulsating on his finger and claw, wishing it was his cock I was gripping instead.

Keeping me pinned to the tree by my throat, he pulls his finger out, brings it to his mouth, sucking the blood and come off it.

"You taste so good. Here." He rubs his finger through my pussy, gathering more blood. He rubs over my clit to drive me mad and traces my lips with my own blood. "Try. See why I can't ever get enough." He shoves his finger between my lips, and I tilt my head, scraping my fangs across the digit.

My body heals from the claw-fuck he just gave me. When no more blood drips from me, he tosses me to the right. I smash against the ground and roll a few feet before coming to a stop.

He marches over to me, sits me up, and positions me like I'm his doll. Grabbing my head, he tries to slip his werewolf cock into my mouth, but he won't fit. I slap his thigh, warning him, but he ignores it.

"We'll make it fit." He grabs my jaw with both hands and with a solid yank, he snaps it out of place.

I scream as loud as I can but moan when his cock slips down my throat.

"That's a good girl," he moans, slipping his cock across my tongue. "Taste yourself on me? Get it while you can."

I do taste myself. I lap the best I can with a broken jaw, the pain easy to manage since my body has been healing every second.

"I'm going to knot your throat one day." He rubs his finger across my neck. "You're going to love it too."

I agree, spit dripping from my bottom lip.

He slips out of me and my jaw immediately clicks into place, healing as if it never happened.

"Run," he orders.

Without a second thought, I do as he says and try to get away from him as fast as I can. I'm weak. I'm exhausted. I need his blood. I'm not moving as fast as usual.

Howling behind me, he attacks, shoving me to the ground again. I'm on my back and he is between my legs, slipping his cock inside again. He's all snarls and growls with every stroke, truly unrelenting, and shows no sign of stopping. His claw digs into my chest. I cry out in pleasure when he carves the A in his name.

"All marked for me," he murmurs to himself. "Everyone will see. Everyone will know you're mine."

I'm scarred across my back, on my chest, and his bite is on my shoulder. There's no mistaking I'm mated to a werewolf.

He curls over me, ramming his cock as far as it can go. "I'm going to knot you. I'm going to spread you so wide, you're going to wish for Death to come save you."

I groan, digging my nails into his back and raking them down. "Why would I wish for him when I have you?" I suck his nipple into my mouth, biting down before letting it go with a pop.

His knot begins to swell, the base of him already struggling to fit inside me.

"Won't. Fit." I have to break up my words in order to breathe. I've never felt anything like this before.

He covers my mouth with his hand, rutting me with small thrusts to push his knot inside. "I'm going to make it fit."

When I glance down, all I see is the monumental size of his knot. I squeeze my eyes shut, tears flowing free and warm out of the corners of my eyes.

His knot pops inside me, locking him in place, and my stomach is bulged. I almost look pregnant. Aziel moans, his cock jerking inside me, and the warm, tingling splash of his come has my muscles relax.

I sigh with relief, the bond snapping into place. Our souls expand from our bodies, wrap around each other, and sink back into us. Aziel snarls, clamping his teeth around my shoulder again as he spills into my womb.

Another orgasm has my throat raw as I scream his name, "Aziel!" My muscles spasm up and down his cock, milking more of his orgasm to be bred.

He licks the wound on my shoulder, giving it care when I least expect it, and lifts me up. My Beloved leans against a tree while I am on top of him. I start to slide up and down until his knot tugs at my entrance.

"I knew I'd fit," he marvels, staring at where we are connected. "You're all mine."

"I always have been." I hold my breasts, playing with my nipples as I slightly bounce on him. "Oh my God, I'm going to come again."

His chin dips to his chest as his eyes hood with hunger. "You're going to come a hundred more times with how my knot is positioned inside you. I love it. Soak up my come. I want you pregnant with my child by the time the moon sets."

I toss my head back, shouting my own howl as a wave of pleasure has stars shooting across my eyes. Reaching behind me and between his legs, I fondle his sack, rolling the soft flesh in my palms.

He groans, another large spurt of come claiming my womb. "You're mine," he growls, ramming into me harder. "You're fucking mine!"

Something shifts inside us causing us to lock eyes. A spark ignites, warming me from the inside out before disappearing. The red haze to Aziel's eyes fade, the beautiful golden hues returning to me.

He inhales, grinning from ear to ear when his hand lands on my stomach. "Already." His bottom lip trembles as he looks up from my belly to me.

The feral side of him is gone. As quick as the wind comes and goes, the moon has given My Beloved back to me early.

My hand lands on his. "How long will we be like this?"

"I don't know. I'm still my beast. It could be hours."

"Even though I'm already pregnant?"

"Even though." He wraps his arms around me, scratching my freshly healed back with his claws. It's hard to believe these were the same claws that made me bleed. "We finally have everything I have always wanted for us."

"It's a good thing we finally ran away," I say, pressing my cheek against his strong chest.

"I'll always run away with you, Louie. I don't care where. Where you go is where I want to be."

"Then, I never want to leave this very place." I poke his chest, slipping my hands up his neck. "If we do, I'll be too afraid to lose you again."

"We aren't lost souls looking for each other anymore, My Light. We're home now."

He is my home.

Epilogue Two

ELOUISE

Getting to know the new coven, or pack as Aziel likes to call them, has been amazing. It's been nice to be considered family when they hardly know me. They feel more like family to me than my own coven did.

And while werewolves slaughtered them, I find myself not caring in the slightest. If my dad were still alive, I wouldn't have forgiven him for everything he did to Aziel.

I have My Beloved now but sometimes I fall into the mindset of how many years we lost due to that day. If we had run away together, he would have never been cursed, and he wouldn't have been groomed to be the perfect killer.

The door opens and slams shut, a blur with long dark hair heading out to the field. Master Monreaux sighs as he enters the kitchen. I'm sitting on a barstool next to the kitchen island enjoying a cup of blood tea.

A few drops of Aziel's yummy blood mixed in with

my chamomile tea is the best. Nothing helps me get to sleep faster.

"Is everything okay?" I ask him, hoping I'm not stepping on any toes.

"Yeah. Minnie is a new vampire. She's recently changed and it hasn't been easy, especially with my father Severide here being the grump he is right now."

"Severide?"

He waves me away. "Long story. How are you adjusting?"

I lift a shoulder and take a sip of tea. "I'm great. It's odd not being in Purgatory and fighting every single second. It takes some adjusting," I chuckle. "But I'm really good. Thank you for opening your home to me. I know that can't be easy allowing another person in when your coven has grown so much."

He opens the cabinet, grabs a mug, and puts on the kettle to heat water for his own tea. "I don't mind. I love that fated mates are coming to us, and I love being a safe place for other paranormals when they feel like they have nowhere else to go. I know I sometimes forget about Irving, our lake monster, but Maven made some upgrades to his lake, and he is having a blast. We probably won't see him until winter."

"I don't think I've met him yet."

"You will in time," he says. "But that's not all that's on your mind. What else is there, Elouise? You aren't at ease."

"Isn't it wild how he always knows that?" Aziel wraps his human arms around me, and I turn to him immediately, wanting to see how handsome he is in this form.

I push the silver piece of hair framing his face behind his ear before tracing his jaw.

I never knew I could love someone so much the way I love him. He consumes me.

"Out with it," Master Monreaux says, pouring the hot water into his mug.

Sighing, I lean my head against Aziel. "My best friend Iggy. He left Purgatory with Aziel. Since his bones were still here, he was able to reclaim them and have a second chance at life."

"And that's bad?"

"No!" I shout at my new Master. "I mean, no. It isn't bad. I'm so happy for him but I don't know where he is. I don't know if he is safe. I have no way of finding him." I trace the rim of the mug with my finger. "I miss him."

"I'll see what we can do about finding your friend. I promise."

"He's a male omega," Aziel inserts, rubbing soothing circles on my back.

Master Monreaux's brows raise. "So he could be in a lot of danger if we don't find him. I'll make some calls and see what we can do."

My eyes water from being so grateful, so relieved. "Thank you so much. Thank you."

"If he is your friend, he is family now. Just like you. I'll see if Maven can't try to figure out where he is with a location spell. Sometimes she needs something personal to connect with who she is searching for which I don't think you have."

I shake my head.

"We'll figure it out." Alexander makes a separate cup of tea. "I'm going out to find Minnie. I am her maker so the only person she might listen to is me. If you'll excuse me."

Aziel opens the door for Master Monreaux since his hands are full. We watch as he heads over to Minnie who is sitting on the swing on the porch, staring out into the field with tears dripping down her face.

"Come on, My Light. Let me rub your back until you fall asleep."

"Can I just cuddle you and softly feed from you? I want to be close to you."

"You better. You know the only way I can fall asleep these days is with your fangs in me. Let's me know you're close." He takes my hand and leads me through the living room upstairs.

I blush as I climb up the stairs. "It's the only way I can sleep too."

"Plus, I need to make sure you don't run away."

I stop at the top of the steps and bring his hand to my chest. "The only person I'm running to is you, Beloved."

He dips me over his knee, one hand on the back of my head, and kisses me until I can no longer think straight.

I'm not sure how my life went from fighting in Purgatory to kissing my beloved in our home, but it's a life I never want to give up.

This is where I belong. Where I've always belonged.

The End.

ACKNOWLEDGEMENTS

Thank you for reading Eternally Lost and deciding to continue flipping through until you got to this page. This book was a journey. It was difficult to write not because the ideas weren't there, but I got into a very bad funk over the last few months. I was worried I was going to have to cancel this release.

Luckily, with so much support from my husband, my friends, and my teams, I was able to power through, giving Aziel the story he has deserved for so long.

I'd like to thank my sensitivity readers. You helped create Elouise to make sure the details were correct. She wouldn't have been who she is without you. She wouldn't have existed without you either. I'm forever grateful. Thank you so much for helping me create my first POC character. My goal is to make Shallow Cove much more diverse and that couldn't happen without you. Thank you, Bryckk, Tee, and Allijay. You truly brought Elouise to life, and I learned so much. I'm forever in your debt.

Thank you to my alpha readers. I just know they are sick of me. I take every second to write, inch too close to deadlines, and give them headaches, but you catch what I can't in this story. I can't see my mistakes, but you do which helps perfect the story. Thank you for all your hard work, quick reading, and dealing with me.

Tiff, my ride or die, my business partner, none of this would be possible without you. I don't think you truly know how much Shallow Cove would not exist if you were not here. You help me create worlds and characters, you are there on my low days, helping me tweak every idea, you are very much the reason the Shallow Cove world exists like it does. You told me to make it a universe. You bring so much value to this, and I will never not know how lucky I truly am to have you as my main squeeze. Thank you for being there for me every single day. You mean so much to me. I love you!

Carolina, none of this would be possible without my amazing PA either. You're an amazing PA. You bring so much knowledge to this business. I know my success started with you because you slid into my messages asking me if I was writing anything new. I told you I was writing Eternally Damned and had zero plans for it. You did not agree, set me up a schedule, made teasers, started getting an ARC team together, and now here we are. Shallow Cove might have ended up staying on my computer until the day I died if you didn't start spinning the wheels. I love you!

Bryckk, my amazing Social Media Assistant. You have breathed life into the readers group, manage my social media teams, and are always there for me to talk to. You helped create Elouise. You were there for me every step of the way to get her right. You added ideas to this story that will forever live on. You are an integral part of Shallow Cove. I hope you know that. Thank you for always being there, for having my back, and for slapping me into shape to write this book.

My husband. I have no idea where to begin to express my love for you. My writing journey started with you finding out I wrote a book (2016 and no, it will never see the light of day again), and you asked if I ever thought of freelance writing. I didn't. You supported me and believed in me, so I took a leap of faith and started ghostwriting. Then, you supported to only be a ghostwriter full time. Then, after many long years and being unhappy with ghostwriting, you told me to take a chance on myself. I couldn't have if it weren't for you constantly believing in me. We are here now. Your unwavering support has led me to live my dream. I love you.

ABOUT THE AUTHOR

January Rayne is a paranormal fantasy romance author who lives in Buffalo, NY with her husband, son, two dogs, and two leopard geckos. Buffalo is freezing, but January loves when it snows as it gives her the perfect atmosphere to write a book for you to get lost in.

Scan here for easy access to follow me on social media: